AMERICAN SLAUGHTERHOUSE

CONFESSIONS OF A 911 PARAMEDIC

DOC CAGE

Published in 2020 by Audax Books
Media & trade enquiries to willaudax@gmail.com

www.audaxbooks.com

© Estate of Luciano Rodrigues, 2020
The author asserts his moral rights.

All rights reserved. No part of this publication may be reproduced or transmitted in any form or by any means, electronic or mechanical, including photocopy, recording or any information storage and retrieval system, without permission in writing from the publisher.

Trade Paperback
ISBN 978-1-7350783-0-4

This book is a work of fiction. Names, characters, businesses, organizations, places and events are either the product of the author's imagination or used fictitiously. Any resemblance to actual persons, living or dead, events or locales is entirely coincidental.

Contents

*Chapter 1 - **911** 1*

*Chapter 2 - **Queens** 13*

*Chapter 3 - **Mexico** 51*

*Chapter 4 - **68 Whiskey** 83*

*Chapter 5 - **9/11** 119*

*Chapter 6 - **Covid-19** 151*

*Chapter 7 - **Roots** 187*

Chapter 1

911

2010

Racing the ambulance down Corona Avenue doesn't move me. New York isn't a warzone. I still have my DD-214 in my pocket. A keepsake. I was discharged from active duty with a pension that goes into a checking account, but it's not enough.

'Rookie, you can't take a left.'

I do anyway. Pablo doesn't object. He nods his head like he's agreeing with something. He pops Percocet like they're Smarties.

'You know…'

He doesn't finish what he's saying. I'm going against traffic down a one-way and the siren blaring. The ambulance hits the side mirror of a delivery truck. Pablo hangs out the passenger window and exchanges *fuck yous* with a line of cars that pull onto the curb to make way. Rush hour and everyone wants to be at home. I shake my head. I'm hitched to this junkie.

'Why you want to ride a bus in this jungle?'

He accepts silence for an answer. We're almost through Elmhurst.

'I'm not living my life. But you did 20 years in the army and pick up as a paramedic. *Hermano*, you should be going places.'

I throw Pablo a look. The Puerto Rican is only thirty and is already shot. He's out of shape with a puppy's face and sleepy brown eyes. If he didn't slouch he'd be six foot. If he didn't eat fast food he'd be slim; instead he's growing a gut. He's glad that he has a scar on his mouth. It allows him to brag about childhood dreams of being a middleweight contender, although I doubt he boxed. He's nine years an EMT and lives paycheck to paycheck with his mom in Ridgewood. It can't end well.

'Pablo, you've got it made. People think you're a god.'

'All I'm saying is that you lived a life. You chose to live. And you're young.'

'Give it time. You'll get there.'

'I drowned when I was nine and was revived by an EMT. I've been paying it back ever since. I wish he didn't resuscitate me. You ever think that killing them would be better?'

Making down Baxter Avenue, I take 82nd Street towards Jackson Heights. Given the traffic, I swing onto 35th Avenue and zigzag my way to Astoria Boulevard. To avoid passing Elmhurst Care Home, I take the long way round, turning onto 23rd Avenue and from there I'm within reach of Overlook Park.

I'm in the habit of making a good impression when I arrive. A clean-shaven man in a crisp uniform with F.D.N.Y patches on your shoulder and you're a godsend. I don't get it. I assume that anyone dressed up is wearing a disguise.

'Cool it. Why all the shouting?'

An old man is on the street. He mouths off as we step out of the ambulance. He points to a ground floor window of a six-story building. There was a ruckus. Screams. The sound of broken glass. Laughing. Then running.

'Doc, what did you say this is?'

I ignore Pablo who trails behind me. Causeway Hill is one of the largest public housing projects in Queens. It caters for trash. You don't ask questions, unless you want trouble.

The front door to the apartment block is ajar. In we go and me leading the way. Down the hall and the door to an apartment is open. I look at my hands. I've no gun. I look at Pablo and he doesn't have my back. A chill runs down my spine. I've been here before. But no, I'm wrong. It's the setup that's familiar. I'm not in Fallujah or Kabul. I must remind myself where I am. I rub a hand over my eyes and believe in the cold air.

Yes, I'm in America.

A blond lady is on the sofa. She's naked. Stark naked. She's muttering something to herself. Her face is bruised and her hair is a mess. She doesn't respond to our questions. Pablo goes to the bedroom, gets a blanket, and places it on the sofa. She doesn't take it. She's not conscious of her body, too desensitized to her own beauty to cover up her injuries. She must only be twenty, all skin and bone. If I didn't know any better, I'd say she was into self-harm. A cutter, perhaps.

Although I recognize her trauma, I don't know how to engage her. She looks hungry but eating is far from her mind. I take a step closer and see scratches and bruising around her chest and hips. She put up a fight. There's no point asking anything. Pablo hands me an ID card that he retrieved from a handbag. Sharon Mathers.

'Sharon? Where does it hurt?'

She gives a polite smile as though I woke her from a daydream. It says something. Maybe before all this, she led a privileged life. I look around the room for clues. She's out of place. It can't be her apartment. There's a framed picture of an old couple on the wall. Then there's the décor, everything is old and the place not refurbished in thirty years. Either she lives with her grandparents or she was dragged here.

'Is this your place?'

Nothing. Gloved up, I take a look around the apartment. The kitchen is clean and the garbage can is empty. But the air is stale and I open a window. There are two bedrooms, one is pristine, with the bed freshly made, but the master bedroom is tossed. The mirror on the dresser door is smashed. Broken glass is scattered on the floor and mixes with torn fabric, which, if it were stitched back together, has the makings of a red dress. Near the window I see a broken high heel; also red. I lift up the blanket and the crumpled sheets are bloodstained. Pablo whispers in the corridor.

'Doc, you think she'll say something?'

'She'll talk.'

A pretty girl gets this. It's best that her mom never sees her alive.

It gets me wondering. I wonder if someone might survive her, if she'll ever allow sex to be about something more than pleasure. No. From her, there'll be no rebirth, no urge to spawn and multiply, no infinite generations. She'll never even finger herself again.

'How many were there?'

She adjusts her head, acts dumbfounded. Confused.

'They beat me.'

She says something about it but Pablo and I lose courage and look away. A wave of jealousy washes over me. *How easily they got away with it.* She'll forever be wary of being followed, carrying a wounded twitch, that of a startled rabbit, and not trusting anyone. Being gang-raped would do that to you, evermore fearing a re-enactment.

Pablo motions for me to follow him to the kitchen.

'I can't handle rape calls.'

'It wasn't a rape call. A kid dialed it in.'

'You mean, the old man?'

'Dispatch said it was hysteria… or something.'

'I'm calling the cops.'

My hand is on Pablo's forearm.

'The situation is stable.'

'Stable? Protocol says…'

'Fuck protocol. I just want to see.'

'See what? This is bullshit.'

The thing is that the girl reminds me of the one that got away.

About my distractions, it's innocent stuff, but it stayed with me. I was always given to hunting a younger sort, the type flushed with the diamond of youth and unaware of her cut, her carat's worth. But I'm touching forty and my girth is growing. I've become less attractive and can't take it.

My wife, Gloria.

Her parents come from a small town in Upstate New York. Every summer we spend a fortnight there with the kids. One evening, we're invited to a posh BBQ, meaning that I'm kidnapped by a bunch of people wanting to be heard. Opinions, opinions, where will it get them? Nowhere. Yet, their voices fill the air, everyone either married to their job or to colleagues at work. They're all property precious, their possessions expressing who they are. They talk freely but aren't. They swallow accepted morals and refuse to see emptiness at their door. I have to get drunk fast.

In the space of a few minutes, the lady of the house says the phrase 'in my experience' four times. Fiftyish and without wedding ring, it's obvious that Mary Horrall is the headmistress of a private school. She gives warning when she might say something of note, prefacing her wisdom by announcing: 'don't quote me on this'. And do you know what she's likely to say?

'I find that planting tulips after a hard frost is a great bet.'

Gardening is all the rave. I neck a bottle of champagne and feel like roaring at the bitch to get over herself, to go fuck her tulips, but she'd see it as a challenge. Anyway, I'm sworn off argument. Apart from with my wife, I haven't been in one for ages. Why? Because I don't care enough about people. I may be a care worker but that was a coincidence not a choice. The truth is that people are a nuisance. The irony is they think I'm going to save them.

I tell Gloria that I've a headache and take a peek around the house. It's old world. Wooden rafters. Antique furniture. The manicured lawn has sculpted shrubs. Steps lead through a tiered garden down to a lake. At a boathouse, youngsters are having their own party. The age range is early-twenties, all fresh-faced and sun-kissed from summer. I help myself to a beer and receive a cursory glance before backs are turned on me.

Where are you?

It's a text message from my wife.

I'm walking home. I've a killer headache. I didn't want to ruin your night.

Ping.

I'll leave in an hour and we'll arrive home at the same time.

I don't know why she thinks it matters. I was eager to be somewhere with life and noise and now I have hope. A few guys play soft rock, boys with long hair and no faces. It's an improvised set, the musicians loosely gathered around a guitarist who sits on a bench and croons. Although I'm written off as being the sleazy old guy, I'm not bullied into leaving and pretend to enjoy the music. The chat I overhear is refreshing, less property precious and more immediate: music, Hawaii, skiing in Colorado, university, and relationships.

Nadine has piercing blue eyes and blond hair. I can't picture who her parents might be from the barbecue. She's built sturdily, wide-hipped and with a low center of gravity. I know this as I bump into her, tipping her glass of wine on her halter neck. Although blocky, she doesn't fall. She laughs when I offer to buy her a replacement.

'Everything here is free.'

Nadine returns with a Budweiser for me. At university, she's conflicted in her course of study (pharmacy, but thinks she should be doing physiotherapy) and trails off, once it dawns on her that she's yapping to a stranger. I lend her confidence, assuring her that I'm listening.

'Nadine, trust me, I know about the care industry and physiotherapy is a dog's job. But drugs are great. Save yourself from hand and back injuries.'

I tell her that I've been to war. Curiously, for a young person, she has a sense of history. *Why does America impose its ways on foreign lands?* It's standard fare and, if only to study her reaction, I delve into memories. Mosul, Kabul, Nicaragua, Bosnia, Baghdad. And so on it goes. We even discuss concentration camps and the bombing of Dresden. Vonnegut is overrated. Yada yada. Then we dance. Although she's half my age, we dance in step. She makes me feel comfortable in my skin, fashionable, almost. My confidence grows. My erection rubs against her jeans. Have I the steel, the metal to win her?

I'm about to suggest something when Nadine's boyfriend puts down his guitar and joins us. It catches me off guard. I thought Nadine was alone. *Stupid, stupid me.* She introduces him as Van Meer, to which Van Meer curtly nods. First name, surname, or nickname? Who cares? Van Meer is only a boy, perhaps a year younger than twenty-year old Nadine. He's tall and skinny with a long face, long hair, and a beard covering his cheeks. He's laid back, his louche demeanor giving him an unwarranted authority. Barely entertaining our conversation, he looks around, happy to hear compliments about his singing voice and for people to fan his ego. He grabs Nadine around the waist and blows into her neck like she's a trumpet, as I stand beside him like an old man and he paying me no heed. She looks up at her savior with a glowing smile.

Total humiliation.

I was only ever a conversation piece, never a viable object of desire. Nadine is out of my league. It's the next generation's turn to be desired. I never considered her reputation, what her peers would say if she fucked me. I'm not the possessive sort. I don't need to be the only one, but all the same I thought that she might allow me to gun her. Imagine it, me, exhausted after two minutes, dozing off to sleep with the smile of a cat that got the cream. Alas, no. My age makes me invisible. Nearing the big Four-O infuriates me. It's a ridiculous age: you're still horny but don't realize that you're wasting away.

It gets worse.

Mary Horrall appears at my side.

'You found the lake house. And you met my daughter. They tell me that you're in the army.'

'Incorrect. I cashed in.'

'It explains why there's a whiff of death off you.'

How did she give birth to Nadine? Her mom ropes an arm into mine as though we're friends. My face reddens. I'm more appealing to the mom than the daughter. Time made its inroads. I'm Mary Horrall's mirror image, both of us worn looking. I feel sick.

'Is you nickname "Doc"? Or are you a qualified doctor?'

'I was a military medic. 68 Whiskey. I'm a civvie now.'

'So, you're actually Mister "Doc" Tony Cage.'

Her vagina is a desert but my dick will always have a home. My strategy can change. Maybe I'll box clever and be the funny guy and somewhere along the way nubile girls like Nadine will tire of the theatrics and lack of respect from Van Meer and his kind.

I'm a nervous wreck when I reach home. *I'm unfit for human consumption and no longer a threat to women.* I poke my head in the kids' door and am consoled on hearing their short snorts. In the kitchen I put on coffee. Although far away, I can hear Gloria snoring. It grates. She chokes a little and then wakes up for a moment. She makes me think of war. A knife stares at me. I try to ignore it but am holding it in my hand. *Accept growing old, or commit suicide?* What's it to be? The knife sparkles. A thought occurs. *Without attraction between the sexes, life loses relevance.* I knock over the mocha pot. The knife follows to the ground. Crash. Gloria mumbles something. I shout.

'Shut up. Just fucking shut up.'

Silence. She's either wide-awake or falls back to sleep. I slam back a few neat ones and pick up the knife. My wife has grown fat and ugly. I'm stabbing the knife into the cheese board. My wife is killing me. I cork the bottle of JB and go to bed, gripping the knife in my hand.

Ever since that night a few weeks ago, I knew that I was searching.

Back to now. I found her. I'll tell you what I did so that you'll have a sense of this unwholesomeness early on.

I leave the kitchen and return with the medical bag. I remove a vial of Ketamine. Pablo looks at me sideways when I grin like I've a great idea.

'She doesn't need it.'

'It's not for her.'

'How does that work?'

'We're partners, right? Take a hit.'

'Doc, you're wild. Why did you become an EMT?'
'The great question.'
'You offering me Ketamine?'
'It's new for you guys but in the military we use it all the time. It's risk free and fun.'
'And the medical director?'
'It's on my head. I'll report it stolen.'
I'm filling the syringe but he's still undecided. I flick the hypodermic needle.
'A free shot. I got it covered. It's either you or me.'
Pablo rolls up a sleeve.
'What'll you do?'
'Run her down to Jamaica.'
'*Hermano*, you're steering patients. How much you getting?'
'It's the nearest hospital.'
'Nope. Elmhurst is.'
'Okay, I'll bring her there.'
'And nobody is any wiser?'
'We're partners. I'll come back for you in an hour.'

I give him enough horse tranquilizer to sedate a stud. Then I pop a Viagra. I rehearse what I'm going to say as I return to the living room. In the end, it doesn't matter how it pops out. She'll do as I say. But I can't fix my eyes on her as I tell her what we're going to do. I drape the blanket over her shoulders.

As I lead her to the ambulance I wonder when she last washed. I'd like to ask but don't. I lie her down on the gurney and notice that her legs are bruised, the colors ranging from pink to bluish brown. I catch her eye but both of us lose courage and look away.

'This is to secure you as I drive. So you won't fall.'

I fasten the restraints, pretending to be a caring human. She becomes aware of my prying eyes and turns her head away. It's true that I'm feeling hungry. Lambs in spring and thin girls make me ravenous.

Everything is set in motion and nothing seems inappropriate. I'm calm. I drive slowly. I'm humming a tune, singing along to Michael McDonald's "Sweet Freedom". I feel alive and breathe through my nose. It's dark and the traffic has cleared. Ever since 9/11, I thought about jumping ship and leaving the army. Stay at home. Get a job. Be a regular Joe. Drive the kids to school. Go to a ball game. Life in Queens. I did it. Here I am.

It's a derelict area I bring her to. Practically a dump. The lack of streetlights leaves us cloaked in a silvery darkness under a half moon. I secure the block, looking for signs of life as I cruise around. Military scouting protocol. There's nothing doing. We're all alone. The hairs on my neck tingle. I park at the back of an abandoned building and flex my sphincter muscles to see if the Viagra has kicked in.

I step outside and there's an eerie silence. The street lies empty. The place is due a makeover and will be transformed into posh condos in the coming years. I look to the sky for a breather. It's nighttime but I can make out a cumulonimbus cloud passing overhead. I'm not in a desert. A wind stirs; the symptoms of a downpour are there. New York life.

I fear that she might be on alert, so stealth and surprise are vital. I yank open the ambulance door and see horror in Sharon's face. But then she smirks. *How could she know?* Hatred brews. I'll have the last laugh. Pee trickles down her leg. Her fear is well-founded. She tries to jack-knife her body into a defensive position but the straps on the gurney won't let her escape.

'Let me help you.'

I bend over the trolley and do the needful but she gets the steel on me and pushes me over. I'm back up and on her in a flash. She doesn't get out of the ambulance. Grabbing her by the throat, I fix her a look, releasing a tight smile. *You think you know my type.* I punch her in the face. *That's how it's done.* Her face explodes in blood. I give her one in the stomach. She falls back onto the gurney, winded. Her rasping is startling. She's fighting for air, fighting for life. My heart thumps. My penis is erect in my pants but I can't get it out until I've neutralized her. She kicks her legs, flailing wildly. She knows what must happen but resists. Her instinct for survival hasn't dimmed. I wonder if I have the strength to overpower her. I get around the gurney and give her a few in the face. With all fight lost, she gives me a dreamy look. A bloody smile. Maybe she's concussed. I work myself up to the task, stroking my cock, in-between slapping her face to ensure that she's awake. A hint of resistance returns. *No. Please. Don't.* I move like lightening to execute my plan, tying her wrists to either side of the gurney to make her seem more open to me.

I put on a rubber so it's only the other guys semen left inside her. Having made it difficult for herself before, she takes a breath, and then her gut tightens, an inward knot. She's remarkably tight, despite that her pussy is overstretched. She's at peace or else falls in and out of consciousness as I pummel her. With all resistance gone, I catch sight of my dick in the reflection of the ambulance window. Love is art. We're an elegant indecency. I'm banging her and wanting objection but instead get harmony. We're riding the same wave, in and out, the unity of penis and vagina, as I pluck at her soul, in to the root, up to the hilt. All the while, Sharon stares at me. Afterwards, she doesn't put up a fight as I strangle her to death.

On the drive back to collect Pablo, I call it in. Sharon Mathers, DOA. I don't feel bad. She doesn't matter. I was only a vulture, feeding on leftovers. Pablo is paralyzed in the bed where Sharon was gang raped. I'm not worried that I cause a racket as I steer the second gurney into the building. He's so K-holed that he won't be sober for days. He'll lose his job. I'm sweating. I nearly drop him on Sharon's corpse as I get him into the ambulance. He notices someone on the other stretcher.

'Who's that?'

'Just another dead body.'

Chapter 2

Queens

2007

My return.

The happenings of a day.

Sunday morning by my house and I'm walking up my street. The American flag greets me, flapping from our porch. The day is full of well-groomed old men, pensioners, and wisps of hair flying. Their spouses are long dead, as they potter off to church with an umbrella or cane in hand. On account of my uniform, they salute my return from overseas.

Then, there's my wife.

'Where's my present?' Gloria demands, no sooner in the door.

For a moment, I think of that word, 'present'. I'm not the kind of present she wants. Seeing no gift in my hand, she gets back to banality.

'Peach or magnolia?' she crows.

It's how she greets my return, our conversation picking up where we left off. She wonders what color to paint the living room. The luxury of her dependencies: no dismemberments or being burnt alive etched in her mind. She doesn't realize that I find everything faintly ridiculous. I sink down on the settee, and fight for attention.

'Afghanistan was crazy.'

Gloria ignores me. Instead, I'm forced to notice her. Around her once slight frame has sprung up a plump body. She's crouching down to match a color chart to the skirting board and her ass is raised up higher than her head. It's a bizarre sight. She's like a giraffe doing the splits to eat off the ground. Each ass-cheek is bigger than her head. Did her body ever fit her? Was she ever proportional, arms to legs, ass to torso, brain to body? Imagine what an axe could do to her skull. Without an axe, it'll be a long march until death do us part.

'So this is it,' I say.

'What's that?'

'You heard me.'

'Doc, I give up. What are you saying?'

'I said, this is us.'

Now that I have her attention, I repeat myself.

'This is the extent of us.'

'What does that mean?'

'Gloria, you're thirty-six but act ancient.'

'Doc, we're adults, don't do this.'

I laugh as I point at her and she becomes conscious of her flowery dress. She fiddles with the color chart in her hand. Her life is a cream-colored creation. Where would she be without her props?

'What do I care about pastels? I'm back from a fucked-up war. People are being murdered, families destroyed, girls raped. And your atrocity is paint.'

'Someone has to look after the house, to keep a semblance of normality.'

'It's a house, not a person. It can look after itself.'

But that's not it. For Gloria, distractions go to the core of her identity. DIY is a 3-letter word that once spelled 'sex'. Skirting boards and paint is her latest thing. She also likes to discuss deodorizing the carpet. She's lost in trivia. I can't see this out. The pattern is too obvious. Is she ever truly present? I've lost interest in our chat. She has worked herself into a monologue, one long complaint. I have to get out of the house.

'What about your plants, jungle man?'

It stops me. I'm almost out the door but redirect to the kitchen to check on the plants. Kurtz is seated at the island, having overheard our argument. I stand by the kitchen door and watch him. Why am I never greeted ecstatically on return from a tour abroad?

'How you doing, son?'

'I'm keeping things green, sir.'

Kurtz is my eldest. He's only six. I named him after Colonel Kurtz in *Apocalypse Now*. He's a 9/11 baby. He has laid out a bunch of weeds on the island. He's trying to impress me. I trained him like a soldier. He protects the back garden at all costs. I go to hug him but he shrinks away from me so I toss his hair.

The garden calms me. Surrounding the plant bed, the Lamb's Ear is as resilient as ever. Believe it or not, but it's native to Iraq. I could shake the plant by its woolly leaves and it would still survive. The Foxglove also thrives, but, unlike the Aster, it hasn't started to flower. The oriental poppy that I newly planted will make the difference when it blooms in the summer. It will attract butterflies. I draw breath. Look at this, the world that I create. Remarkable. There are no weeds. Private Kurtz deserves a medal of commendation. The roses are blessed with a layer of mulch. I lean in to sniff one. Not much of a whiff, so I cup my hands around a yellow rose. I sniff deeply. Inhale. The ecstasy. I'm in another world. I come to my senses and touch the soil, to feel the moisture, the temperature of planet earth. I look around. Weeds: nope, there are none. Kurtz deserves that air gun. A corn-gluten herbicide works wonders. I smile.

How easy I am to please.

Compost and I am happy.

Welcome to Afghanistan.

It was only last week.

Another day, another shit hole, another sweaty body. The shower is broken and I've a week's worth of stubble. Everyone wears the same fatigues. Who cares? No hope of meeting Miss America out here. It's why Abigail cleans up.

We pulled back from the Forward Operating Base and are twiddling our thumbs. Sitting around, we tot up the body count. We bombed a Taliban target but today they claimed a few of our guys. We're still winning as, for every few hundred of them, they get one of us.

Anyway, there she is, Abigail, all legs and ass, a girl on a mission as we gather around the Green Bean. Tonight's target is a guy who must be from B Company. He looks fresh, most likely on his first tour abroad. They're all the same, young idealists, titillated by gore and brave talk, unaware that the cunt they're talking to is the world's greatest war hooker.

'Hey grumpy.'

'Good evening Abigail. This beats Korengal Valley.'

'Not if boredom kills us.'

'You don't look bored, Private.'

Abigail gives a fake smile. The slut. The guy she's talking to steps forward and shows me a hand. I don't take it.

'We just blew in. I'm Sebastian. I'm from Belmont.'

'Fresh meat from Belmont, cool,' I say.

But I don't know if it is cool, as I don't know where Belmont is. Do I care? His type prays for war to fill the boredom. It allows them to hold court back home at the bar. He wears one of those jungle jackets, the ones with little pockets on it as though he's a cameraman instead of rank and file. Perhaps I've him pegged wrong and he might be a journalist. So what. I'm already walking away.

We know the score, Abigail and I. Free love. After running around together in K Company, it made sense to get it on. Like me, her time is running out. She's mid-thirties and it shows. The harsh sunlight from Iraq to Afghanistan means you can't escape crow's feet. It irritates me that I want her, as I have a policy on anyone over thirty. On the plus side, in the dark, her firm body passes for late twenties, and her ass, I estimate, for eighteen. Sometimes, I wonder where she's from. But I'll never ask. I'd hate to lower myself by registering any curiosity in her. When we fuck, I wonder if she even likes me. It's animal sex. Hungry.

Functional. Desperate. A thought flashes through my head: imagine if we were something else. Then, as quickly as the idea comes, it evaporates, and we're back to now.

Abigail sees sex as a duty of sorts, a comfort to those at war, a vocation in hostile territory where companionship is hard to come by. She likes to joke that she's my home away from home. When I fuck her, I feel dirty afterwards, and have to shower to wash the regret away, to rid me of my hunger for human flesh.

My only consolation is continuity. I have one regular sexual partner at home, and another at war. I remember the first time with each. In the beginning, Abigail was loud and raunchy, full of fake rapture, until I told her to shut up. A silent routine then established itself. My wife, by contrast, when I first plugged her, gave a snort, a contemptuous, affected sneer. I should have spotted the signs early on. Not long afterwards, dreams gave way to practicality and we got hitched.

The problem with Abigail and my wife is that they're too familiar. Sex with them leaves me as uninhibited as if I'm knocking one out over a statue of the doe-eyed Virgin Mary. No respect remains. The animal instinct is gone. Sex has become boring, a domestic chore no different to washing the dishes. There's no life or death vibe. It's just sex: me and my dangling meat. Anyway, fucking isn't enjoyable if you half-like the person. It's why I like doing it with someone I hate or who hates me.

The ambiguity of being me.

First night back and I can't sleep. When I close my eyes, there are guns and knives, and I see the faces of infamous warlords wielding them: the Butcher of Kabul or the Sheikh of Slaughterers. On closer inspection, their eye sockets are hollow.

In my dreams, I sometimes fight with the goodies, but other times I'm drawn against them. I'm always one of the leaders. I jump up in the middle of the night if I'm about to be killed, my subconscious protecting me. My enemies never get me, as long as I wake up in time.

In the morning, I replay the night's fleeting scenes: the images of gore, my near death, and raids on targets. I put order to it, fighting my foes on my terms, in the conscious world. I'm something of a military strategist. I read all about the great battles, ancient and modern. I even bought an elaborate children's toy soldier set, with militia pieces and an undulating landscape.

Over breakfast, I'm deep in thought. It's not enough. I go to my study and set up the pieces to replay my nightmare, to re-enact the ambush by al-Zarqawi, and see if it was well thought out. My nerves depend on debriefing my dreams. Doctor concurs. She calms me. Doctor listens when I talk. Dealing with post-traumatic stress disorder is a battle of wits: the conscious versus unconscious mind.

Kurtz saunters in.

'Sir, what are you doing?'

'Playing.'

'Can I play?'

I look him over. We have history.

'Sure. But you're military.'

'Why do you always get to play guerrilla?'

I look at him sternly.

'Because I'm your father.'

He huffs. We play on a desert landscape, which is lit up by an overhanging lamp. Our war is going well, at least for me. I spring a surprise attack from an inaccessible flank, and get behind Kurtz's troops from beneath a ridge. It's my Omaha move.

'Boom, boom, boom,' I roar, as I blast his troops to smithereens. 'Your men are dead. Surrender. I win.'

I've made a mess of the board. Dead soldiers lie at our feet. Kurtz is startled. Is it because of my bravado? He stares at me, and then cowers. Now there are tears. He runs from the room. The little sperm-head is a crybaby. I hear Gloria consoling him.

'Daddy didn't mean it.'

It drives me bonkers. I didn't get a break growing up, so why should he? Gloria comes in, with Kurtz tucked safely in the crook of her arm. The little serpent.

'What's going on?'

'Nothing. We were just playing.'

'It was my move. You can't hide men under camouflage. Dad cheated.'

'I did not, you little runt.'

'Enough,' Gloria shouts. 'You're both banned from playing with the board for a week.'

'I can play on my own,' I say.

'Nobody plays. I'm confiscating it.'

'But I didn't even kill him. Look, he's only wounded.'

Gloria glowers.

I buckle.

My shoulders sag.

Sure enough, Gloria slams the board shut, and begins picking up the pieces. Kurtz and I stand there watching, staring at her fat butt. Fine. If I don't get to play, I won't buy Kurtz that air gun. Then we could have played for real. The way that I used to.

It's difficult to tone down, to not be on constant alert. A mere pedestrian, once again.

I'm not long in the peaceful world when my sleeping enemies turn up in broad daylight. I see murderers, torturers, and rapists in the faces of people on the street. Maybe it's only me who recognizes warlords around New York. They stare right back at me, strangers do, and without shame. *Look, there's Dragon.* I see his face in a fruit-seller at Jackson Heights, and then again, in a waiter near Rego Park. Dragon looks straight at me as though he's really asking me something. Something beyond my coffee order. Perhaps my forgiveness. I keep this to myself, that I see warlords in my corner store. That shadows have faces. That I have no allies.

Even Doctor doesn't know.

When I return from a warzone, my usual routine is to take the electricity out of my caution. I try not to be startled. I train myself not to look around for exit points as I wait on the subway platform. But I'll never stop standing next to fat people. Their blubber serves as a shield to hide behind in the event of a gunfight. My wife, who never considers my life expectancy, scowls when I veer towards fatties. She's biased. She says that if a terrorist unleashes a volley of bullets, that the fatty has as much right to live as I do. This misses my point.

If I stand behind a fatty only one dies.

If a fatty stands behind me, we both die.

It's all to do with body count.

Another misunderstanding: Gloria thinks I'm free when I go to war. She says it's much harder to mind the kids.

'Going on tour is a holiday camp. You've no responsibility to shoulder. No blame for the kids going AWOL.'

Indignant, I cut her down in her tracks.

'I hear your parents' voice in you. Don't be such a little girl.'

Gloria bites her lip, and swallows her retort. So predictable. The world of control.

'You must show solidarity.'

I say it compassionately, although I know that the real word isn't 'solidarity' but 'subservience'.

When Gloria's parents surface in our conversation, I lay it on real thick. Call it role-play. Gloria is her mom, and I'm her dad. I spotted it early on in the relationship. It's part of why I married her. She was brought up being spoken *at*. Gloria puts up and shuts up.

Her dad is a real hotspur, a windbag full of opinions that nobody listens to. His family is his only audience. At home, he's a little Hitler. The only difference is that Hitler had success with the plebiscite. I guess it happens to many families: dad works tirelessly in some company, a faceless human, he's there so long that he's just a cog in the wheel, a minnow. He gets passed over for promotion, and sees his life out in the margins. He hates being at work, but he's happy to boast about the company's share price on the golf course. In his heart, he knows that he's a nobody.

Gloria's two older brothers were also rubbished until they stood up to their tyrant father. After high school, they both fled as far as possible from Yonkers, one going to work in Newark, the other in Bridgeport. They never returned. This meant that little old Gloria and her mom became dad's full-time fodder.

In our courting days, Gloria hinted at her mom being beaten, once her brothers were no longer around to hit. Mom took the punishment to ensure that the trail of beatings didn't flow over onto her only daughter, precious little Gloria.

The belligerent old fool was always eager to lay down the law. Once home, Gloria's dad would look for any excuse for a rant: her untidy room or money wasted on unnecessary household expenses. I suspected that Gloria's mom was smarter than her dad, but didn't let on. From a psychological standpoint this interested me: how she could tolerate being belittled by a moron.

Low self-esteem?

Perfect.

Like mother, like daughter.

Although Gloria's mom was her inspiration and role model, it was inevitable that the mom would vent her own frustration on her daughter. I once overheard her scolding Gloria in the kitchen:

'You change your mind like a little girl.'

Gloria protested like it was the greatest of insults. It was a week later when she foisted the charge on me. 'Doc, you change your mind like a little boy,' Gloria accused, and all because I had decided that I'd rather a peanut butter sandwich instead of banana and jam. Her gripe offended me, as friends were present, and they choked back a giggle. Later that night, I enquired about it.

'What's with the little boy insult?'

'I didn't insult you.'

'I heard your mom say it to you.'

'That I'm a little boy?'

'No, that you change your mind like a little girl.'

She tried to laugh it off, but I knew better. Then, she capitulated.

'Dad used to say that if you can't act grown up, you don't deserve to form part of the decision-making process.'

'So you hated being called a little girl?'

'Correct.'

'And does your dad think your mom is grown up?'

'No.'

I liked what I was hearing.

Perhaps Gloria married me as harmony lay in repetition, each generation following the next. Gloria's dad beat into mother and daughter that the outside world is a big bad place, and that sanctuary is found in the family. It's the lesser evil.

It's why Gloria saw me as a catch. I was like her brutish dad; it allowed her to put her years of training to good use. You see, all in all, Gloria has no self-worth, and the thought of being alone was too much for her to bear. She was built to be harnessed. How convenient.

Sometimes, I think that I was never meant to meet her, at other times, I think that she was destined for me.

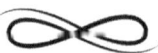

When I return from a tour abroad, it's Gloria's size that surprises me. She's larger, plumped out, shapeless, and lifeless – like a squid – having made no attempt to defy time. I'm sensitive to her growing mass. I never planned on it. I can't figure out if it's me or her that I find lacking.

Back from a deployment and I have to remind myself why I do it. Why I live in this family. And there it is, the constant truth. It was only by getting married that I believed I might become a functioning adult: by signing up to a rulebook of behavior from which I might only digress.

I've gotten away with too much. At home. At work. Everything is so mixed up that I don't know if going to war is the bit where I get away *with* it or *from* it.

Doctor is also confused.

No sooner home and I misjudge dishing out the right amount of blarney. I'm not in the habit of chatting someone up for real, and find it unnatural that I have to get my wife's consent to avail of a bit of marital sex. God knows that I've paid for it.

'You look good tonight.'

'Just tonight?'

'Especially tonight. That green dress . . .'

'What about it?'

'It's lovely . . . it makes you look elfin.'

We're efficient with our words.

'Doc, what do you want?'

'Does it take a lot of work to do that?'

'What?'

'That,' I reply, pointing at her face.

'How do you mean?'

'The make up. To make yourself up like that.'

Beneath the carrot-colored makeup she's caked in, I can't tell if she's blushing. I guess the worst.

'Sorry honey, I'm out of practice. I'm not used to being me, the real me. It's just that everyone is their plain old unmade selves where I've been.'

I go to touch her, to stroke her hair, but she shrinks beneath my hands, cowering like a dog. She doesn't have enough self-possession to say, 'Don't touch.' Just then, the doorbell rings and instantly there's a key in the lock. The floor shakes. Deja, our neighbor, has let herself in. The Afro-American giant barges into our bedroom and fixes me with a lesbian look. Deja is the muscle that Gloria never flexes.

Deja weighs 260lbs.

Deja plays right guard.

Deja comes from an Ogoni tribe.

Deja sports biker tattoos on her forearms.

Forearms that she crosses tightly.

'Is he bothering you, honey?'

My wife doesn't say. But this isn't the Gloria that I know. In my absence, she has been coached into being braver by this dyke. Did I fail to mention that Deja is a fat lesbian? She stands with hands on hips, her chubby paws sinking into her fat.

'Déjà-fucking-vu. Make yourself at home. Nice boots. Are you off playing dickless football?'

'You hassling my little girl?'

Deja uses her outdoor voice indoors. She's not afraid of me.

'Since when did a compliment turn into bother?'

'Doc, have a little humanity.'

'I work in humanity.'

'Where has your post-coital softness gone?'

'My post-coital what?'

How to relate, how could anyone? The emotional investment is draining. Our stupid chat. This nonsense. The absurdity. How can Deja speak of a post-sex softness if there's an absence of sex? Yet, there's no stopping her.

'Democrat in my ass,' Deja wheezes. 'You're a raging fascist.'

'What would you know, homo-fatty. Deja, you heard the one about the well-endowed lesbian? Fat fingers.'

Admittedly, it's not my best effort. But if I cared to, I could light a fire under her. It's only a question of redirecting my energy.

'Christ, you girls spend months and years slapping on make-up. Meanwhile, girls are being raped and chopped up. I can't even tell the color of your skin beneath that shit.'

Gloria holds her hands to either side of her head and then there's thunder.

'Shut up. Just shut the fuck up.'

Her scream is the only gag order I respond to, as her outbursts are so rare. I fall hush. Gloria is crying. She spoils her make-up. Women. Fucking hell.

'Forget it. I'm not going out. I don't want to be seen in such a state.'

Deja releases a satisfied grin, mocking me with a look, and rubbing Gloria's back. This is the way of things at home: a lesbian gets more of my wife than I do. My only hope is to act penitent. Not now, but later on. Another day. When Gloria is calmer. I bungle Deja out of the house – no easy task – and return to Gloria, who has left me vexed. Who is this weeping wife of mine?

'Honey, it's not adultery to be happy. We can act like we enjoy one another's company. Let's have fun being us or, at least, act like we tolerate each other. Life doesn't have to be magic to get through it. Just be happy.'

Gloria looks at me through weepy eyes. I must look like a mirage to her. *And how do I see her?* I imagine Gloria with her hands bound over her head and her naked back to me. There I stand, with whip in hand, and I'm flaying her to death, my wife's blood splattering my face.

'I did nothing to you,' Gloria protests.

'All I'm saying is that our agony could be joy. A smile would be a good start. Who knows, a kiss might follow. It's easy: I'm happy, therefore I have love. I'm sad, therefore I have none.'

'You're so transparent. You always act like you want a makeover, when we both know you just want to get your hole.'

'Who put you up to this? Oh, I get it. That lesbian cow. Has Deja been licking you out?'

'There's no need to bring her into it.'

'But she just barged into our bedroom.'

'She's been a great support with the kids when you're not around. You shouldn't hate her.'

'I'm not the evil one. Anyway, you can't hate what can't be liked, and that fat dyke doesn't have enough personality to hate.'

My palaver backfires. Gloria mutters something that I never heard her say.

'I hope you fucking die.'

Knowing what I know and the ways of death, I don't think it nice or necessary. She didn't even bother to dress it up with the usual build up, of first saying that she hates me. No, instead, she laid it on real thick and full of exaggeration. *I hope you fucking die.* It's odd hearing her swear, and it makes me wonder if her curse might work. I'm at a loss for words.

First there are hiccups, then tears.

I'm jealous of people crying. It infuriates. At airports, I study good-byes, always drawn to a stranger's tears. I envy the way people long for one another. I once poured water into my eyes, to see how it feels. I've been told it isn't the same thing.

I leave the bedroom. I feel good. I didn't cave in, and can now spend time on myself. I'm already out the door, and on my way down to Shooter's Bar, returning to my inner sanctuary.

I forgo much to live here, and for that reason alone Gloria could try playing ball. That she doesn't see our mundane existence for what it is, I admit, keeps me curious. It's exhilarating that, after all these years, my wife still bewilders me. She lives in hope, not accepting hell.

Later on, after sinking three beers, I end up at the cinema. The queue is full of couples.

'How many?' the ticket-seller asks.

'Just the one. The wife stood me up.'

The ticket seller empathizes and waves an usher over. He treats me with compassion, as he leads me to a seat. Later on, back at home, Gloria is in bed and I'm in the living room watching TV. I flick through the channels and stop at a station with a man imploring me in a passionate voice. At first, I think it's a comedy but then I realize it's a religious show. He makes promises: 'God will save you if you are willing to ask.' How easy it would make things. I call it a night when he asks me, 'What are you going to do?'

I'm going to come clean.

I've a glitch that I'm semi-aware of. I want to feel part of something, a family, and feel loved. But I need the punishment of loneliness. Solitude. It is, I admit, a unique capacity: enjoying being sad because you pushed everyone away.

No sooner returned home and I notice how I manufacture fights to be alone. Then I feel safe. Maybe it's a childhood thing or a realization that domestic bliss only exists in TV soaps. Happiness isn't reality, pain is. Blood is real. Everything else is improvisation, and bad acting.

Doctor disagrees.

Doctor is always happy.

I say, control the inevitable collapse and you're in charge of destiny. Example: when Gloria and I go on a trip, no sooner in the car and I start a fight; then we fly through the journey in half the time. When we arrive, her tears have run dry, and we're closer.

See.

Reality is imperfect, unlike the life in my dreams. It's a platonic pining for love I prefer, over a real, physical love. The kind of lover I want is where girls don't change, and don't grow jowly, with bingo-wing arms, fat butts and saggy tits. It endlessly disappoints me that women fail to be special. But not only women.

Nobody is doing God's work, so I also cease trying.

Gloria accepts my complexes. She knows who I am: that I'm above humans, that I need to acclimatize when I return, and that if she leaves me stew, I'll come back to her. But lesbian Deja can't understand. It's all to do with dick psychology and what would a dyke know about that?

I'd rather be brooding at a bar on my lonesome, ashamed of my actions, than sitting with my wife and chewing a T-bone. Is there a cure for this? Is it too late to move to a new situation, to be a new person?

Wanda is the cure.

Like me, Wanda isn't a qualified doctor but all the same, she's something. A psychotherapist, who can't prescribe shit. She's free for service members but given DOD rules, you'd be a fool to confide in her. Nobody can help. Even Google spews out wishy-washy answers to bullshit questions. *What is a toxic relationship? Can someone with PTSD fall in love?*

We have outings in normal settings, like cafés. She said, 'bravo you', when I first suggested it. Call it Cognitive Behavior Therapy with a twist.

'Doc, great to see you. You look refreshed.'

'I'm using my wife's moisturizer.'

We share an awkward hug, stabilizing ourselves across a table by gripping the other's midriff. I inhale her. Something floral. Then I'm thinking of mass. Volume. I felt her love handles. Wanda has porked out two sizes. The low-slung top she has on draws attention to her droopy boobs. She wears mommy jeans, although she isn't one. Then she does something that I despise; she man-fists me in the chest. For her, this is to remind me that she was once a service member, before she made a sideways to counseling, tired as she was of being around testosterone-filled jerks.

We order coffee and I observe how good Wanda is at being herself. So composed, so sure. I love her self-knowing, and the way it washes over me. I relax. I smile. It's the sureness of a person in his or her own skin that puts me at ease in my own. Horses are the same, they can read a human's mood, and fall under its spell. But show fear, and a horse will bolt. You must dominate them, no matter how fake the sentiment. It's all to do with power relations. The same theory goes for women, or course.

'The last time we met, we spoke about Iraq.'

'Iraq is a desert. The mud flats are dry but along the banks of the Euphrates and Tigris rivers, papyrus, lotus and other tall reeds thrive. Did you know that the Mosul Dam captures the snowmelt from the mountains in Turkey? If they opened it, they could irrigate the place.'

'Doc, tell me about Tony Rivera.'

I disguise the truth.

'I was part of a Medevac crew in Al Anbar province. The helicopter pilot didn't obey procedures. Captain Michelson graduated from West Point Military Academy and should have known better. What went down was this: a unit had attempted a rescue operation in Tal Afar but they were ambushed. Operation Sure Fire. All dead, save for one. We shouldn't have gone in.'

We swooped in. It was a nothing place. There were four houses, a bombed out vehicle with our dead soldiers, and nobody else about. A soldier had lost his leg. The remains of the Humvee he stepped out of lay on its side. The bottom of the vehicle looked like it had been ripped open by a can opener. The commanding officer said to bring the Joe back alive. For us to go in without cover meant his family must be people back home. I'm in the bird with Rivera and a Special Forces Medical Officer. He was psyched up, the 18D. The officer must have known the guys.

'Corpsman, are you on this?'

'I'm on it, sir.'

'Lets go. Lets see how big your stones are.'

Private Rivera is in front. I run behind. The 18D officer is in the middle. We zigzag to cover, in case there's a long gun. We get there. We're against a wall. We have our man. He must have stepped on an IED. He's unresponsive. He should be in a body bag. There's gunfire, sporadic stuff. It's a lone jihadi, a straggler. We give cover as Rivera goes around the safe house to get him. And he does. He nails some dude. There's only the sound of the bird and the officer shouting. Rivera doesn't come back.

'We must run an IO into the bone.'

'I'll prepare an IV line, just in case.'

The backup is needed. The officer switches over to my IV line, and squeezes a bag of blood.

'You got a pulse?'

'Negative.'

That's when I switched off, zoned out. *Where's Tony Rivera?* The house he went into is a shed with a tin roof. I go inside. I see the fighter he dropped, some kid who hung behind after the initial attack that took out our troops. Rivera shot the jihadi in the back of the head. The external wall is made of brick but the internal partitions are of heavy blankets. The windows are unopened. The place smells of meat. My nose leads me to the kitchen. A head lies on the floor and Private Rivera is looking at it. He's transfixed. The neck is shredded like mincemeat. Flies feat on it. I hold my shirt over my nose.

Wanda nudges me from the memory.

'Doc, what happened?'

'Rivera wanted to take the head with us. I didn't.'

'Why?'

'It was a Caucasian head. Must belong to somebody. Rivers says I have no sorrow. A bit rich, I thought. We agreed a compromise. I said if the fridge works we put it in there. It worked. The Special Forces douche is shouting at us from outside. Forget the Joe who's hanging on, as we're trying to save a dead head. It's crazy. With a soup ladle, we roll the head onto a baking tray. Rivera holds the freezer door open and in it goes.'

In the helicopter, the bodiless head is in my mind. Did it come from a small man or big man? The head was bloated. His eyes were wide open and gave me the standard plea. *Save-me-I-don't-want-to-die.* I felt sad but don't know why as I didn't know the poor bastard and mourning is for others. Then I wondered how on earth the freezer was working. There aren't mains in the desert and I didn't hear a generator. Did Rivera hoodwink me? I tried to put it from my mind as I had enough on my plate with the one legged guy in the hellcopter. The Golden Hour was gone and I was breathing for him. I had to keep it together. The bird lands and I'm shouting 'Tango 1' as I hand him over.

I'm slow snapping out of it. Wanda rests a hand on mine.

'What about Tony Rivera?'

'He was gone.'

'Why do you think you're telling me this?'

She angers me. I never told her about seeing Dragon in my nightmares. I don't tell her about the warlords running around New York. I know why. It's because they're involved in a conspiracy of my mind. Nobody can understand how they freak me out. But this was real – self-acceptance issues – and I thought that a therapist would get that.

'Dad put fish guts in the freezer to stop them rotting. It kills the smell. As a child I was into destruction, detaching things. I removed wings from flies, or spliced the bodies of wasps in two. I'd put their remains in the freezer.'

'Why?'

'Waste not, want not.'

Coffee arrives, brought by a slim waitress in a white t-shirt with 'Yes or No?' emblazoned across her chest. I think yes, but she ignores my look. On the back of her t-shirt is printed: 'Care for service?' We take a break from talk therapy. I watch Wanda's hands hover over the accouterments, touching each, and then engaging first with the milk jug, and then the sugar bowl. So precise, so sure. The coffee cup chimes as she taps the spoon against the rim. The ceremony of hot drinks is so ecumenical.

Wanda goes off on a tangent, discussing office politics. She thinks she's being passed over. Aware of the forces at play in the military, I'm in a position to give her my two cents worth. Yes, she should remain her feisty self.

'If you want to make it, you'll get there.'

'You honestly think so?'

'You cured me.'

I reassure her, placing a hand on her arm, stroking it gently. Amusing myself.

'Thanks. It's not that easy finding someone you can rely on. Everyone has their own agendas.'

'I know.'

We smile. I'm her friend because I make her feel good about herself.

It costs me nothing to say that she'll get promoted. I'm not even focused on our chat, as I'm shocked how butch she has become.

I'm a cowboy, sitting with my back to a room, ever conscious of getaways and exit points. I'm alert to what people carry. *No bombs for me, thank you very much.* A poster on the wall reads: 'Art is dangerous'. At the table next to ours sits a sultry-looking girl, who becomes animated when joined by a skinny friend. They touch their faces and pinch their arms, yearning for their own flesh. Models, is my guess. An image flashes across my mind of these girls running naked through the wilderness, their pussies tarred in honey, and hungry bears on the prowl. Where's the YouTube of that?

'Doc?'

Wanda interrupts my wildlife fantasy.

'I'm here to help you understand the relationship between thoughts and feelings.'

'Between what's real and what's not?'

'Doc, there's no record of Tony Rivera in your platoon.'

'If you don't believe Iraq happened, what do I care?'

'How many tours have you done? You pretend everything is fine, but it's not.'

∞

New York is an outfit I'm unused to. I'm out of place, an animal in the city. My time at home is perishable. I soon go off. The possibility of eternal happiness is too much to bear.

The truth is, no matter how long I'm back, I'm never really home. Home is hostile territory. Once I dust down my routine, I despise everyone else's. Time passes on a familiar loop, every day and week the same. There's no rebellion. The milkman delivers milk; the newspaper arrives every morning. Rubbish bins are put out on Thursday nights. Family activities are at the weekend. The quotidian norm sucks. I crave damage.

There's a knock at the door. Stupidly, I answer it. It's our nosy neighbor, Mrs Daniels. She's involved in Neighborhood Watch. Every movement interests the old cow. She sits at the window in her living room all day long, she and the cat both, watching the world go by. There's no excuse for it, but I'm only wearing a string vest and boxers. I become self-conscious because, by contrast, Mrs Daniels is over-dressed. She looks posh, smells of sherry, and does her best not to give in to her hunched back, thanks to the support of a hospital crutch.

'Mister Cage, you're here?'

'It's my house.'

'Have you noticed that the air is very heavy?'

I sniff the air.

'I'm used to breathing.'

'It's the smog – too much industry in the city. The price we pay.'

'What price do we pay?'

'The lack of fresh air, Doctor Cage.'

'Only God can help us now.'

'But you don't believe in God.'

The old bat has pushed her way into the kitchen and looks out at the garden. She's not bullied by the silence. The great unspoken between us is that we both know New York is a desert but we enjoy the solitary confinement. I don't articulate our secret, preferring, instead, to observe a silence. Mrs Daniels pipes up again.

'You could do some good.'

She thinks I'm a do-gooder. It irritates me.

'Why would I do that?'

'Because you care for people.'

I've been here thousands of times.

'The smog could be controlled if people knew about it,' she adds.

'Let me guess, you want me to provide gas masks for everyone?'

'That would be nice.'

'You know what, Mrs Daniels, I'm tired.'

I enjoy watching her beg. She's always harping on, prevailing upon me to help somebody or to save the world. She looks dejected. I like that – that I shut her up. With her words spent, she tries to squeeze past me, leading with the crutch.

'You and Gloria are refurbishing.'

Her head is already inside the living room by the time I crowd her out. I push her back to the hall door and fearing that I might kill her. She wheezes for air as she struggles against me.

'We're just doing a spot of painting.'

'The Kowalski's are also doing renovations. You should compare before committing to anything.'

'Before committing to paint?'

Though I rarely see our neighbors, I know all about the Polacks. Without having set foot in their house, I know that their makeover will be identical to ours. *Peach or magnolia*, that is the question. I hate them. I hate me. We are, all of us, too conventional and our senses dulled. There is no daring. The axis never shifts. It's the lack of movement that makes my neighbors seem so potted, fixtures no different to plants. And in loathing them I come to loathe myself for my plantedness.

'Say hello to Gloria.'

'Was there a message?'

'Say hello to Gloria,' Mrs Daniels repeats. 'It's lucky that she has Deja. And you, when you're home. Now young man, don't be a stranger.'

And with that, she's gone. Who is my seventy-something neighbor? Where did she come from? And, as for the Kowalski's, what do I care about their lick of paint? All this useless information leaves me empty. Our encounter was pointless. Nothing is what most people do. Nobody is who everyone is. It reminds me of my fear as a child. 'I am nobody now, but just you wait, one day, things will change.' Setting out this goal was to remind myself that I wanted to be someone, somewhere. But now that I've grown up, I'm beyond who and whats. It's too late; the dream has passed.

I slam the front door. I no longer want to belong to this. The civil obedience, the servility, civility, the way everyone accepts their lot and swallows rules, puppets to peace. Few break ranks or are conceptually free. The masses think they know right from wrong. Clowns. Comrades. Original, we are not. But once abroad, back in a war zone, I wear my colors with pride, and am the first to prop up the stars and stripes. Abroad, I would die for my country; back home I despise being one of them.

∞

I used to be curious about what would become of me. Now the adventure of being me has come to an end. There's nothing new after thirty; the enigma of life is gone, all my dreamy urges spent. Me, I'm one of the living dead.

Maybe my fate will change. I say it, but don't believe in destiny, so unless I actually do something, I'll plod along as I am. I'm resigned to the fact that I'm not destined for glory. I'm down with it, but what I don't like is the way that fate is flashed in front of you, as though your situation might change if you took a left turn. Bullshit. And don't blame bad luck or religion. Believing in things is nonsense to fill the void.

And speaking of hope . . .

Drum roll, please . . .

When I was 16, I dreamed of being someone.

I don't anymore.

Blame *Platoon*.

I wanted to be a hero. When the film came out, I said that I found it overly dramatic. I lied. I even cried at the end when Taylor kills Barnes. I enjoyed how it showed the hell of living. Friends kill friends. There is no salvation. I'm destined to serve the world, never the reverse. And so I drag on, accepting my lot in life, sticking with things, my talents: being a master of mystery and documenting the world I piss on.

∞

Back in the day.

I saw what pregnancy did to others and didn't feel the need to express myself that way. Despite my protests, dead set against peopling, I couldn't stop it happening. Gloria was having none of it. There would be no abortion. She was incubating.

'I'm not built to last,' I protested.

'Don't worry, you won't last. It's not about you.'

'But it is. I'm not in Darwin's plans. I am not fit, and therefore should not survive.'

'But you think I am, right?'

'Sexy? Sure.'

'Well, I want to continue, I believe the world isn't such a bad place to live in.'

'That's because you haven't considered an alternative.'

It was cruel, robbing me of my right to be erased with the passage of time. There I was, scared of only one person in the world – me – and I went and created another. I was always wary of reproduction, of having myself thrown back in my face, of having another adversary.

I remember seeing Kurtz as a fetus. He looked like an extra-terrestrial, splashing about in another world. A gift from God, Gloria said. I didn't have the heart to tell her that God was my dick. I was stunned, not with delight but with revulsion. I almost punched my pecker right in front of the gynecologist. Instead, unwilling to draw attention away from the miserable tadpole, I stumbled into a tray of instruments, hoping that a scalpel might slice off my cock.

I had no urge to make animals, to perpetuate myself, to last. None. I was content to leave it to the Arabs and the Indians to continue the human race. The reproductive urge that afflicted the masses was like the plague.

I never wanted to walk the yellow brick road.

I wanted to disappear. However, I admit it touched me when the little slug said the word 'dad'. My throat welled up, and I felt like a protector of people, doing my bit for mankind, making babies, independent beings.

It was the first time I felt that I was making a concrete investment in time, making time count. But then, I reverted to type, the feel-good feeling washing away, and being replaced by nausea. They say that the first child is the curiosity: *what will we create*. After that, it's old hat. The midgets are all the same.

Once Kurtz was born, Gloria abandoned me. After she plopped him out, she opened her thighs less, and I fell into the background, as she had a new object of adoration. I felt like a spaceship undocking itself from the mother ship as Gloria and I became separate individuals, with different lives. We began the next life-stage: parents being managers of a human factory.

Sometimes they must wonder if they are from me, the kids, Kurtz and Bob. I wonder if they'll blame me for landing them here, sentencing them to life and to eating shit.

Early on, as babies, they were joyless, merely deposited here on earth – eating, shitting, farting and crying. Though I'm not overly curious about them, now that they are older, I wonder if they see us separately, as individuals that is, Gloria and I, or if I may hide in our togetherness. I wonder about this as it may affect memories of their father. Against the kids' rebellions, Gloria and I back each other up as a team, but we break apart either as good or bad mom and dad. The score out of ten for best parent must stand: Mom 9.5, Dad 0.5. And that's being biased.

We're crowded; we can't co-exist, the kids and I. I can't flog them hope. Hell, maybe. They are always at war, my boys, Kurtz and Bob, their fratricidal screams haunt me.

I see traces of me in the older one, Kurtz. I think he has premonitions of what's to come. He seems aware of the racket. He adapts well, employing a cordial manner to get by, as he sifts through people, tapping into their usefulness. People serve him. I know what he's doing, the rascal; he's trying to test people, to figure out the boundaries, to see how far he can push things, and how many degrees off 'normal' folk will accept.

It's touch and go if Kurtz survives; suicide by twenty, most likely.

Would the bookies take the bet, the odds on my six-year-old son's suicide? If not, I'll take out a life insurance policy geared towards his untimely demise.

At school sports day, I see how much the loner Kurtz is. There he is, with his knobby knees, wearing his mask at play. I act cautious, the model father. I roar him on in fear that he'll otherwise put his apathy down to me. But he gets fed up. Of everything. Of all sports. He could, if he applied himself, win. But nothing is worth the concentration. He knows this – that winning could be his destiny. It therefore amuses him to underperform, to throw the race.

I'm there for Kurtz at the cross-country race. I tell him to keep his elbows out, to keep other runners away. But out on the course, he goes his own way, converging with the route as he likes. He ignores my yelling, and makes into the woods all alone. This is his life, marginalized and mocking, playing the absurdity of it all: faking life, faking nice.

Kurtz thinks rules are for others. And because he's fearless, he has choices, alternatives to following the yellow brick road. I rarely scold him as you get what you make. Watching the boys' race, I make small talk with three mothers.

'I guess that boy won't make it at cross-country if he doesn't stick to the course,' I say about Kurtz.

'Yes, it's sad,' a skinny mom agrees. 'You never see a champion swimmer or tennis player coming through anymore.'

'Kids are more all-rounded nowadays,' an overweight mom says.

'No. That's not it,' Skinny Mom corrects.

Skinny Mom is justifying her own child's non-sportiness. I know this as her lame daughter runs up to her, crying and explaining that she couldn't see during the race as her glasses were fogged up. With the daughter gone, Skinny Mom gets back to me.

'It's to do with specialization. If a particular sport demands fast-twitch muscle fibers and our kids haven't got those fibers, we must accept it.'

'We'd be better off learning chess instead of taking on the Jamaicans at sprinting,' I agree.

All the mothers look at me.

'That's a bit unfair,' the Fat Mom says.

'Sport is about inclusiveness and trying,' says a Yummy Mommy.

'But trying to fail, when it's a given, seems odd to me,' I say. 'I'm a if-you're-shit-at-it-don't-do-it kind of guy.'

'Do you have a child here?' Skinny Mom asks.

'Sure. The lunatic who ran into the woods and got lost, he's mine. And you?'

Skinny Mom frowns. Oh yes, I forgot that hers is the limp thing with the fogged up glasses.

'Four eyes. The wimp in the glasses – she yours? You don't look alike. Does she take after the father?'

'You don't look like a father,' she replies.

I let it lie. Maybe it's her time of the month. We're back to the other thing. Kids.

'It's not about genetics,' Fat Mom says. 'I know a goalkeeper who only had one eye.'

'Mental strength counts for so much,' Yummy Mommy agrees.

Realizing that we'll never get on, I walk away without goodbyes. I see Kurtz emerging from the woods, looking dazed.

Kurtz and Bob scuppered my plans at engineering a way out. My hurt is raw. Maybe I'll issue them an ultimatum: die off. I'll ask them to succeed where I failed, to cease procreating. I'll threaten to shoot them if we don't strike a deal. No endless yellow brick roads, no reincarnation. Or else I'll sneak them off to hospital to be neutered. Next year. Castrated or circumcised, it's all the same, just cock-tampering.

∞

Wanda gets up to leave. She turns to me with a ghostly face.

'I've porked out, haven't I? Be honest, Doc.'

'Wanda, you look as firm as ever. Magic moisturizer all over, right?'

'Doc, you're a star. I appreciate your honesty.'

My therapist gets over her minor outburst and relaxes. But she knows the truth. She's conscious of her fading looks. Look at us, kindred spirits, trying to conquer time.

'What moisturizer do you use?'

'Doc, are you serious?'

Wanda sees how serious I am, digs in her handbag, and retrieves a 20ml sample of something. She unscrews the cap. With my face jutted forwards and my eyes closed, she goes to work on me. Once done, I open my eyes and test my face, feeling it with my fingers, and smile.

'Keep it. I've loads of them. It tenses up the facial skin.'

I pocket the elixir.

'Can I ask you something personal?'

'Sure, Doc. Shoot.'

'Am I a handsome man?'

'The hottest of hot.'

Wanda smiles on giving me her blessing and then she's back to punching me in the chest.

We stand up again, but this time I say that I want to stay behind and motion to resume sitting. I stop mid-hunker to air-kiss Wanda goodbye. Still half-standing, I watch as she leaves. My parting move is deliberate; I want a good view of her butt. I had spent upwards of an hour guessing how her backside had fared under the clock.

Her tight jeans allow me read her contours. Her openings. Wanda shifts weight from one foot to the next, the meat of each bum-cheek creasing her pants as she negotiates her way around the tables. All is revealed in gait. She's so certain in her stride. So confident, so sure. She'll be promoted to head psychotherapist. But she has grown a builder's bum.

If the mood takes me, I'll café hop all day. The most trivial of things might keep me seated for two lattes: perhaps a waitress with a ballerina's gait, or someone with a bizarre habit. Cafés allow me strike up chance encounters. Validation of my cruising, of my cachet, comes when

I say that I'm a war medic. It obliges strangers to accept my valuable role in society. Everyone switches on, wanting my sad stories and acts like things matter. And for a few minutes, these nobodies are my best friends.

I marvel at the way everyone sits for everyone else in a café, everyone each other's muse. As I watch strangers, I attribute life stories to them, granting fantastic fetishes and intimacies to random nobodies: the granny to my right jerks off her dog; the waitress has a fantasy about the fat chef; the man in the business suit is a pedophile; the mom in the corner took her son's one-year-old cock in her mouth, curious to see if it would harden.

I sit back and reflect. *Wanda and her search for Tony Rivera.* Imaginary friends are real.

Fate.

Or daft?

∞

Apnea is the feeling.

A lack of oxygen.

Occasionally, I venture into Central Park. Rich New Yorkers, how I pity them. There for an afternoon and I ache to return to my no-nonsense neighborhood, complete with hardy stares. All these posh jerks and their impotent lives, they don't know revenge, only regret, losing respect for themselves in increments, and shunning nature's call. The law of the jungle is alien to them.

Here's one now. Look at him, the man sitting beside me in a café on the Upper West Side. He speaks shamelessly into his phone, misguided into believing that I find his life worth overhearing.

'One fifty. You're kidding. It can't have dropped that much. Wait. Wait. I SAID WAIT. I want you to verify that and call me back.'

He hangs up and gives me a look. He orders a coffee with the same tone of authority. He's a composite of a bad soap actor and my dad.

41

Yes, my dad, the man who I take after. The phone rings. He listens for a moment. Then:

'Never mind. Go ahead. I understand the deviations. Is there a task for me to write up the minutes? No. Then make a task. Yes, that's what I said. I'm authorized to authorize you.'

He hangs up, and throws me another look. Am I curious? I clear my throat, all nice and noisy. Then, turning to meet his stare, I spit phlegm into a napkin. He turns away. He's not the polished article. He stares into his coffee cup. No *cojones*. I look around. To my left is a pair of girls, giddily falling over themselves. God help me, they're everywhere.

'My hair is so curly it's not funny,' says one.

She runs her hands through the offending hair, trying to pull it straight.

'You need to iron it at a higher temperature,' the other girl consoles.

I need air. Pulling on my jacket, I turn to the girls and, in a loud whisper, say:

'Girls. Get over yourselves. You don't matter.'

But here's the thing: I leave the café knowing that they *do*. Hot chicks have a voice and, what's more, a license to be listened to.

∞

When I arrive home, my wife is in the bedroom. I remain in the kitchen, and boil the kettle.

'Where were you?' Gloria calls out.

'Out.'

'Where?'

'Shopping... with Doctor.'

'You went shopping with Doctor?'

'Yes. It's all part of it.'

When in doubt, say you were shopping. It's the acceptable thing to do.

'What did you get?'

'A new sweater. It's V-necked.'
'What color?'
'I think it's . . . navy.'
'Good for you. Sounds hot. Will you wear it tonight?'
'I sure will Misses Hotness.'
'Great.'
I pretend to want her.
She pretends to be turned on.
I don't believe her.
She doesn't believe me.

She didn't even care to notice that I returned without shopping bags. All I got was a porno mag in the newsagents.

It's a week since my return, and we're about to have our first night out. It took that much time to recover from our last abortive attempt at a date. I remember the first time we did it. It was in her friend's bed. She was fearful that we would stain it. I did. I shot too early and pretended to be embarrassed. All I wanted was a happy ending. I loved the thought of spreading my seed over her friend's bed. I understood, then, why a dog pisses on a lamppost. It's to celebrate the joy of it's own unique DNA.

If only I disrespected Gloria a little more – pushed her to breaking point, forced her to limit her investment in me. Alas, back then, she thought me a worthy suitor. She took an interest in me and maybe that's what did it. Nobody else bothered to look under my skin. But it still irritates me. I only ever wanted to borrow girls, never keep one. And I never planned on being a breeder. Perpetuating the human race wasn't in my life plan. Doctor and I, we explain it like so: with other girls, sex was casual, and meaningless. But Gloria wasn't smart enough to realize that she was only a number.

A waft of perfume greets me. Gloria is fastidious in her preparations. She's long at it, at making herself up, and I know better than to disturb. Through the bedroom door, I see her at work, at her make-up table, and wearing only a slip. Her pink dress commandeers a chair all on its own beside her. She won't put it on until the last minute to avoid unnecessary creases. That, or else she's trying to match her face color to it.

'The mouse was about,' Gloria calls out.

It's her joke, calling me a mouse. I don't tidy up. I leave traces of me behind. Crumbs. She doesn't understand. Doctor gets it. I do it to prove to myself that I actually exist. Not up for debating her dress, I remain by the door, loathe to enter the bedroom.

'The kids?' I ask.

'Deja is babysitting. They're are in the living room watching wrestling.'

'Wrestling. But that's utterly violent.'

'Harmless,' she mutters. 'Doc, you might have brought your cell. I couldn't reach you.'

'Bring my cell shopping. For what?'

'In case there was an emergency.'

'Good Lord, how did man survive before the phone?'

She picks up on the cynicism, but ignores it.

'Come in,' she summons. 'Let me look at you.'

I wander into the room like a scolded puppy. She's primping and painting, preparing her restaurant hair. She tests its functionality, running a hand through it, and checks that it corrects itself in the mirror. Perfect, it bounces back into place.

'Shower and shave. You look more handsome clean-shaven.'

She says all this looking at my reflection in the mirror. She resumes work on her face. Then she hears my downcast sigh. Then she sighs. She complains that she has three boys: Kurtz, Bob and me. Maybe I'm being ungenerous. She's trying. The mood remains fragile. After all, it's my prerogative to throw a tantrum, to even the score.

∞

This is the bit about revenge.

Every dinner out has its cost; even the sweetest smelling perfume turns sour. The next morning, Gloria is prickled by something.

'I'm depressed.'

'It's called a hangover.'

Melodrama is her forte. We slept like angry spoons, curled up facing away from each other. I call our bed Cyprus. We fight over the center, over who hogs more territory.

Gloria has planned ahead. She pre-arranged to have the kids collected, and I hear one of their school friends call out as they're whisked off to the swimming pool or a soccer match or something. We have the morning to ourselves. And I dread it.

'There's no time for me anymore,' she whines.

'Huh?'

'No *me* time, Doc.'

Gloria nudges me in the back. She wants paying attention to. I feign not hearing.

'Doc?'

'What?'

'Are you listening?'

'Of course I am. We have all morning for you,' I groan, acting sleepier than I am.

This is referred to as coming to one's senses. I call it Hell. Even from my side of the bed I can smell her morning breath, full of stale booze. I could be living in a bachelor pad. The sheets haven't been changed in weeks and there's nobody to tidy the mess. I roll onto my back so as not to see an empty whiskey bottle and soiled clothes on my side of the floor. I peek down at my crotch and pick at dried semen, my cock a never-ending fountain of cream.

'We only have three hours,' Gloria moans.

'Three hours is gold. Let's go shopping and fix that depression of yours. Let's buy a dress.'

I'm trying, yet she sighs. She's climbing up a mountain and starting to overheat. I have to walk her back down to a safer altitude; otherwise the feelings might overcome her. If I don't nip it in the bud, Gloria might throw an all-out hissy fit, and ruin the day. She comes to life like this once a month, although it rarely coincides with her period. It's a something else that I've to deal with, a double dose of monthly moodiness.

I could also pull a long face, but we have to be mature about it, to take turns. Sometimes, when I especially hate her, and it's my turn to cook, I might jack off or pee a little into the sauce. If she isn't going to take it in one hole, she may as well take it in the other. But this isn't one of those occasions. I'm not cooking.

Gloria begins sniffling. The melodrama. From my distant outpost of the bed, I hear her work herself into a lather, from whimpering to full-on uncontrollable tears. In the early days, I enjoyed licking away her salty tears. Now it makes me irritable, her practiced art, the art of being a woman.

I roll over, and put an arm around her. I wait. What will she do next?

'You don't love me,' she announces.

'Of course I do.'

'You need me, but you don't love me.'

She's being niggardly.

'Out of bounds. Next point please,' I quip like a television game-show host.

'I'm handy for you,' she says.

'How so?'

'I run the family when you run away.'

'It's called war and it pays for the kids' education and your coffee mornings.'

'We can't go on like this.'

'Sure we can. You're overreacting.'

We both know that I need the vestige of a family, to have a grounding of some sort, to appear functional. Gloria reminds me of who I am, as, without her, I'd have no reflection. I'd be shown up as the fish out of water that I am.

What brought on this sudden attack? Perhaps she feels unattractive, vulnerable or disposable. I too miss the beauty she once was. OK, she was never knockout material, just average. But when the average go off, they become truly rank. She has aged dramatically, worn out by time; there's so much extra dead weight. There she is, sprawled on the bed, on which she seems to have grown overnight, doubled in size. Her face is flushed red, and puffy with tears. It's true: she's vile. How did this stranger come to share my bed?

She has on a pink nightie, its color faded after numerous washes. I never imagined having the misfortune of sharing a bed with a woman who wore a pink nightie. When she inhales, she balloons. It's comical.

Gloria feels unloved but must also be aware that she's ugly. I sit up in bed to allow her to recover. To be charitable. To perform an act of kindness.

'What did you think of the restaurant last night?' I ask.

'You're trying to change the subject.'

'No shit. Hey, did Claire tell you about her new man?'

'He's already left her.'

'No,' I say in mock exclamation.

'All men are the same. You're bastards.'

'Had his oats and left? But come on, mid-40s Claire was hardly a keeper.'

Claire is my wife's new friend, someone that she appears to be nurturing. Usually Gloria's friends treat me with suspicion after I return from a deployment. It's as though they can sense something in me. As for them, they always smell of cooking or whittle on about it. Their gut is their g-spot.

Gloria introduced me to Claire, telling her that I may be someone of interest, like a curious insect. Usually I don't merit an introduction but, one day, I materialized alongside Gloria and her new friend. Claire goes 'Oh, I know all about you, you charmer, Doc.' But apparently I'm not for everyday use. Gloria says that I'm a near extinct animal (or rare delicacy, when she's in a jokey mood). I must stay hidden, and only emerge for rare appearances.

'Gloria, what do you want me to do?'

'Be different.'

Why can't she love me for who I am? But then I realize that I'm asking more of her than I allow myself.

'I'm just me. You bought the product: me. Why do you always make me feel like I've killed someone?'

'I should have married Aaron.'

'Remember the bit where you didn't want to marry the runt?'

'I should have anyway, despite you.'

'As I remember it, you wanted a new life with me. With foreskin. I rescued you.'

'You drowned me.'

Gloria gets me wondering what kind of transgression marriage is. Is it a selfish act done out of revenge, to decommission the other, to remove them from active service? We fall silent, Gloria and I. Perhaps she's thinking about Jewish cock. Peeled asparagus springs to my mind. Then Gloria releases a heavy sigh. Crying tires her. She sits up in the bed alongside me. It creaks under the strain. Her venom has abated; the silence has a neutralizing effect.

'Doc, are you okay?'

'How do you mean?'

'The tablets you're on, the ones in your bag under the bed.'

'What were you doing rooting around in my things?'

'The kids needed to borrow your bag.'

'I didn't want to worry you, that's all.'

'Are you sick?'

'I won't die on you. I promise.'

I turn and smile at her, and she responds likewise.

'So what is it?'

'What?'

'Your mystery illness.'

'The doctor gave them to me for gallstones. He caught it early. I'll be okay.'

'I hope so,' Gloria says.

We fall silent again. We don't need idle chat – chat for chat's sake. I'm not worried that she has come upon the tablets. I know she's not curious enough to chase it up herself. They're for a touch of clap that I got off some stupid girl. $30 later and the bitch still lingers in my groin.

Gloria never suspects a lover. Perhaps she's too scared to do the math, to find out that she's in the 'subtraction' part of the equation – the one who will be cut. Or, maybe she knows how preposterous it is to imagine me having sex with victims of war.

'Doc, make me toast.'

It's a cry from our loved-up days of old. She's sweetening up. There are certain solids in our life, holding points where we both feel safe, on safe ground. And these places are sacred, off-limits: toast, cigarettes and foreskin.

Then I remember why I married her. She isn't posh, and doesn't need to be propped up by fake pretentions. She has just the right amount of breeding. Beauty fades; character doesn't.

They say that marriage is about property, only we had none back then. Anyway, Gloria wasn't a whore. It is, for us, about a lasting friendship. At least, that's how I have it down in my head. I mean, you can't talk to a pair of sexy legs forever. You need a girl with a mouthpiece, someone who can help you make sense of it all. With Gloria, sense will prevail, unless I get the better of her. Our children, for example, bear sensible names: Kurtz and Robert.

We don't need to pretend to each other. We've grown into what we've become. Our status in life was hard earned and incremental, tirelessly working to hive away a nest egg, although her parents helped us out with the house.

'Toast?' Gloria whimpers.

Indignation mounts. We hit a wall. Then I capitulate. Restitution is made as I bring tea and toast to bed, as well as an ashtray, cigarettes and a lighter.

There we sit, side by side, propped up in bed and sipping tea, eating toast and smoking. Gloria tips ash into the ashtray or reaches for the toast, as I notice the afterglow of fake suntan on her arm and say nothing. It's spring and her arm is two shades darker than mine. She rests her hand on mine and squeezes. Without turning to face her, I raise my cigarette and slot it in her mouth. When she draws on it, I remove it, tipping ash in the ashtray. She exhales.

We know that words cannot explain us.

Chapter 3

Mexico

1990

WILD GAME.

It's a fitting goodbye, Dad and I sitting tightly, knees touching, in his little gloss-painted bedroom at Elmhurst Care Home. Although it's not a hospital, the place has an infirmary about it, flushed with the smell of cleanliness. The colors are wishful, heavenly: sky blue chairs and an orange tablecloth. Colors to stave off depression. The plastic flowers are an afterthought, and overcook the cheap feeling.

I'm visiting Dad to tell him of my intentions, and to extend an olive branch. I'm unsure if I'll see him again. One of us is bound to perish. He's pleased when I tell him, for the first time approving of something that I'm doing. It hits a chord.

'It's the right thing to do,' he says.

'Why didn't you tell me to go before?'

'It had to come from you. I knew you'd find your own way home.'

'Home is America.'

Dad bites his lip and mumbles.

'Perhaps.'

Miraculously, our chat ends on a positive note. This in itself is a bad omen. Something's amiss. It's alien to me; I miss his rage. Without it, there's a sense of foreboding, a sense that we're at an end.

Opening the tin can is a ceremony Dad enjoys. He listens intensely. He's no different to the cats for whom the food is intended. He licks his lips.

I up-end the tin of cat food into a Tupperware bowl, throw in some defrosted peas, and mix in mayonnaise. I sneak off to the kitchen to toast some bread and, once returned, heap lashings of the cat food mix on the toast. I drop some on the floor but scoop it up and put it on Dad's sandwich. Then I watch him eat.

'The other is better,' Dad says.

He only stops stuffing his mouth to say this halfway into his second sandwich.

'You prefer the rabbit stew?' I ask.

'Sure. And the other one.'

'Lamb stew, or the one with wild game?'

'Those too, all of them..'

'Which one? The wild game was the one I think you liked the most.'

'Yeah,' he says. 'Is it Walmart?'

'No, it's expensive stuff: Trader Joe's.'

That shuts him up. We eat in silence, he, surely figuring on the cost of our delicacy. That's when I break the news.

'Dad, I'm leaving New York. I'm going down.'

'Down where?'

'To the Land.'

'To the Land?'

'You heard me.'

'*La Tierra*. It will put you in your bones,' he says.

And that's when he adds:

'It's the right thing to do.'

We feed ourselves; we feed the silence. Things need thinking. Maybe remaining silent makes Dad thinks he's wise. Or is being diffident and evasive a conscious move on his part, to ensure his manliness? Perhaps he's figuring out what I might be thinking. But at that moment, I'm wondering why they don't make cat food with catfish in it.

My thoughts shift.

A father's expectations for a son: what are his for me? All I know is that I desperately want to fail him. But without knowing what hopes he holds for me, I've no target to miss. He never gives direction nor enquires after my dreams. He wouldn't sully himself with my desires. Willful ignorance, I suppose. He blots out all my possibilities so that he won't be riled by his own pitiful failings.

I want to be everything that Dad hates. We're strangers, he and I. At best, we speak like fellow bricklayers, stopping for a morning break on a building site. The nurse catches me as I'm about to leave.

'Your dad is supposed to be on a salt-free diet,' she scolds. 'You had no right letting yourself into the kitchen. There are hygiene regulations.'

She whittles on until finally she runs herself dry.

'So, go on, what is your dad's favorite?'

'Mary, we can't reveal that,' Dad says from behind the nurse.

Dad thinks it's a bit of fun; that we're bonding. I look at Nurse Mary: mid-30s and liberal, I hope. Dad and I have been through a whole repertoire of foodstuffs: hedgehog, dog, pigeon and even raven. I've fed him just about every kind of road kill I could find. I once gave him the boiled after-birth of a mare and told him it was tripe.

Waste not, want not.

Or revenge?

Either way, I feel no remorse.

How many times did Dad say that he'd ram food down my throat, if I didn't mop up every morsel off my plate? Didn't I first learn about places around the world due to their lack of food? Ethiopia, Calcutta, Bangladesh. Then, there was the never-ending threat of the starving black babies if I didn't finish eating my peas. I was brought up believing that everyone abroad was starving. The Third World, I believed, was everywhere but home. All combined, it made me terrified of travel.

From my satchel, I fish out an empty tin of cat food, and motion to the nurse to be silent with a finger to my lips.

'Trader Joe's finest,' I say.

I give her a wicked grin and watch her raise her eyebrows. She's dumbfounded and tries to ignore the truth. With a huff she starts preparing Dad's bed. She moves like a Hoover, cleaning and rearranging things at a touch. I decide to make myself scarce. As I leave, it occurs to me how pathetic we are, Dad and I, celebrating my departure over lamb-flavored cat food toasties. Dad senses motion.

'Let me see, let me see. Come here,' he demands, his arms outstretched.

I let him touch my face for the first time ever. I've lost my puppy fat, and am all skull and bone. Insomnia is my staple diet.

'This is it.'

'It sure is,' I say.

They're my parting words. It really is goodbye. I turn my back, and walk away.

Sad as it is, I don't shed a tear. Dad used beat me for being teary-eyed, and now my tear ducts are a desert, the jets long since clogged up. I try to be upbeat. I got a roof over my head out of him didn't I; what's left will be spent on home-care. It isn't cheap. His longevity must kill him, every day costing money.

'Say hello,' I hear him cry from the corridor.

There's an air of desperation in his voice now that I've left.

Nothing's left.

Mom doesn't want to see Dad, and Dad can't see Mom. Our family has ended. I made sure that I ended up on the right side of the family. I have two passports. My Mexican one states that I'm a Rivera, after Dad. But I changed my surname by deed poll, and swapped my American passport to Mom's maiden name, Cage.

∞

Fresh out of EMT school and I needed to get out and walk in the real world. Although I'm trained to save lives I needed to see hardcore. To experience life. To see death.

Mexico was the ticket. Don Miguel Angel and my father came from the same town and ever since the arrest of *el Patrón* the previous year I got a notion into my head. The first week in Mazatlán and I don't sleep.

The monopoly in the drug trade is over. New drug cartels have sprung up and protect their turf. It's a shaky truce they keep. I'm alive to every movement. Anything that moves is a murderer: a slamming door, a cat or a drunk. I check the window latch every few hours. My nerves are frayed. Mexico's drug empire was divvied up at Acapulco, where *plazas* were doled out. My surname puts me on the side of *el Patrón's* nephews, the Barrera brothers. I walk lots. Being a moving target makes me feel safer. I tread with caution. Nobody is a civilian. Everyone can be a murderer and half the population is your enemy. I'm out of my league with the stares. Combat is in every stranger's eyes. The surge of the place, the latent energy, willing and waiting to be unleashed at any moment. One minute, the oppressive sound of silence, the next: gunfire, broken glass, helicopter blades, sirens, screams, engines revving, tears, and death. It's a constant festival of fear, where the unexpected is expected.

The children who grow up in a drug cartel will repeat the cycle and destroy like their fathers, with the same blinkered ideals, the ingrained hatred, the pride: no retreat, no surrender. Sometimes I see strawberry smudged on a child's face, and I think it's blood. Except it's strawberry. But other times it's blood, and I'm laughing as the child cries.

Get out of here quickly or be sucked under.

∞

I stayed. I integrated. I went to the beach. It took me time to trust love, to accept that it might be reciprocated. I was fearful of letting my guard down, of being known to another. I should have known better and only have myself to blame. I should never have become vulnerable. The fortuneteller said as much. The witch. The bitch. Maybe I'll kill her.

Owing to Isabella's psychological malaise I have to break up with her. The fatal moment is half way down the Malecon, the world's longest boardwalk on the beachfront. Isabella knows nothing of my quest, that the end of things is on my mind, and delights in the romantic setting, her arm in mine, and me out for revenge; revenge for what my lover

55

might do to me.

'I think we need a break.'

'You tired? We can get a coffee or something.'

'No, Bella, I mean us – *we* need a break.'

Isabella stops and plants her feet squarely, to be properly grounded, and rooted to what I'm saying. Then she shifts, placing one leg slightly in front of the other. One standing position to take information, another to go on the attack.

'Break up? Why?'

'I feel like we're suffocating each other.'

'What are you talking about? We're getting along great. Where is this suddenly coming from?'

'It's not sudden. I've been thinking.'

'You have?'

'I think it's best for both of us.'

'You're acting very strangely. This is the other you, isn't it?'

'No, it's the me me.'

'Doc, it's not your heart speaking. It's your head, your wonky thinking. It's taken the nice you hostage.'

Isabella thinks she can rescue me, rescue us. As though to emphasize her point, she swaps legs, jutting the other one forward.

Just as she's on the attack, without warning, she breaks down crying. I look about, fearful what passers-by may think. I guide Isabella to a bench but she won't stop being weepy. Her tears put a wedge between us. Tears make me angry. I move in for the kill, emptying senseless words into the warm night's air.

'Isabella, you have it all, everything.'

'No I don't, I swear. I have nothing. Only you.'

'But you could. This is all just a game for you.'

'What do you mean?'

I look at her, saying nothing. I'm thinking about it all: her, me, us. I'm only her charity case, a challenge, or a temporary lapse.

'We could be in the movies,' she says.

I don't know what she means and don't ask.

There's no holding me back now that my thoughts have bubbled over and come to the surface. It happens increasingly, my imagination is more intense than real events. *Who puts these thoughts in my head? Who is making me go crazy?* It all comes back to the same thing: I'm from my dad. But still, how can I know when I'm being the real me? This outburst, for example, is it the real me or am I more me when I'm calm and composed? It's frustrating not knowing where my center lies. Yet one thing is sure, the strawberries are killing me.

∞

It surprises me that I had the patience to complete the Emergency Medical Technician course in New York. What surprised me more was that I might be allowed a seat in the world and play a small role. I didn't think my life would allow it. I completed the course despite myself, or in spite of everyone else: my parents and that girl, Erin, all of whom had filled in the landscape of my life until that point. It was time for me to find room to grow freely. But then again, there were few other options.

Mom had already been taken away. Then it was Dad's turn. He didn't seem to mind being sent out of sight. I couldn't mind him any longer after I was accepted to York College. For my part, it was a deliberate move to get away from him. It made sense to sell up and for Dad to go to a care home. I became a nomad.

When I turned eighteen, everything happened so quickly, that I hadn't time to officially change my surname from Rivera to Cage. Anyway, 'Tragic' would have been a more appropriate family name.

When things started getting extremely strange at home, around the time I turned fifteen, I became more withdrawn and more reflective, rather than heedlessly ploughing into things. It was beaten into me, through my thick skull: reflect a little. And so I did. I began applying myself to my studies, so much so, that one day, I figured that I must be mildly intelligent.

At high school, the only school teacher that I got on with took great pride when I received my results. It was as though he had proved to his colleagues that they were wrong about me, that I wasn't a waster. Or perhaps he had some kind of wager on me. I hope so. I can picture him pressing a finger against his glasses to push them higher up his aquiline nose, and then boasting to his colleagues, 'There, I told you so.' He left me with parting words to the effect that, in everything, through all the ups and downs, there is a greater scheme at work. When I heard that, I knew I had outlived his teaching. He must have either been a religious fanatic or daft.

At York College, fear of the world was replaced by investigation. Big ideas were floated around as everyone was told to chase carrots. Save a life and get paid. I learned to hold my own and met different sorts of people. It was as though I was suddenly free of shackles, and could start assembling my own Lego tower to myself, my masterpiece, me, mister Cage.

∞

When I first met Isabella outside a cinema on Avenida Camaron Sabalo, the most curious thing about her was her voice, her posh Mexican accent. She knew it set alarm bells ringing and was at pains to stress how grounded she actually was, how she wished to be pauperized, to try it out. I dreamt about her but imagined she was out of my league, or so I thought, until, I told her that I was going to be a paramedic and wanted to save people. It's then that she began to show a determined interest in me.

One day she comes up to me and says:

'You know the cinema where we met? Want to go back there?'

And the penny slowly drops.

I had slept with my fair share of girls, which, by implication, meant that girls must have also been at it, dipping themselves into a bit of cock. But having lost the home that I grew up in, there came an impetus to finding lasting attachments, to have someone to share stories with. That said, I wasn't inclined to have a girl define me, squaring off a relationship and being off limits. But this was different. This was Isabella. And she was class. The trade-off was simple; being with Bella was better than being single. She had a keen wit and was a lads kind of girl, the kind you could rough it with, and the type that everyone, both male and female, wanted to fuck.

The consequence of dating Isabella was earth shattering. I fell in love. That summer in the resort city of Mazatlán we made a go of it, of us. We moved in together to try it out, to see if we jelled, and if we really wanted to be together.

Isabella was slim, with long thin hands and a bony face. She was the pride and joy of her parents, the father a successful businessman and housewife mother. She had been to New York and knew the sights better than me. How she spoke about New York left me appreciate my own city: the timeless buildings, the memorable bridges, the can-do attitude and the rule of law. It had the freshness of a new world, she gushed.

In Mazatlán I rented a room by the week in a boarding house but when we moved in together, instead of taking an apartment in a posh area, she wanted to slum it with me. For her, it was a chance to act bohemian. We sat in cafés in little pockets of the city that existed hundreds of years ago and learned about each other. Ethnicity aside, there were hints of my mom off her, although Mom was a poor WASP, a misnomer of sorts. It was fun for a while, drinking and walking around what was one of Mexico's most romantic cities, but soon the novelty wore off. Isabella wanted to know more and I couldn't tell her.

Where once, it was us against the world, then everything changed.

∞

It was a Tuesday afternoon. I was roaming around the Golden Zone with the sun beating down on my face and a warm breeze blowing in from the Pacific, when I began to feel horny. Isabella wasn't around

– she had gone shopping and then to get a haircut. The problems of having money for free.

I can't think what it is that drew me to Le Muse that day but I gave myself credit for resisting until then. One minute, I'm wandering aimlessly on Avenida Del Mar, the next, I'm in a taxi to a dating house. Outside Le Muse the scent of cunt lingers in the hot air. Even the cracks in the walls are made of cunts. And all the cracks are filled.

What harm, I think – Isabella is having a haircut and this is my equivalent. Still, perhaps in hindsight, I didn't have to buy myself a fuck. Maybe I was just bored, or maybe I was looking to get tangled in a mess, to flirt with danger, to engage in strange relations. Or maybe I wanted a local *concha*.

Whatever.

Call it a reward.

I've kept my nose clean for too long, I think, and needed a little discomfort to prove that I was alive.

It's a lazy afternoon and the entire world is down at the beach. Only the truly desperate are inside, away from the sunshine, unable to wait until nightfall to taste pussy. The girls distribute themselves among the tables, one to each client. Without cursory pleasantries, a lady plunks herself down onto a stool next to me.

She's a brunette with blonde streaks and, like most of the others, is dressed in lacy black. Hers is a little chiffon number, a *peignoir* that reveals her peaks and troughs and leaves little to the imagination. Her curves aside, she has hammy thighs that flesh out when she sits. I think about how large she'll look sat atop of my pencil-thin cock.

In the corner of the bar, I spy a thinner, tamer looking sort who's more to my liking, and who sits looking distracted and alone. *Why hasn't she indulged me?* She's has on a frilly mini-skirt to make her coquettish. *What's she waiting for?* I feel cheap, that she doesn't itch for me. Money is money, so why not me? I hate girls without a need; they're unbreakable. Unbendable.

'I'm Maria,' the girl beside me says.

As though I care to know her false name. Maria has been rubbing my thigh, and sees me gazing over her shoulder at her colleague. She's used to it. She makes do.

'And who are you, Mister Mysterious?'

'Call me Doc.'

'Doctor?'

She laughs, not believing the nineteen year-old boy. And there was me, hoping I might indulge in a bit of pseudo-class with a charming hooker. I become self-conscious. I may be nineteen but I'm a man. A touch of hair gel makes my hair stretch into the air. Despite the trimmer attributes of the girl in the corner, I start warming to Maria, although she's a cunt who smells of toilet lavender.

I say little as I look at Maria, scrutinizing her body parts and imagine using her as an instrument. Though corpulent, it's only her bad breath that turns me off. I quickly knock back one, two, and then three beers. Platitudes are few, but Maria makes me feel wanted, as she kneads her hands into my thighs and urges me upstairs. When it comes down to it, the exchange is brief.

'You like me?' she asks.

'*Si.*'

'You want me?'

'*Si.*'

'Or is it her you want?' Maria says, throwing her head over her shoulder.

She's referring to the skinny hooker standing alone at the bar. I feel a little guilty. I don't know why, but I decide to show Maria loyalty and boost her morale.

'I feel something special for you,' I say.

'I am special. Let me show you.'

I throw another glance over Maria's shoulder. It all becomes clear. The prostitute at the bar was pre-ordered. Her suitor just arrived, a balding man in his sixties, dressed in smart cream slacks and a sports jacket. He has a thin moustache and walks with a cane. After greeting his prize, he pulls a white linen handkerchief from his top pocket, and wipes the lasciviousness from his mouth, a mouth that oozes spittle.

'Five hundred pesos for all you can do.'

Perfect, I have just that amount.

I watch Maria mount the narrow staircase and try not to lose my hunger. I tumble her onto the bed, and that's that, once I step out of my jocks. Sure enough, she hoists herself onto me like a spavined mare. My lack of respect for her works wonders, my confidence giving me a firm erection. She's as obedient as a dog and as dumb as a cow. It's like fucking the hole in a piece of cheese, and just as pungent.

Ten strokes later and I spill it into her. She hardly notices. I'm only her next heroin fix, her pussy traded goods, rosebush commerce. She flops onto a bedside bidet. Only now do I notice her cropped pussy, the bristly sort, like a weekend's stubble. With one hand, she gives two brisk scrubs of her minge and is done, off the bidet, and with a towel wipes herself, packing away her dewy softness into the same panties.

Then it's time to pay up. The joys of forbidden fruit. I hit a snag as I re-enter the bar. I left my beer tab unpaid. I owe almost as much in drink as I do for the fuck. It's a smart move, cleaning me out upstairs and downstairs. Fucked twice.

I have no choice but to bolt. Reading my move, the burly doorman walks in from outside, blocking the exit. He's used to this kind of carry on. Without creating a fuss, I turn on my heels, marching back upstairs. I'm back downstairs in a flash and a stuffed wallet in my possession.

Outside the brothel, I pile into a taxi and urge the driver to leave quickly. It's no good. Mine was a costly mistake. Three pick-up trucks speed down the dirt road after us. Warning shots are fired. The taxi pulls over and mister muscle from Le Muse pins me against a pick-up and gives me one in the stomach and another in the face. Lying in the dirt, I feel someone rummage in my pocket, as I watch the taxi drive off.

'This belongs to Señor Salazar.'

The hired muscle is holding my passport and a stranger's wallet in his hand. There's no point denying it. I'm surrounded by six meatheads.

Back at the brothel, I barged in on the old man mid-fuck and robbed him. It turns out that Señor Salazar is linked to the Sinaloa Cartel and is friendly with El Chapo.

I'm about to be given a beating when I make my plea, although naturally I can't tell them who I am, what I do, or lead them to my money, or I'll get a bullet.

'I'm from America. Check my passport. Anthony Cage. I have money.'

'You sound Mexican.'

'I'm half half.'

I talk the hired muscle into driving me home to fetch what's owed. After much imploring, he agrees to wait outside the apartment as I go inside and beg Isabella for the money.

'I told you, I went on a bender. Can you be a bit understanding?'

'A bit understanding?' she parrots.

She looks at me like she doesn't know me.

'Tell me it's not my Spanish that you're having trouble with.'

'It's not.'

'So, what's the issue?'

'Look at you, Doc, it's your life.'

'I seem to remember it being *our* life.'

She ignores, preferring to continue investigating.

'How come he handed you drugs if you had no money?' Isabella asks.

'Because I told him that I did have money.'

'And when you hadn't, why didn't he take it back?'

She's getting tedious, pedantic even.

'There was an element of trust.'

'Trust? Between a dealer and a user? Show me the drugs then.'

'I told you, I lost it when I tried to run. Then he caught me.'

Isabella doesn't believe my story but looks out the window to confirm that there's a goon in a car. I think nothing of my story. A lie is only a lie when something is at stake. A few pesos won't break the bank.

'Doc, I don't even know what you do.'

'I work.'

'Do you really? It sounds suspicious.'

'It's not. Isabella, it's like you suddenly don't believe anything about me because of a small fuck up.'

'You come home bleeding with a gangster and a broken nose.'

'Trust me: that guy will kill me. He might kill both of us, if I don't pay up.'

'You don't know shit, do you?'

I change tack, and become indifferent, resigned to the imbroglio exploding in my face. I'm tired of our to-and-fro, as she constantly quizzes me as I dig myself out. Maybe that's what does it, what fires me up, the working class me, offended by her spoiled sense of self-righteousness and desire for control. I pace up and down the room. She knows what I'm thinking, why else the capitulation? As she gives in, she starts officiating over the finer details of the transaction. She doubts me, and I must coax her over the line.

'I'll come through. I promise.'

'You'd better. It's my dad's allowance. I need that money back.'

'You will.'

It galls me, her stewardship of my life. I can't help myself. I need to know more, to put out feelers, test the water.

'Isabella, I've had a hard life . . . '

'What's your point?'

The point is already made. She doesn't do pity. Indeed, she will never be a nurturer. She's too cold. And if I'm in this for the long haul, I reckon that I've already endured enough cold in my life. I can't help thinking how similar she is to Maria, the prostitute: money the route to all performance. I'm fed up playing with an heiress and holding out for a rich reward. Isabella dislodges me from my thoughts.

'Doc, are you listening?'

'I told you that you'll get it back.'

'When?'

'Friday.'

'Friday morning?'

'Sure,' I say.

'What day is today?'

'I don't know. Tuesday?'

'No, it's Wednesday. That's two days.'

'Whatever, *fresa*.'

She doesn't respond to the slur about her upper-class social status, but the look she gives irks me.

'What happened, Doc?'

'Time happened, *fresa*.'

And then she's crying. I won't console her. Walking away, with her money in my hand, I stop and look back. We make eye contact. Her tears leave me feeling like a murderer.

'You didn't even notice my haircut.'

∞

That was the start of it, what prompted my preppy girlfriend's suspicions. Though I showed no contrition, this first indiscretion came at great cost. It weighed on Isabella, my lifestyle – the drink, recreational drugs, and a niggling question about ambition. There were also question marks over what I do for money, added to which, she has become nasty. She's out for revenge. But revenge for what? For undermining our hopes of being together? Of stamping on her dreams? Whatever. She scrutinizes us. As a reactionary measure, I also begin questioning us. Everything about her bothers me: she might say the wrong thing or wear the wrong outfit. I even pick apart her choice of shoes. In no time, I have it in for her.

Although our relationship preoccupies me, I have no template to work off of. Love was new to me and, without the requisite knowledge, I couldn't make a valued judgment. But this much I did know: love is about being vulnerable, and men hate appearing weak. It's not love per se that we fear, we men, but the possibility of being undone, and love holds that threat. Furthermore, over time, Isabella would learn how inferior to her I really was, unable to match her lofty expectations, unable to be her Prince Charming. Puzzled by it all, by what girls ask of men, I started babbling, promising anything. I promised her the usual list of things that men promised: drink less, flirt less, wash more. A superficial emptiness crept between us.

We start to become insecure, as little things became big things: leaving the toilet seat up, not washing-up, staying out late and the like. It does my nut in. I know I have to break with her. There are no alternatives. I'm too working class.

When I have it decided – our break up being the only outcome – and long before breaking the news to her, I lay awake through the night, frozen in fear. I watch her sleeping beside me. She resembles a porcelain statuette. She looks harmless. It infuriates me. Life is unjust. I could set life straight by punching her in the face and denying it when she wakes up covered in blood. Anything to kick-start the inevitable fight. Instead, I shove a stranger's dirty panties down the side of the bed hoping that she'll discover them. I want the fight; I'll relish the guilt.

When I finally manage to sleep – always just before the nine o'clock drilling begins in the apartment next-door – I dream that I'm trapped in a forest with no way out. At other times, I'm bringing our newborn baby to meet my parents.

The drill next door startles us awake. It's the drum roll for our fights.

∞

Here then is where we are: sitting on a bench on the Malecon.

'We need a break. It would be better.'

'What's better?' Isabella asks through sniffles.

'It would be better to put a distance between us. Until we get calmer about all of this. I wish I met you ten years from now. But now is not good for me.'

'What's that supposed to mean?'
'That life is about timing.'

∞

Common sense prevails, and I move out. The day is etched in my mind, the last look from a lover: eyes welled-up and under-hanging lip. A taxi comes for me during a downpour and I get drenched. I take a small room where I used to stay. I get back to squeezing my spots. There's no more drilling from next-door, and I can sleep. But then, just as I walk out of her life, Isabella walks into my dreams. I'm mystified by how she still controls me. I have to escape her ghost. I can't risk sleeping, of meeting her there, in my dreams. I'm afraid of being under her spell. I must re-focus without her being in focus. I look in my belongings for a trace of Isabella. I want to savor her. I find pubes on a razor and sniff them before throwing it out. Look what a fool love is making of me. The blasted thing doesn't make sense, being lovesick.

This isn't living.

I revert to basics and relearn how to stand up on my own two feet. I stroll down Avenida del Mar, the promenade where Isabella and I came to an end. It's evening and I make down a slipway to the beach. The water laps at my feet. Groups of young people drink alcohol and laugh. A yacht is anchored and it's lights bounce off the flat sea. Nighttime is calm, a break before the day's influx of tourists. A couple looks at me, probably because I'm looking at them. Or can they read in my face that I'm not quiet right? Self-conscious, I turn away. A female jogger trots by, daubed in red lipstick. She also looks at me. But girls are always quick to give me the eye.

With my feet in the water, I walk for miles, arriving at the Fisherman's Monument. Isabella and I once snapped photos of us here. I'm lost. What is one to do?

I go to a bar overlooking the beach. The waitress tells me that tequila will pick me up and I sit and sip it, hoping that the alcohol will give my life color. It's an intimate place, but the darkness provides me with a comforting blanket as I tend to my frayed nerves. At the table beside me, a son arrives to meet his father. They greet one another with a respectful hug. I turn away, finish my tequila, slamming down the empty glass and move on.

I enter a jazz bar, and zone out. I don't know the sounds, the beat being new to me, but it feels like being in a comfortable dream. A curvaceous female singer, who wears a long body-hugging black dress and a tattered pink boa, enchants me. She's bathed in a halo of smoke. She wears the same bright red lipstick that the girl jogging on the beach did. I've stopped liking the color red.

In a bid to hide from my old life, I return to the jazz bar over the coming days. I'm the youngest by ten years. It's my private bubble, a safe place, a dream existence where I don't think about Isabella. But then, one night, the lady with the boa sings Nina Simone's '*Ne me quite pas*', and Isabella floods back into my mind. I stagger onto the street, thinking of Isabella's warm cunt, and who might be filling it.

Of course I miss Isabella, but isn't my entire life built on missing people? The pain of loss has made me irritable. We don't get on, this world and I. I stand on the Malecon and punch the clear midnight air. But the world doesn't feel pain, only I do.

After Isabella, it takes a long time before I really lust after another girl. Perhaps a full three weeks before I get my cock back to working order. What breaks the spell is a note I receive from Isabella. It's merely says: 'I want you back.'

Her note is so uninspiring that I instantly turn off her. I'm brought back to what she said the day we broke up: 'We could be in the movies.' I don't reply. There's no concession from me, no quarter given, and there is Isabella, on her knees, yet she doesn't have the guts to top herself. She can't commit. How pathetic. In my life I've known other girls with more conviction. Isabella may be posh but she's truly ordinary. She's not better than me. It triggers my release. My revulsion. Our bond is broken. Isabella is finally evicted from my dreams. Her godliness is gone and

I'm no longer a fugitive on the run. I'm a free man.

I return to my ways of old: to the language of indifference and to sleeping around.

∞

I lied.

It suited me to tell a lie, to lay blame on us. What is true, however, is that Isabella undermined any hope we had of sharing a future together. The witch said as much.

The beginning of our break up?

The strawberries.

Witchcraft or female intuition – whatever it was – it's undeniable that the fortuneteller's prognosis offended me. The *bruja* opened a wound. Having our futures read was supposed to be a bit of fun, something to bring Isabella and I closer together, in the same way that we shared love letters and bed bugs. Instead, the malicious old hag ripped up our life, and robbed me of any security or self-worth. And all for a measly three hundred pesos.

Quite the pairing we were, Isabella and I. I'm sure I already mentioned that she was a catch. But I failed to mention that I was too. Nineteen, tall and dark, with a cheeky grin, I suppose that if I put my mind to it I could have had any girl.

It surprised me that Isabella was just in it for the sex. I thought we were more than that. I felt betrayed that there was no higher realm, nothing between us other than the physical. Isabella was only made for pleasure. The rest was a lie. Learning this made my discovery of 'love' into a twisted, artificial creation.

It was Friday 13th, the day on which the witch's spells ought to be most potent, added to which it was just after a full moon. The clairvoyant had a special offer for couples: two for the price of one. Isabella was keen to be told how compatible we were.

We took the desert road towards El Chilillo and pulled up outside a house in the middle of nowhere. One minute there's nobody but when I looked again a woman with rheumy eyes was standing by our parked car. Senora Veras was slight and shifted her weight from one foot to the other like she was hovering on thin air. The skin on her face was drawn tight with deep lines running through it. She wore a black apron over a green dress and had her hair wrapped in a colorful cloth. Her green eyes were startling and unsettling. She was mid-forties with a wiry frame and, if she had a drink in her hand instead of a carving knife, I would have believed that she led a partying life. Without a word, she sized us up. Then she smiled, without showing her teeth. She put an egg in my hand and rolled my fingers around it. She walked back to her house and, wordlessly, Isabella and I followed. She trod gently on the world, waking toe to heel, as though stepping on broken glass. Her garden was full of prickly Aloe Vera and a plant, hanging from the porch, caught my eye.

We arrived at a garden shed. A shelving unit made of sculpted chicken wire and papier-mâché stretched along the back wall. The undulating structure held hundreds of figurines from floor to ceiling: Mother Mary, black minstrels, baby Jesus, furry key rings, toy animals, and all sorts of kids' junk like *Hot Wheels* and superheroes. I was slow to notice a trickle of water curling down the uneven display unit to a fishpond.

The fortuneteller showed me her palm and I placed the egg back in her hand. She studied it and I felt ashamed when I noticed a hairline crack. With a nod of her chin, she indicated for us to sit before her altar. The witch cracked the egg into a bowl and studied the yolk. I didn't know if it was good or bad omen but my life was clearly under inspection. The mood was heavy and things had yet to take a turn for the worse.

Isabella took out money. The *bruja* nodded to a saucer and Isabella put it there. When the witch left the room, I whispered to Isabella that we should leave. She refused. The *bruja* returned with a bowl of strawberries and a rooster under an arm. She fed a strawberry to the hen.

It looked so peaceful, the red strawberry so pure against the murky red color of the fowl's neck. It happened so fast that we were caught by surprise when she sliced off the rooster's head. From the floor, the head continued to eat the strawberry, as its corpse flapped around and blood spewing. The witch picked up the head and looked in its eyes. She turned to me and uttered her first words:

'You need help.'

I forced a smile, wondering what kind of voodoo spell book she got her tricks from. The fortuneteller nodded to the door and I left the shed, as Isabella chose to go first. While reading her palm, the *bruja* asked her to imagine herself in the countryside.

'Close your eyes. Imagine you are walking through a field of strawberries.'

'*Fresa?*' Isabella asked.

'Yes, *fresa*. You like strawberries don't you?'

'Who doesn't?'

'There you are, as free as a bird and all alone in the field. The sun is shining. You have an empty basket in your hand. The strawberries are ripe. You stoop to pick some up. How many do you put in your basket?'

'You want me to count them?'

'Yes. But take your time. When you are finished picking the strawberries, I want you to look inside the basket and count them.'

Isabella counted a dozen *fresa*. Then it was my turn. I went into the shed, and sat at the altar in front of the *bruja*. She walked me through the same routine, first sprinkling tealeaves on my palm. Afterwards, I told Isabella that I also counted twelve strawberries. She clapped her hands as though we had done something right, and hugged and kissed me. But I pulled away knowing that we were at an end.

The number of strawberries revealed a person's libido.

The palm-reader told me that, in the long term, Isabella and I were ill suited. Isabella, it seemed, was a nymphomaniac while, apparently, I was dead below the waist. To cover this up, I lied to Bella, and told her that I had counted twelve strawberries, when in fact I had counted none. I don't care for strawberries. They don't sit well with me, as they're too acidic. But the psychic bitch never bothered asking me whether I liked them or not.

What kind of liturgy was she spreading, ruining lives and breaking up couples, and then acting all pious and deterministic and so on?

Anyhow.

I tried not to think about it, but the presentiment lingered; it was an indubitable fact: we were doomed. I couldn't hide from the truth. I was too proud a person to watch us slowly deteriorate. I vacillated between believing the witch, and writing her off as a fake. But, all the while, she nagged, Isabella did. I became standoffish and uninvolved and we broke down together.

I wanted to be rid of her. Control my fate, rather than have it spring up on me. I had to dump Isabella before I lost her to another. The portents were there – the strawberries hovered inside my head like swooping vultures. Time was running out. Procrastinating wouldn't help and, besides, a slow death is not for me. Any day she might turn, and then it would be too late. I had to get in first. There was no point stalling the inevitable.

When I fell in love, I didn't realize the program I was installing in my life: how I was building myself up, only to be undone by a force outside my control. I needed to protect myself and to ensure that I couldn't ever be ruled, indeed *ruined*, by love again. I was furious that I had allowed myself to become so vulnerable, to allow a girl do that to me: to make me love when love was poison.

From then on, I, Anthony Cage, would not be taken in by any cunt. To do so would be to show weakness. I'll go it alone, I decided. I'll mean nothing to everybody, free of attachments, and complications. I'll live outside people. I knew what I was signing up for: nobody. And nobody can have me happily ever after.

To celebrate this radical decision in my life, I brazenly went back to Le Muse, made peace with the place, and requested Maria, the prostitute. It was my way of breaking free, of cementing things. I also got the lowdown on Señor Salazar. I admit that when I fucked Maria that I thought of Isabella.

'There you go, that's because of you.'

I shouted it to Maria when I came in her. She can't have known that it was a parting message for Isabella. Call it a form of revenge, a way of telling the world that I wasn't frigid, my insurrection by erection. After fucking Maria, a weight lifted. There came a brighter day and, as my head cleared, I saw who I might become. There was no longer any need to restrain myself from doing anything.

∞

The end of summer came, and the rain came with it. A torrent descended on Mazatlán. The warm asphalt along the main drag has a distinctive smell as raindrops sizzle on the avenue. Everyone is caught off-guard, leaving me looking oddly prescient in a rain jacket. But then, fifteen minutes later, and the skies are clear once more, and it's like summer might return.

Today, it's a clear dry day, and no clouds threaten. It's one of those days in late fall where the bark of trees darkens overnight. The leaves have fallen, and the bare trunks reveal a damp color. With the in-between nature of the seasons, the high priests of Mexican fashion haven't yet decreed that winter wardrobes be worn; at best, a sweater is required. And this is why I notice her.

She's conspicuous in a pair of yellow rain boots, strolling through the city park by the aquarium. There's something off. I feel inexplicably drawn to her. I feed off clues, morsels of truth, and eroticism. I don't urge myself, but I can't control it, can't stop myself. Call it a force of nature, or whatever, but I'm off. I'm up off the park bench, and take a parallel path, walking in step with her. Out on the street, she dives into a café. It's there that I pounce.

'Do you speak English?'

'Yes?'

'I don't mean to impose but I can't help noticing the rain boots.'
She looks down at them.
'The puddles, they haven't yet established themselves.'
'Why wear the boots – is that your question?'
'Aren't you being overly precautious?'
'Why wear clothes?' she asks, looking me up and down.
'Do you mind if I sit?'
'As you please.'

I hold my breath, and slip into a window seat across from her. She's an American *Chicana*, but claims British parentage, and speaks English with an odd, neutral twang: globalese. Her mom, once married to her father, now has a wife. She's easy with it, and together they hate her father, with whom she lost contact after he returned to England. Now she has two moms, she matter-of-factly says, and stares at me like I might challenge this assertion. I don't.

Instead, I notice the tattoos. I imagine they were from her rebellious youth and having to swallow an unusual family setup. Five numbers, '3' through to '7', are tattooed on the underside of both forearms.

'Is it fashion or is there a reason why?'
'Do my mud boots disturb you that much? I wear them in case of lightning.'
'But rubber isn't a conductor of electricity.'
'Precisely.'
'I don't follow.'
'It's to stop lightning being transmitted *to* me.'
'Into you?'
'Yeah.'
'From the earth?'
'Right,' she nods, as though I'm slowly catching on. 'The earth has a charge, a current running through it.'
'That's odd.'
'What's odd?' she asks.
'It's odd because I get you. I do. I often feel electrified.'

She nods cautiously. I'm drawn to her because she seems offbeat and quirky. I imagine she might be able to help me; to pinpoint what's up with me. Or maybe I picked up on the rubber boots because I associated them to fetishism. Just as I'm building up to confess all, to blurt it out, I freeze, embarrassed to be so frank. She, meanwhile, seems to have no such misgivings, happy to rave on about the sun and moon.

'What do you want?'

Being so blunt catches me off-guard. She sees that I'm speechless and gives me a warm smile. *Who is she?*

'If you can't tell a complete stranger intimate things, then who can you tell?'

My youth harps back. I'd heard the very same line a long time ago.

'I don't know what you're asking me.'

'You approached me. Why? You must tell me.'

'Why must I?'

'It will liberate you. Equanimity.'

'Equi what?'

'-nimity.'

I play for time. We haven't had much of an introduction, and what introduction she did give, I doubt very much. She's a typical Mexican-American but the British origin story must be bogus. Maybe the married lesbian mom too. I shift the focus back onto her.

'You said you're from England, but you're really American, right?'

'I'm an opera singer.'

'But also a Latina on holidays from America?'

'I'm also a poet.'

'I notice that you don't feel the urge to reciprocate, to enquire things of me. I'm Tony Cage. I'm just a typical Yankee.'

'I'm sure you are,' she says doubtfully.

'And you are?'

'Call me, J.'

'J for Jade?'

'Or just the letter J.'

'OK, you've lost me.'

'That assumes that you first knew what you caught.'

J smiles. She's twenty, possibly twenty-one. She's petite, no taller than five foot four, with black hair and an oblong face. Her melancholic eyes have sockets so deep that you could fuck them. I pry into her background, with question after question. She picks out parts of her life to discuss. Falling off a pony. Parachuting. Breeding tadpoles. It's a footless feeling I have, of floating. Of being led into her world. At fifteen years of age, J too had her problems.

'I tried cutting off my excess fleshy bits.'

'Which bits?'

As I ask, I'm inspecting her midriff.

'Not there. I like my belly,' she says, patting it.

'I hated my earlobes and the chunk of fat hanging under my baby toes.'

'There's fat there?'

'Don't you know yourself?'

It's true – J has no earlobes. What about her tits, I want to ask. Are they unnecessary 'fleshy bits'?

'Do you want to see things?' she asks.

'What things?'

'It's a surprise.'

The arty get-up, the tattoos, the boots: it's touch-and-go if I have the bottle for this, if I have the guts for her, but then I think, what the heck. J invites me back to her studio apartment. I feel a shot of panic, gunfire in each heartbeat. Am I ready for this? Or am I misreading the vibes? I'm uncertain if we're about to do something. Perhaps all the weird talk is foreplay. Perhaps it's not. I don't know, and not knowing is titillating.

'Have you ever thought about the relationship you have with things?'

'No.'

But it's a lie. I have. I'm shocked that she even asked me. I'm scared of what it might mean, if we are the only two souls who think about the life in things. Are we the perfect match?

J asks me to close my eyes as she introduces me one-by-one to the objects that she lives with: this is a book, this is an oriental figurine, feel this plate, this plant I've had for years. And so on it goes. Bizarrely, I find it cathartic. We're on the same wavelength. Like a blind man, I continue on my own around the room, feeling the shape of her things, caressing the contours of objects.

I open my eyes and see that J is sitting on the bed, watching me. I pick up a jug and run a hand over it. I wonder if she's thinking how I might feel her body? The ritual of touching objects has the effect of condensing the bedroom down, sub-dividing it into the minutest of parts, focusing my attention, reducing life, to the tiniest of things. The little things make the big things complete. She's watchful of me as I touch each item. From across the room, there's a healthy tension between us. She's watching to see if the objects rebuke my friendship in the way, say, that a pet might reject a stroke.

Do the things that J owns speak to me? Yes. They are the clues to who she is, the ingredients that make her up. But the end-goal is one that I don't understand. Is this a charade to slow me down, to increase my desires and whet my appetite, so that I digest her in bite-size portions? Is it? Well then, the candle would fall off the mantelpiece, the books off the bedside table, the painting off the wall, when fucking goes on in her bed. I say this to the objects. Then I shoot J a look. Reading my mind, she blushes. She straightens her blouse, composes herself, then, just as quickly, sulks.

She asks me to leave. She scrawls a telephone number on a piece of paper, and bids me farewell, with the words: 'All in good time'.

Out on the street I'm lost, floating. At the same time, I feel heavy. Our alchemy, was it a put on? Can animal attraction lie? I feel humiliated that I'm under her command, me, the obedient dog. It matters not, I have her number. The pursuit has only begun. And anyway, don't I want a master?

A destiny.

∞

When J and I next meet, I'm introduced without warning to sadomasochism. We're out to dinner in a posh joint. I've splashed out and invited her. To oblige – and perhaps to mark the occasion – she ditches the plastic boots. Beneath a fitted dress she wears flat slippers.

'I thought that we mightn't meet again,' she says.

'Yet here we are.'

'Yes. We are. Here.'

J has the measure of me. As I bite into a piece of bleeding steak, she stabs me in the leg with a fork under the table and simultaneously tips over a glass of red wine to excuse my agonizing shriek. I stare at her, wordless. The table is reset. When the waiter departs, and me staring confusedly at her, J reaches her hand under the table, squeezes my balls and says:

'I'm meat hungry now.'

The time has come to knock the mountings off the wall. Back at her apartment, she removes her clothes and wraps a black plastic refuse bag over her head. She holds out her arms so as not to bang into things as she approaches me. She unhooks my belt and I take off my trousers. She pushes me backwards onto the bed.

Fucking without her eyes on me allows me to study her body. Her skin is wafer-thin, and along the length of her arms I notice her shimmering blue veins; they twitch as if silverfish are swimming through her. Her lithe frame is spotted like a Dalmatian's, with upwards of a hundred homemade tattoos dotted around her body. They all show numbers. Maybe they're a safety measure in case she explodes, so that she can be pieced back together, number by number.

My eyes water, and she blurs before me. She looks like a sheet of paper with a strange algorithm. On her chest, over her heart, I make out the numbers '999'. Upside down, it reads '666'. How preposterous, I think, and begin fucking her harder. I want to see if I can make the house collapse and the devil appear.

She directs my hands to her neck, and urges me to squeeze. I throttle her. Through the black bag, she begs for more. I let my hands and body bear down more heavily on her. Without oxygen, the bag is sucked in around the contours of her face, outlining her features. Her face is like a black plastic sculpture. I could be fucking and killing a black baby, all at once. The witch springs to mind. The bitch. I kiss her. I kiss the plastic bag, and roll my tongue over it. I wonder if I'm smudging her strawberry-red lipstick.

J writhes and, to hold her in place, I thrust harder, sticking it in her, up to the hilt. We fight for a few moments, and then I let out a primal roar and spill my seed into her. I desecrated her. I am a lion. If I liked, I could break her brittle bones, or ring her twiglike neck. Under me, she's a helpless child.

I collapse on top of her. J gives a kick, and manages to loosen my grip on her throat. Near asphyxiated, she whips off the bag, sits up in bed and draws in lungfuls of air. I don't ask how she is. We share no words. When she has recovered, she waves me away. I get dressed and leave. She once chillingly warned me: 'I'm for fucking and forgetting'. The new mantra of my life. There's no going back. She's too much of a puzzle. As for me, I've learned the lesson.

I can be savage.

∞

Witch voodoo.

A chicken almost sends me to the grave.

Returning home to my room one evening, I treat myself to a firewood-roasted chicken. By the early hours of the morning, I've stomach cramps that feel like I'm being eaten alive from within. I'm doubled over in pain, too weak to stand or to call for help. I can't even get a drink or race to the bathroom. I piss in the bed and vomit on the floor. I'm feverish and have the sweats.

I have salmonella poisoning. It looked so harmless the previous night, as I ripped apart the chicken's ribcage and drunkenly devoured the flesh. But right now, I swear that if I survive I'll never eat chicken again...

I survive. It must have been a message. I return for more. I buy two raw chicken breasts, bathe them in a delicious marinade and half cook them. Then I leave them on the counter overnight. The next day, I eat one chicken breast. But nothing happens. I feel fine.

I'm irritated, so I buy a half-kilo of shrimp. That night, I put the remaining chicken breast on the windowsill. The next day I walk around with the piece of chicken in a jacket pocket to let the bacteria grow. I let the shrimp stew in my other pocket.

At the main drag, I sit in the window of a café sipping a *café con leche* and nibble on chicken breast. I peel a few shrimp and pop them in my mouth. I'm building up for a religious experience. A crucifixion perhaps?

I'm on tenterhooks as I observe myself, eager to spot the first signs of food poisoning. By early evening, my stomach gurgles. But the thing is, since my earlier food poisoning, my stomach has built up a tolerance. At first, it puts up a good fight, as I'm forced into emptying out the danger, with a bout of the squirts.

Later on, it kicks in, but I'm prepared for it. I've bedside liquids at the ready, damp cloths, toilet roll, a plastic bottle cut in half for a bedpan and a bucket to vomit in. I even prepared my last will and left my air gun to a childhood friend, Paul.

Later still, I almost croak.

I writhe, kick and scream. The demons have taken me. The pain doubles in strength and I become hoarse. The neighbors call the police. The police call the fire brigade. They break down the door.

I'm obstinate, adamant that I don't need help. They can use my body for medical research if they leave me alone. They don't know what to make of my rants. To call a priest to perform an exorcism or fetch a doctor? I'm too delirious to make sense. I forget my name, then almost remember it. And then, I kind of forget it again.

A man from the American consulate arrives. He has misunderstood. He thought a murder was on the cards. I'm not someone to help make his name.

'Who are you?' he asks.

'Cage.'

He looks at my dark green passport and whispers to the policeman. I grasp the basic message: I'm confused and am not who I say I am. It's not an American matter.

'What brought you here?' the Embassy man asks.

'Good question,' I say. 'You answer first. If you fare well, I'll have a go.'

'We're trying to help you.'

I give him a blank look. He gives up. With a shrug, he's gone.

The others start to pry, to make sense of me, the police and the fire brigade. They seem to care more about who I am than the possibility of me dying. How can I not know myself, they ask. They ignore my insults. Then they discover the chicken and shrimp. All becomes clear: what I've eaten, who I am. An ambulance crew arrives and manhandles me into a cot, fastening the straps to stop my flaying. The whole way to the ambulance, I curse weakly, as the beginnings of a crowd gather around.

At the hospital, they puncture my vein with a needle. It's so exquisite, an object piercing the skin, the needle. The thermometer, cold in my mouth, strikes 101 degrees Fahrenheit. I'm put on medication and a drip for a few days. All these objects inside me, prodding, and all I can think about is J. The hospital staff wants to know if I have contacts in England — why I have no idea. Forget J, instead I could plead for Isabella, yet I refuse to mention either of them. Isabella would love to nurse me. But I don't want to climb down or show weakness. I'll die first. There's nobody, I say. I have nobody.

I caught a curious strain. It's a hybrid of shellfish and chicken poisoning. They've never seen anything like it. They ask me if I would allow them to keep a sample of the bacillus. My insides going public, becoming part of science? Apparently there's learning to be found in me. Yeah, sure, I say. I imagine a killer germ named after me.

But truthfully, I think differently. During my convalescence at the hands of these celestial nurses and their squeaky rubber soles, I realize that I may have killed the virus but had best not try that stunt again. Unless I'm really bored.

Chapter 4

68 Whiskey

1995

Nobody gets away with it.

I go to see Raúl Barrera, nephew of *el Patrón*.

If Mexico is my second home, then visiting my father's childhood friend, is an attempt to meet my own people. But it also means that their war is my war. I recall seeing *el Patrón's* arrest on TV in 1989 and my father commenting how they used to play together as boys. It didn't surprise me that Dad never mentioned that his friend was responsible for torturing Kiki Camarena to death. He was always going to side with his Mexican friend over a DEA agent.

El Patrón being on television triggered a curiosity in my roots. Don Miguel Angel looked psychotic. He had been on the run before his arrest and sported a thick dark beard and had a matching thatch of hair. His eyes floated around his head like he was high. All said, he looked barbaric, a primitive man. He seemed to be constantly speaking to himself as the TV cameras followed his extradition to the US. It's then I wondered about going there and studied a map of the world to learn about Mexico. I learned that people kill each other over drugs. That soldiers and helicopters can't stop the drug lords. That it's lunacy, the country taken hostage, and that it gives America a headache. I had to see the anarchy with my own two eyes.

In Mexico hatred bubbles beneath the surface, until it erupts. In jail, the cartel factions are segregated, their privileged status allowing each side to wear their own prison clothing.

I ask the guy that I've been getting my drugs from to speak to someone higher up. The next night, one of Raúl Barrera's men approaches me at a seafront bar. Juan wears a suit but no tie. He's fortyish, tall, athletic, and has a healthy head of hair. Without introducing himself, he asks if he may join me. We settle into an easy chat. He's courteous and educated, cunning and dangerous. I have him pegged for a cartel lawyer. He takes my dark green passport in his hand.

'Rivera.'

'Yes.'

'You're one of ours?'

'My dad is from Culiacán. He and *el Patrón* were childhood friends.'

'You're Mexican?'

'Yes.'

Juan returns my passport. He smiles politely. Dryly. We relax. He opens up. I think. He's hard to read. He'd make a good actor.

'You've been running drugs to tourists all season. You're young, maybe idealistic.'

He prods the table with an index finger as he lectures me. Beneath his smooth skin and coiffed hair is the machinery of a savage. His cartel slaughters people every day, yet he is mannerly, indeed posh.

'Juan, I didn't ask to see anyone from my father's town as I wanted to make my own way in Mexico. I'm not political and fuck the authorities, if that's what you mean.'

I say it with steel but no sooner urge myself to be wary. Act dumb. Maybe I am. He moves away from touchy subjects, favoring educating me about Mexican history. I'm bored. I zone out when he goes on about the Mexican-American War and the notion of 'manifest destiny'.

'The Americans wish to impose their high example on us. But this is not their country.'

The next day a large black car fetches me. I ask where the driver is bringing me and he replies with something about the weather. Around he drives, until he's sure that he's not being followed. I'm brought to an industrial area of the city and the car pulls up outside a warehouse.

In I walk and the steel gate automatically closes behind me. A man, as smartly dressed as Juan, greets me. He's out of place in this warehouse. It must be a vetting point.

'I know where someone is,' I say.

'Who?'

'That would be telling.'

He smiles and two men with guns join us. They're not polished, one wearing a muscle top and the smaller one with a Hawaiian shirt and a protruding gut. The fat one pokes me in the ribs with a pistol. He looks like he might kill me for fun.

'I want to help.'

'How?'

'I told you, I know where someone is.'

'And I asked, who?'

'Not one of your men.'

'Is that so?'

'Yeah.'

'What do you want?'

'To meet Raúl Barrera.'

All three men laugh. The man in the suit takes my hand and puts something cold in it. Meeting my eyes, he closes my fist around it. I look down and see that I'm holding my first silver bullet. It's time to come clean.

'There's this guy I ran into. Salazar.'

Pass go. On I go. Raúl Barrera is holed up in a hacienda nearby. It's a big house in a street full of them. I bet his neighbors are investment bankers or corrupt politicians. Entry to the cul-de-sac is controlled by private security. They have semi-automatic rifles and shelter behind a fortified bunker. Once we pass this checkpoint, the next line of interrogators, at the gates to the mansion, become confused. What do I want? They're suspicious. They don't buy my story. Then Raúl Barrera emerges from the house to greet me. He's given my Mexican passport, which he studies carefully. 'Antonio Rivera,' he repeats to himself.

85

'Just like your father.'

'Yes.'

'My uncle would be so pleased. What a pleasure.'

Raúl has a mongoloid look, a low hairline and deep lines in his small forehead, just like the Hulk. Beneath bushy eyebrows, his eyes are jolly. His shoulders are rounded. Naked, he'd be soft and pudgy. He's like a kid trapped in a psychopath's body. I bet he would laugh as he tortured you. He's the incarnation of the word 'demonic'.

Raúl leads me through the house, to a table in the shade by a swimming pool, bordered by green grass. Two children play in the pool, a boy and girl. A few men with semi-automatic weapons patrol the perimeter wall. There are also surveillance cameras but it's the fluorescent green grass that catches my eye, a manicured lawn the likes of which I've never seen.

A pitcher of sangria is served. Raúl fishes out the fruit from his glass, sips, and smiles.

'You should visit my uncle.'

'It would be a pleasure.'

To visit him in a jail cell in the US? I don't enquire what he means and get to the point.

'I have information.'

'Compromised?'

I'm confused and it shows.

'You're twenty?'

'Nineteen.'

'You ask to meet me and want to give me information. Why?'

'I have my own reasons.'

'A teenage informant? This isn't the place to play games. You understand?'

'I do. With respect, I was looking forward to meeting you but I thought I should bring something.'

'A gift?'

'Hopefully.'

'You'll dog me if he gets it.'
'Actually, no.'
'Actually no?'
'Yes.'
'No, he won't get what's coming to him or no you won't go to the cops?'
'The latter.'
'The latter?'
'I won't squeal.'
'How do I know?'
'What if I came?'
'Came?'
'I could come along.'
'Why?'
'To watch.'
'Why would I trust you?'
'You wouldn't have to.'
'How does that work?'
'I'd be an accomplice.'
'No wires.'
'You can search me.'

He scratches his head, looks at his children splashing in the pool, and then studies me.

'Do you have political opinions?'
'No.'
'You will if you do this.'
'Probably.'
'So,' he says with a wink, 'where is he?'

A chef sizzles meat on a barbecue. Raúl throws an arm over my shoulder and we go over and order bloody steaks. We understand one another. I check out. Over dinner, we get down to the details.

'How do you know it's not a set-up?'
'I was in the brothel. It slipped out as an after-thought. They had me

down as an innocent American. Salazar's friend, a security guy, didn't realize he said it.'

'Rivera, if it's not religion, then what's your motivation?'

'I'm not religious.'

He laughs.

'What I'm asking is, what's your game?'

'I told you, I have my own reasons. Maybe I just want to know how torture works.'

'How's that?'

'Why people bother resisting interrogation.'

It's the first time that Raúl gives a curious look. I confuse him. But fuck him, right? I don't even understand myself. There are ghosts in me. All I know is that there are different ways of dying, and I want a shot at the worst kind.

∞

We take Route 40 into the Sierra Madre foothills. It's dark as we drive through the old colonial town of Concordia. On we go, three black cars, winding our way up the mountain, past illegal drug farms, and heading towards the picturesque village of Copala. We stop at the outskirts. Raúl and I are in the middle of the convoy. Men from the other cars approach our window. They agree that we should wait as they tour the surrounding roads. In half an hour they're back and the mission is on.

We leave the cars and wait in the hills. We're waiting to see if there's any movement in front of us, and ensure that nobody catches us from behind. No booby traps.

'He's in the house on the right?' Raúl asks.

We're overlooking a walled compound of two houses, both tastefully built in the Mexican style. The nearest hacienda is a two-story befitting a drug lord, with white stucco walls, arched tile roofs and intricate windows to show off the arches. An elaborate entrance hangs over the driveway so that a car can pull up under the front porch. Across the courtyard is a smaller house, a Mission Style home, and clearly the residence for the hired guns.

'Rivera. Here's the deal: you must strip. Now.'
'I'm not taking my clothes off.'
'Then the operation is not happening.'
'Why?'
'We're not taking chances. It could be a set-up.'
'But I'm with you. I'm complicit if anything goes wrong.'
Raúl thinks about this and seems to agree.
'Still, humor me. We go no further unless you strip now.'
'I'll freeze.'
'But we'll know that you don't have a fancy wire on you.'
'I don't.'
'Fine for you to say. Call it. What's it to be?'

I'm a naturist on the loose. The night is bitter cold and the wind on my bare skin gives me goose pimples. My skin gleams pink, as we sit in a gulley in the wilds of Sierra Madre. Around me are ten murderers, snug as a rug in their black attire. I never imagined that one day I'd be hiding out in the hills of Mexico, hoping to spring on a drug cartel's henchman, while freezing my butt off, stark naked.

I didn't sleep the night. I felt sick, disconcerted. But then I set myself straight. I know where I stand. I'm an American along for a joyride with these wild Mexicans. Once I cross off that concern, another worry overcomes me: I'm fearful of what I mightn't allow myself. Is this it, the sum total of me? Am I now, at nineteen, a formed man, my mind made up about myself, about what my limits are? Or am I willing to push my boundaries and experiment, so that I can learn more about myself and grow?

'Put this on. It'll keep you warm.'

Raúl smirks as he throws me my underpants and a balaclava. I pull the woolly thing over my head and my breath feels warm. Peering through the eyeholes, I see that we're all hooded up, and then we're off. Balaclaved, we make our way down the hill, spread out, one flanking the next, our eyes pinned to the compound we're honing in on. All ten men are tooled up, carrying phosphorous grenades, semi-automatics, and revolvers on their belts and, I suspect, a back-up handgun or knife strapped to their ankle. I'm unarmed.

I dance barefoot through the overgrowth, a tingling in my bones. I feel heavy, burdened down by decisions and doubts. I urge myself onwards, to be brave, to be free of prejudice, to act freely. I can criticize my actions later on and reign in my free spirit, if I overstepped the mark. But for now, I tell myself to be silent. Be an observer, witness life, promote death.

∞

They celebrate capturing Santiago Salazar by almost kicking him to death. There's nothing I can do about it. I made the introductions; now he's theirs.

Before we captured the old man's son, I heard the thud of a grenade exploding in the house next-door and the sound of muffled gunfire. I don't know how many they got, but my adventure will go down as a bloodbath and not as a single murder.

Santiago had been boiling a pot of tea, a slice of cake already cut, and he had the presence of mind to fling the pan of boiling water at one of us. It got soaked up by a screaming balaclava. Moments later, his pretty-boy face is smashed into the ground. His blood-drenched curly hair is handy to grip as his head is pounded by a wrench. He's dragged outside and brought to a garage. He regains consciousness, with gasping breaths, when a bucket of water is thrown on his face. With the blood washed away, I can see him clearer.

Santiago Salazar is the spitting image of his father, the old man I robbed in Le Muse. He's mid-twenties and has shaggy hair down over his ears. His face is already beginning to swell.

All hope is lost. Santiago breaths a sigh of resignation, accepting that he must die. Painfully. He thinks his clan is worth fighting for and won't give up their whereabouts. He fears breaking his promise, of being broken. It's passive resistance. Death is nothing but the marks on his body will speak volumes. They'll call him courageous and in the afterlife, he'll be a hero. His method is dumb.

Raúl whispers to Santiago, tries to talk sense into him. Take a bullet instead. His gruesome death is not only one man's tears but also his families. But Santiago isn't listening. He holds his head high, his eyes fixed on the distant wall beneath a red Porsche.

'The bible says: "Greater love hath no man than that he lay down his life for his friends." John 15:13.'

Raúl smiles. He's in the habit of reciting the phrase before going to work on someone. During the hour in which he's tortured, his face swells twofold, his puffy eyes turning into slits. Like a rancid fish.

Santiago behaves like a sheep, relenting, and accepting his lot. He's in the zone, his day of reckoning come. After the initial punches, he stops crying out. It's hard to get the balance right, to measure the dose: painful, while not yet fatal. Raúl seems to know all this. He puts on a butcher's apron, which materialized out of nowhere. He looks a sight: black balaclava, white apron, and wielding a knife.

Santiago is stripped and lashed to a pillar. Now he and I both stand naked, facing one another, at opposite sides of the garage, me wearing only underpants and a balaclava, he wearing only blood.

Raúl is in a frenzy, happy to move to the next level.

'You, you,' he says to me, pointing with his knife. 'You want to see pain? Watch and learn.'

With promise delivered, Raúl returns to his work. I can't swallow: my throat is dry. I almost daren't look. He grabs Santiago's testicle and almost rips it from the body. Using his knife, he crudely hacks it off. Santiago lets out a wild roar. As he has already been made toothless, he has no way of refusing the testicle as it's forced into his bloody mouth.

'If you swallow, I'll give you a clean one in the head.'

But Santiago knows the score and unflinchingly faces into it, choosing pain. An autopsy revealing an eaten testicle would indicate compromise under interrogation. Santiago spits his testicle back at Raúl, and it lands squarely on his forehead. Santiago stares at him with a manic grin. He tries to sing, but I can't make out the tune. He's gargling on his blood.

The drug mafias can tell the point at which their men break under torture. It's all down to the history that can be read on a cadaver, how the person manages to frustrate his murderers by resisting and holding out. Bodies un-maimed and given a bullet are a cause for concern – they're the broken ones. Equally, once cut, if there's only a small pool of blood before a bullet, it implies that the tortured person might have capitulated to get a swift one in the back of the head.

Raúl is professional about the business of death. First, he breaks Santiago's jaw. Then he takes an ear. Then the tongue. The blows to his face and body are the only sound, as Santiago makes none. But then he begins to cough, expelling blood. He's gagging like a drowning man. The coughing levels off, weakens, and becomes gargling breaths, as his vitality leaves him.

Unbelievable, the things people are willing to die for. His end is art.

He's returning to earth, to the lush green mountains, to his beloved Mexican land. His blood is already feeding the soil. His tongue was cast onto the floor. My eyes search for it, as if Santiago is a jigsaw to be pieced back together.

His head lolls as he seems to notice, with pride, the pool of blood that he's swimming in, propped up as he is by his bindings. Then he's gone. Santiago is elsewhere, outside himself, floating on euphoria. He lasted. He's dead.

I wince a little. 'To hell with you', were his last words. He had the final say. Tongueless Santiago made his point. You may take my body but still not hurt me. My soul lives on, yes, in you. What you have done to me, my comrades will do tenfold to you.

That day I learned that resisting torture is the only real silence, the only real stare. What I didn't understand was the need for balaclavas once we secured the place. After all, Santiago was never coming out alive. Perhaps it was to hide from the surveillance cameras, or was it to hide from ourselves, to shield us from our actions, to hide from the shame. Or, maybe, it was to leave a little innocence in their other lives, as they are men with children.

They, his torturers - indeed us (as I was complicit) - we told him who he was; his carve up was not in vain. He was martyred for a doubtful cause: power. Santiago won. They (we?) couldn't break him. He held out, and then came the release, the reward. Death. He can return to earth having once lived.

When Santiago's head slumped forwards, we didn't celebrate. I felt dirty and used, an instrument of his immortality. He had taken a stand. There was a strange silence in the garage afterwards. I wanted to wash Santiago to see what was left, but there was no time. I spied the slice of cake that he had left behind. How did it get in here? It had flecks of blood on it, otherwise I would have eaten it. I'm galled. His tongue too would go to waste, unless a dog gets it.

Raúl sheathes his knife, and all ten men wordlessly turn to leave. Suddenly, they face me, my erect cock pointing back at them. They filed past me as I braced myself for the cold.

∞

That was then.

This is now.

Five years later.

Before I left Mexico, another visitor made their way to my door. The cops. They gave me a warning. They knew I was a smalltime drug dealer to the tourists. They were passing the information on to their American colleagues. I wasn't worried about the authorities in either jurisdiction, what concerned me was who had eyes on me when they paid me a visit.

I'd seen the extent to which members of the drug cartels would go. If in doubt, kill. At Santiago Salazar's funeral, revenge was promised. I didn't want to be on a hit list. Mexicans are savages. Even back in New

York I didn't feel entirely safe. I had no home. I needed a new beginning. I had no choice but to enlist.

∞

Sarajevo.

We stormed the house by day. It wasn't much of a risk. Our marksmen are better than a lone sniper. When they barged into the bedroom, our point man shot the Serb in the head, no questions asked. But he also got Aleza who was in bed beside him. I'm tending to her, as she lies naked beneath a blanket that soaks up her blood.

She took one in the leg. Her long leg peers out from the blanket as I apply a tourniquet. Aleza screams when I touch her. I don't speak her language but imagine she's telling me that it hurts. I touch her again and she punches me in the face. I'm laid out on the floor and the soldiers around me laughing. I get back up, wipe blood from my nose, and give Aleza something for the pain, holding the tablets out like she's a wild hyena. There's not much more I can do.

'I'll stay with her until an ambulance comes.'

'Doc, you won't leave the room?'

'Fully understood, captain.'

My plan works. The grunts leave. Next, I have to get Aleza into my way of thinking.

'Do you have foreign blood in your family?'

'Foreigner?'

'Your family, do they come from other places?'

Aleza thinks it's an ethnic questions when all I really want to know is if Russian soldiers once fucked her people, and if it's why she's so desirable. That's the extent of my curiosity in her bloodline. The medication I gave her kicks in and, lying beside the dead Serb, she confesses her mission.

Beauty is her weapon. Aleza lures enemy commanders to her bed. There they die. Maybe it was Aleza herself who gave us the tip off. She's

Bosnian and, unfortunately for her, also Muslim. The religious hurdle aside, turning me on is the furthest thing from her mind, given the carnage she witnessed.

I'm in Bosnia. The 1st Armored Division should be confined to the northeast of the country but we didn't trust the French with our intel, so we came to Sarajevo.

'Do you enjoy it?'

'Killing or sex?'

'Killing.'

'The enemy are dogs. If I don't kill them, they kill my people.'

Her little sister was raped, and then had her throat cut. Both parents were butchered. It's why Aleza became a ninja whore. Revenge. But it comes at a cost. She looks like a girl exhausted after too much sex.

Her face is sculpted like an automobile. More Ferrari than Porsche, she's all sharp angles and edges, the deep gorges in her cheeks accentuating her mountainous cheekbones. To suffer starvation can be so attractive. Her lupine eyes consume my gaze. They would make anyone believe her pleading cries: *please help; they're slaughtering my people, so stop thinking about fucking me.*

In a warzone there's no time for pleasantries and, what's more, there's no reason to be mannerly. I wonder if I could interest her in earning a few dollars. I stand up and poke a finger through the buttons of my pants. She lets out a heavy sigh and turns away, preferring to face the dead man. I don't know why she's acting like such a bitch after I saved her life. I only wanted to worm a measly bit of pleasure out of her plight.

'It only takes a minute.'

She remains tight-lipped. She isn't up for a friendly orgasm. She won't open up, body or mind. She'd kill me if I stick my dick in her without permission. I bet she steals the wallets of her dead victims. I work another angle, satisfying my curiosity.

'You only get to go in the ambulance if you answer my questions.'

'Or what?'

'I leave you here for the Serbs to get revenge.'

Aleza turns back to face me. I clench my teeth. I'm not bluffing. I'm suffering burnout. Every war is a blur. My commanding officer, Captain Sloan, says that nobody is special and, once you accept that fact, you'll either be liberated, or eternally confused. What he says, goes. Uniquely for a man with soft hands, who never made the college football team, he manages to keep it together. Captain Sloan is posh, right down to his habit of wearing a military V-necked sweater at all times, even in the desert heat. But he's also sensitive. He knows that since my last stint in Iraq that I've been finding it tough going. Massacre here, genocide there, who cares? I once found a booby-trapped bomb *inside* a wounded child. Counseling has been suggested more than once.

Captain Sloan says it's not war that we're fighting, but meaning. We're competing with other events on the evening news. Show business is where the news is. 'If it bleeds, it leads' – nope, not anymore. Our priorities are muddled up. Real news has become the sidebar story, as celebrity trivia is center stage. Only false universes count. There's a blurring of boundaries between fact and fiction, and skepticism about what's reality. Mortality is only a plotline. Personally, give me a starving Bosnian Muslim about to be slaughtered over Big Brother any day of the week.

Wars and reality TV do have some things in common. The 'contestants' - real or otherwise - are always being (mock) rescued, but in wars the 'actors' don't always survive. In this regard, I take off my hat to General Mladic's only daughter. She invented a hybrid news piece: she mixed war with reality TV. Her dad is a genocidal warlord. But his daughter outwitted him. She saw the futility of her situation, as her father tried to become the next Hitler. She wanted to ensure that her poisonous bloodline stopped, so she topped herself. Touché. Now everybody in her family has killed someone.

War complicates. Nobody is up for the fun of war.

'Ask your question.'

'How many men have you killed?'

'I don't know.'

'You lost count or you can't remember?'

'I can't be sure all are dead.'

What am I doing here? I prefer wars where I have to wear sunscreen. The Bosnians don't even have a beach. It's baffling. Why does anybody want to fight over this godforsaken land? Operation Joint Endeavour is bullshit.

Captain Sloan says we're not allowed to take sides. Impartiality is our slogan. We're here under the auspices of NATO as part of the Implementation Force in Bosnia. The Serbs are carving up Bosnia (and the Muslims), as the pro-Nazi Croat Ustaše do the same from the western flank. Serbian expansionism and Croatian nationalism are choking Bosnian Muslims in the middle. It's Europe's biggest land grab since Hitler.

My commanding officer is fed up with the politics of this operation. We're deployed alongside the Russians in a peacekeeping brief. He tries to laugh it off, showing that he can poke fun at himself. He even wrote to the makers of the board game, Trivial Pursuit, suggesting that they incorporate his question: What do a Slovene rock band, a yogurt revolution and a bad game of football have in common? Answer: They precipitated the downfall of Tito's Yugoslavia.

I have a better idea for a game.

'Do you have a job?'

Aleza shakes off my gaze and looks beyond me, indeed, through me.

'This side-line, the murdering-hooker thing, that's a mission, not a job, right?'

She looks at her wounded leg, and raises her head again.

'Factory close long time ago. We no work. No food. We know not what do.'

'Who are the "we" that you are referring to?'

I find it remarkable that she's in the habit of using the collective pronoun. We. Who does she mean? Has she blanked the fact that her family has been snuffed out? She looks down, as though ashamed. Then I hear sniffles. An act? I proffer a hanky. She focuses on me with a look of steely determination. It says, 'Fuck you and your sympathy.' Sure, have it that way, so I pocket the hanky.

'"We" is my people. Muslim people,' Aleza says, as though I butchered them.

'Would you like to come with me? For something to eat?'

'No. I bury my family.'

She's lying. With her parents gone, she's free to do as she likes. Why hold back?

There's something in her that I find hauntingly desirable. Perhaps it's her ability to flare up, and be lethal like a python. Or maybe she's more scorpion-like, what with the way she kills her lovers. I'd like to experience the erotic danger but not here and not now, as an ambulance is on the way. I'd also like to know the survival rate; how many men survive having sex with her? While on the subject, I'd also love to know if she has sex with her victims before slaughtering them.

Conquering her kind and staying alive would be like playing chess against a grand master. You need to worm your way under her skin – show a little vulnerability, to get her onside before dominating. It's like taming a lion. What's more, Aleza has a glimmer of the man-beater about her. At first, I imagine that you'd have to take a beating from her, before changing the tune and becoming her abuser. Then again, it might just be the mood she's in, pissed off that her family was annihilated. Maybe otherwise she'd be gentle and full of gaiety.

∞

It's odd, but I'm suddenly self-conscious. *How did I become me?* Perhaps my last girlfriend was right about me. Still, how could she have known, how could she see through me? Me, a faithless man, pretending to help the wounded. Why do they always send me, a lone operator, to these wars? Why do I accompany soldiers on risky missions? Why do I volunteer? Aleza sits up in bed. She asks me something. I wave her away. Dismissively. I'm done. I'm fed up. But she persists and points outside.

Is it the ambulance? I snap out of it and rush to the window.

I hurry back to Aleza in the bed. Just to talk.

'Crunch time. Aleza, if you had to rape a nation to death, which one?'

'Why you ask?'

'Because you are in the business. You fuck and kill. I want to know what it takes for real attraction to exist. Must there be an element of rape about it?'

'Is the ambulance outside?'

'Answer my question.'

Aleza gives me a nervous look and then looks at the window. There's the sound of men on the street. Her saviors or the enemy?

'Aleza which country do you rape until death?'

'America.'

'Why?'

'Because I hate.'

'You hate Americans. Good choice. But rape is based on attraction, so you ought to rape someone that you are attracted to. You rape the sexy ones, like you. Would you like if I raped you to death?'

'No.'

'Aleza, I don't understand you. You do not pass go. You stay here.'

'Please, no. Don't leave me.'

The shouts from the street are getting nearer. They're Serb.

'Aleza it's your fault. It's woman's fault. You're too strong.'

I don't know what I'm saying. All I know is that I'm blurting it out. I have to stop this halfwayness, this starting and stopping, half-halting my way through life without having the bottle to finally, fully, either start or stop it. Aleza looks at me, imploringly. I turn on my heels and start running, leaving her in bed with the dead Serb and his comrades about to make an interesting discovery.

∞

Back home.

I've taken a mistress of sorts, a new plaything, while stringing along my on-off girlfriend.

Becky isn't much, but is at least something. She slides out of one bed and into the next, never asking questions, as she drags around her three-year-old. Before me, Becky dated three other soldiers from my base. Sometimes I call her by Satphone, less to keep her up to speed than for me to keep up to speed with her. I yearn for stories of mundane life back home. She's my sounding board. I know she'll keep things trivial and mix in a bit of madness. It's what makes men love her, her insanity, but so too her pliable body. She works in a bar, and with the tips, earns more than me. Her life is casual and easy. I'm conscious of my novelty wearing off.

'How's Brewer's Bar?' I enquire.

'Full of the usual Joes. How's it going there?'

'Same old. It's hell and I love it.'

It's difficult to move beyond pleasantries. Say too much and she cries, say too little and she thinks I'm hiding something. I can only lose. It can only end. Yet I persist in the folly. It's male-female relations the world over. But it's awkward being your lover's hero.

'I wish I could be with you,' Becky says.

'Me too.'

It's a trap. It isn't enough to tell her about war life. She wants to share my adventures and not just listen to them.

'Can I visit?'

'It's not that kind of place.'

'But you never take me anywhere.'

'Where do you want to go?'

'Somewhere with you. Doc, are you listening to me?'

'Lima Charlie. But Becky, you can't come. You wouldn't understand.'

She huffs. A silence descends. I've insulted her.

∞

Back to here.

My angle of attack shifts.

The blood of locals must be thick. Out on the streets of Sarajevo, they wander the sub-zero streets wearing few clothes. I kick a frozen piece of shit along the road, mistaking it for a stone. Even the piss in the open gutter freezes. The stench of decomposing bodies, ever present in summer, is now, in winter, less apparent. The dead survive for longer, resisting decomposition.

I shouldn't be alone but a combat medic has special dispensations. I'm not on a tight leash, indeed, as a war medic, I'm not supposed to be involved, being a kind of auxiliary support to the soldiers.

My trouser legs are muddy and wet with sewage and blood. In a gutter, a dog is licking the blood off the face of a dead man. His master, I hope.

A white-painted UN truck approaches, so high off the ground, so virginal, so pure. A soldier in a blue helmet is propped up in the hatch. I raise a hand and he stops.

'Let me guess. You're going to collect a girl with a gun wound?'

'Who are you?'

'I'm out of place, I know, but I'm 1st Armored Division. US army.'

'Wait.'

The French soldier dips into the bombproof vehicle to discuss me. He reappears at the hatch and wonders what I'm doing wandering the streets alone. I mumble something about humanity – the pity of Bosnians clinging to me, clinging to life, and how the crippled and starved are a world away from us as we cruise around in a UNPROFOR vehicle, two feet above it all. It's the talk of someone who has served for too long.

'What about the wounded girl?' he asks.

'Stable. She's already evacuated.'

'You a combat medic?'

'Yes, sir. 68W.'

The French soldier smiles. The back door is opened and in I jump.

Inside is a mix of grunts: two Brits, a Frenchman, and an olive looking soldier, either an Italian or a Turk.

'How long you been stationed here?' the British soldier asks.

'Two months, sir. A few more months and I'll be relieved.'

'Back to America? What are you, age wise?'

'25, sir.'

'You have family?'

'No. No wife, as I don't want to get a Dear John letter, sir.'

I nod to the Major's wedding band and there's laughter as I'm suggesting that back home his wife will shack up with another. The British Major smiles. I imagine he's conjuring up an image of his sex-starved young wife back home. He almost makes me pine after my own deeply meaningful union.

We talk some more, but I'm disinterested. It's safe chat. Boring. Comparing the military in the US versus the UK. The truck lurches and I grab the bench with my hands. Then we screech to a halt. I spring upright, alert. But it's nothing; perhaps some people blocking the road. I squeeze the bench again. My right index finger throbs; it's my war wound. The top of my finger is swollen and bulbous red, in marked contrast to the whiteness of my other fingers. It became infected after some nail biting.

The vehicle starts to move and I enjoy its comforting hum. We settle into a silence which is only broken when the British soldiers become immune to our presence, and resume mouthing off, yapping about the difference between army grub in Bosnia and back at base. They're trained to discuss things that don't matter.

Through my finger infection, I feel camaraderie with the natives. I know what it's like to hurt, to bleed. My own little sacrifice. It reminds me to check my nose and I do, picking the dry blood, and I curse Aleza under my breath. But I like to be forced to take notice of myself. Ever since meeting J back in Mexico, I've become more aware of surfaces, of touching things, and the grounding sensation when I graze my hand against different materials. I'm also in the habit of tasting sweet-smelling shampoos. I'm an amalgam of things: part-man, part-shampoo, and not forgetting the splinter in my finger. All these things complete me and help me feel part of the world.

'You got a nick there, soldier?'

It's the other Brit who says it. I hold my finger up and we all look at it.

'It's nothing. I won't die, honest.'

He laughs. I pop my finger in my mouth to soothe it. It turns out that the British major is accompanying an English journalist, who is dressed like a soldier in fatigues.

'What are you hoping to write about?' I ask.

'About the war, and you guys.'

'Grunts. What do you expect to learn from us?'

'The brave work you're doing.'

'We're not so brave in this,' I say, referring to the armored vehicle.

'You can still take incoming.'

'If we get hit today then at least we won't get hurt tomorrow.'

The soldiers smile. They're easy to get onside and compliments are cheap.

'What angle do you take in your stories.'

'Trauma.'

'What trauma?'

My interest in his work catches him by surprise.

'I want to meet people with trauma.'

'Why?'

'Because it's real. I want to report it. Write about it. For people back home.'

'How would you do that, sir?'

I'm genuinely puzzled, my face scrunched in thought.

'I'd need to find someone caught up in this mess. Victims of war. Then I could show trauma in action, in real life.'

'You must be a good journalist, sir'

'Why do you say that?'

'To think the way you do. Working the angles, I mean.'

'Just doing a job, my friend,' he says, and I see his chest rise. 'A good journalist needs to feel a sense of outrage, that there's a travesty of justice.'

'You're very brave, sir.'

'Me? No. I'm only an observer. Observe and report back is all. I'm not part of it, unlike you. You're the heroes.'

We smile. We're bonding. Initially they saw me as a strange sort, a lone soldier, but the journalist's respect for what we do on tour had me perform an acting role. He's impressed how I'm living up to the mythical image of an obdurate soldier on the frontline. The shy Turk or Italian, who had been attentive to the conversation but was too timid to join in, now pipes up.

'You looking for survivors?' he asks the journalist.

'I sure am.'

'Are we survivors?'

'Yes, we all are.'

The soldier grins.

We haven't moved in half an hour, being at a standstill once more. I fall silent with my thoughts. I close my eyes and pretend to have a nap, as I listen to the banter of the British duo, which is tailored for my ears, when, over their prattle, the commotion outside kicks up. Like a dignitary, I hammer on the side of the vehicle and ask to be let out.

'Soldier, the door is not opening.'

It's the Major who confirms it. The driver reports that a group of people has blockaded the way. Muslims. They surround our UN vehicle, complaining about promises made to safeguard them in the United Nations Protected Areas, where in reality they're being slaughtered.

'Major, I need to leave. My unit isn't far away.'

'It's a narrow street.'

He says it like we're liable to come under attack.

'I have agoraphobia. There isn't going to be a surprise attack. They're Muslims, not Serbs. They're starving and afraid.'

'You toured in deserts?' the journalist asks.

'Kuwait.'

'Your agoraphobia might be a form of PTSD.'

I fear wide-open spaces, the void, the devil infinity. I get waves of it, overwhelmed by vastness. Undulating countryside and horizons are my enemies; places without borders, endless space where chaos can run amuck. It's why today warzones are confined to cities. Public places cry out to be filled by war. The streets giving rise to the pinnacle of human performance: live theatre – life or death.

'If you want to meet trauma, then come with me.'

I tap on the side of the vehicle again. I've caused a rift between the Englishmen. I make my case, pleading with the journalist - who introduces himself as Adam - to roam the streets with me.

'We're not hemmed in. It's not an ambush. I need air. About my condition, it's not PTSD, I just feel safe in a city. Cities have edges.'

'Edges?'

'Boundaries. Once I'm hedged in, I feel safe. Look down a street, to the left and right, and the road is hemmed in by right angles. The curb. The walls of buildings. Nature isn't visible. Without edges, which differentiate one thing from the next, I'm at sea. The untamed wild is uncontainable. I need solid boundaries, limits that can be erased, nuked, and blown into oblivion, like a leveled building.

'You think we'll be attacked?'

'No, I don't. I think that fear is controlling you. All I'm saying is that destruction makes me feel mortal. And feeling alive is important. But that only happens when faced with annihilation. I love when things are reduced to nothing, otherwise I'm left wondering about this world that we build.'

My words touch the English journalist and we step down from the vehicle, into the frozen muck.

My eyes adjust to the grey light as I turn a full 360. Adam and I pull away from the mob. He snaps photographs of Muslims banging on the UN patrol vehicle. I notice a man across the road watching the Muslim mob. I recognize his eyes, they're the very same as the dead Serb that we assassinated. Ballsy of him, I think, flaunting his hatred in public. The Serb hasn't noticed me. I don't know what urge it is that has me follow him – instinct, I suppose, and the fact that I'm a tad curious. Adam doesn't notice where I'm leading him but has his camera at the ready. I take off the safety on my handgun. The Serb is about to enter a gated yard, down near the railway station, when he sees us. He puts his hand in his pocket but doesn't draw his piece when he sees Adam's camera.

'What's going on?' he asks in English.

'We're lost. We got stuck in a UN truck. We decided to walk instead.'

'It's dangerous. Sniper's alley. Be careful.'

I ignore his goading remarks. The Serb looks shifty as he steals darting looks, checking to see that we've come alone and that we haven't been followed. Though he's clearly worried, he pretends to be glad to see us. I peer in the half-opened gate to the yard. Two strong-arm men lurk inside and, on receiving a nod from the Serb, they crowd the entrance and block my view to what seems to be a breaker's yard.

'What is this place?'

'Garage. Must get car fixed.'

'But there are no cars in there.'

'That doesn't mean they won't fix it.'

'Is it a mechanics garage?'

'Yes.'

'Where's your car?'

The Serb fixes me a look. What do I really want? He doesn't step out of the way of the steel door, and I don't feel emboldened enough to press him any further. I've seen enough – a large walled yard with a lot of idle machinery, bench-tops and a mass of crashed cars off in a corner. Interesting.

∞

I tell Captain Sloan that the British Major wants me to remain in

Sarajevo to recount our heroics about rescuing the Muslim hooker who took a bullet.

That night, I return. I scramble through scrub at the back of the yard, where earlier I spotted a hole in the wall behind the crashed cars. The sound of machinery puts me on high alert – chainsaws, and the cutting of metal. It's a ruse. I peer through a hole in the wall, and realize that I've landed in a nightmare.

To one side, which earlier that day was empty, is a line of mesh containers. People are crammed inside, to the point of being crushed to death. They look too weak to stand, but without space have no choice. A forklift stands at the yard entrance. These human lobster pots were unloaded from trucks like cattle. I've unearthed one of the much rumored death camps.

I'm witnessing something important.

Something clandestine.

Just-in-time genocide.

The caged are categorized. One cage is filled with solemn-looking men (Muslims?), another with a more agitated mix of youths, while a third is filled with gypsy women and children. I judge the gypsies based on their colorful clothes. It's Auschwitz all over, people sorted in cages according to a hierarchy for ethnic cleansing.

The mass killings have already commenced. The door to the cage containing the women and children is open. Half look like they've already been clubbed to death. Their remains are piled high in a rubbish skip. The human slaughterhouse runs like a smooth factory line. Henry Ford would be proud. How brisk and meticulous the butchers are in dispatching life, and yet so sanitized, wearing dark overalls lest they be covered in blood as they club and machete their way through the victims.

They're being murdered for their beliefs. They meekly accept their lot, with all hope lost, resigned to the inevitable. There is no protest and little energy left for it. Hands are raised to cover their faces. The beatings bring the victims to their knees, where their skulls are then cracked open. They seem so lonely in dying, each with their own farewell thoughts. Surely they lose their faith in the face of such abandonment.

It's systematic slaughter. Two men wrench more prisoners from the cage, while others line up with bats, ready to club them as they emerge, like slaughtering seals. Once snuffed out, a half dozen men load the corpses into the skip. The dead take up marginally less space than the caged. A line of armed men stand sentry, to the ready, in case they have to waste bullets.

Peering through the wall, I don't feel threatened but, rather oddly, relieved. But relieved about what? My self-confidence grows. I feel important. I'm the gatekeeper of this place. I'm the eyes of the world. But my sense of detachment catches me off guard. How composed I am.

Suddenly, there's commotion, not from the remaining wretches, who are reluctant to emerge from their cage, but from the henchmen. A lookout runs into the yard, and the murderers fall hush. My heart is in my mouth.

Have I been found out?

For whatever reason, the mercenaries make to leave. Before doing so, one finishes off the women and children in an opened cage, mowing them down in a hail of machine-gun fire. Only then is the sound of industrial machinery cut off. It was a noisy ruse to hide what was really going on. The place is suddenly deadly quiet. The men in the unopened cages fall silent, afraid of receiving the same fate. The murderers dash off. Where before I was merely a calm observer, now I become utterly transfixed. An element of panic stirs within. I sense the opening of an opportunity.

A heroic deed beckons.

From beneath a crumpled pile of machine-gunned bodies comes movement. A dirty white sock appears from a pile of dead meat. Then a leg protrudes. A girl's leg. She doesn't know if she should surface from beneath her dead gypo mom.

The sound of cars screech off into the night. She may only have minutes before they return. She can't know that this is her only chance to escape. I've mixed feelings, not knowing which instinct grips me – courage or desire?

Quickly, I clamber through the hole in the wall, lowering myself to the ground the other side. I fall awkwardly, twisting my ankle, and let out a small shriek. I look up and see hundreds of pairs of caged eyes fixed on me. Not one blows my cover. It's as though they're without tongues. I ignore them and focus on my target, the leg poking into the air.

As I near the open cage, a putrid smell of feces and death invades my nostrils. I almost slip in a pool of blood. I have to concentrate. I hone in on the girl's leg. I can make out the gooseberry fuzz on her skin.

Grabbing her leg, I wrench her out from beneath some corpses. She doesn't resist. She behaves like a lamb resigned to the slaughter. What emerges is a vulnerable teenager. I hoist her up onto her own two feet. She cowers, hands to her face, small and untrusting like a shrew.

Erin?

Though perhaps 15 years old, she's not yet fully formed, with child-like, button-like, breasts that press at her blouse. Her gaze is perplexed. Her tired eyes try to erase the world from memory. She wants no more if it. Rescue doesn't occur to her. This life has lost all of its charm. Although maturity ought to be years away, her innocence was lost long ago.

Having been squashed between bodies for so long, she immediately collapses when I hoist her onto her feet. Perhaps she hasn't eaten properly in weeks. Or maybe she's simply parched.

I try to take her hand and lead her from the cage, but she won't open her fist. It's less to do with me, and more to do with a piece of stale bread that she's holding. Just then, she seems to remember the bread and turns to look back, seeking out her slaughtered mother. But I'm wrong. She isn't staring at anyone who could be her mother, but rather at a little boy, younger than she. It's her little brother, I suppose. He got one in the jugular and his head now swims in a pool of blood. It's he she was keeping the bread for, I guess.

She's rooted to the spot. I have to press my advantage over her.

'They are dead. I want to help you. Come, quickly.'

I coax her from the cage with platitudes.

'I'm here to help you, dear.'

I test the water, and refer to her as 'dear'. As we begin our escape, the caged people come to life, speaking in tongues, begging – I can only imagine – to be set free. I'm afraid of them, and suddenly feel relieved that they can't get out. We must hurry.

'Come along. We'll get you cleaned up,' I say. 'How old are you, dear?'

I don't suppose she understands. She flinches as she hears ammunitions popping off nearby. The shelling of Sarajevo has resumed. I squeeze her hand. It's decided. I'm her savior; me, the rescuer. Initially she resists my support, but then, as she zones out, she finally relents. We depart with her tucked away in the crook of my arm.

I've claimed her. Now she will evermore exist through me.

I feel my heart pound, uncertain if I'm afraid of being caught or if I'm terrified by my endless possibilities. Because now, I own a nobody.

I bring her to Adam's safe house. The journalist is holed up with a war widow. It's how Adam came to be here, having helped the widow track down her husband in the beginning of all of this. That was back when the personality of the country was being initially overturned, when the annihilation of a rival race was thought to be the only way to stop the bloodshed.

The widow's husband was shot and dumped in a mass grave. Adam helped her sort through the bodies, the rats dancing around their feet until they found him. She now lives for her eleven-year-old son. Her house is bare, shorn of anything of value, everything sold or stolen.

'Have you food?' I ask the widow.

'I have food.'

She clasps the girl's hands before huddling her inside. She doesn't care what religion she is. The girl smells like shit. In an hour, the widow has fed the girl what little food she has and washed and clothed her.

'What you going to do with her?' the widow wonders.

'Take her out of here.'

'Save her?', Adam asks.

'Our lot will get her out of the country or something. Refugee status.'

We leave at nightfall.

I bring the girl to a house around the corner from where the journalist is staying. The fact that he's staying nearby means the neighborhood is secure. It's a disused shop that was long ago ransacked and won't attract any more looters. When I came upon the place earlier in the day, the thought lingered in the back of my mind that it might be used to keep someone.

By candlelight, I lead the girl down to the cellar, closing the trapdoor behind us in case anyone might hear. Uncertain how to begin, I start mumbling about also feeling the pain of war. I look at my swollen finger, lick it and show it to her. She doesn't seem to care.

She surveys the room, which is equipped with a bed and blanket, basin, bucket, table and mirror. She catches sight of herself in the mirror and stares as though uncertain of who she is looking at. Watching from some remove, I size her up. She has a pale fresh face, but is emaciated. Veins protrude from the inside of her bare arms. She has a boy's slim hips, as yet unsculpted. There's something of an androgynous look about her.

I suppose that makes me a latent homosexual. Impossible. I love beasts of passion – wildlife programs and loose women, preferably just out of nuthouses. It's their vulnerability I like – how I can prey on them. Dominate.

The girl looks up. In the mirror, she notices my eyes feasting on her. She holds my gaze for a moment, then looks down, remaining motionless, stock still, hoping that I might forget she's there. Instead, I gain heart, gazing more intently. Oh, my desire has found a home, a hole.

I gently turn her around to face me. Me, with my pants already down, stroking my cock. I place her hand on my member, urging her to maintain the rhythm. She isn't surprised; she knows the drill. Perhaps she thinks this will be all.

With my hands on her shoulders, I guide her onto her knees, urging her mouth onto my throbbing penis. She sets to work, her head bobbing back and forth, working the shaft with her thin lips.

'Don't worry, I won't come in your mouth,' I find myself promising.

With each plunging motion, deep into her mouth-hole, I feel warm and safe. The rhythm becomes more frantic, as I control the speed of her bobbing head with my hands. I almost pull the ears off her. She gags but continues. As I shoot into her she throws up. When I pull out, my cock is covered in bile.

Her tears add to the after-effect. I soothe her. I promise that I won't hurt her. I think about all the fun I'll have with her. But first I need time with my own doubts, before reckoning on my next move.

I leave her some bread and matches, and instruct her to use the candlelight sparingly. I'm unsure whether she understands. I lock her in, happy to have collared my very own plaything.

∞

I'm going to be a centerfold story in a British newspaper. I'm an interesting guy, according to Adam. There's a temporary ceasefire after a mortar was dropped on Sarajevo's marketplace, killing 69, and leaving shrapnel in another 200. With the body toll in Sarajevo alone topping 10,000, it's uncertain if the football field can accommodate another 69 bodies. The fallout rages a few days, the Serbs copping a lot of flack, but then it's back to business as usual, back to the killing spree. Then a temporary ceasefire is struck, allowing NATO to gather intelligence and figure out which side was behind the marketplace massacre.

It's when Adam reaches out to me, inviting me to accompany him to Dubrovnik.

'I haven't been back since it was bombed a few years ago. Back then the journalists holed up in the Hotel Argentina, a plush 4-star out of town place that overlooked the walled port. From the panoramic lobby, we watched the shelling of the defenseless city, as the European overseers explained the difference in sound between incoming or outgoing fire.'

'Does Dubrovnik have a beach?'

'It has pebbles, not sand. I got off my weekend dispatch so if you're commanding officer allows, we could leave ASAP.'

'Before there's any retaliatory slaughter, you mean? I guess you're right, a little normality is needed to counteract the insanity. Laugh a little.'

Adam finds me insensitive and doesn't comment. Although Adam is the serious type, I thought that he might loosen up once on the road out of town. Not so. He wants to see Dubrovnik for journalistic reasons, to study the impact the war is having on the coastal town. I'm just going for the pubs, pussy, and the beach.

'Is your dad proud of what you do?' he asks, once we're on the open road.

'Is this for your article about me?'

He, driving, turns to look at me. To judge me. It's like he's got me wrong and is confused about me. Time to feed him lines.

'Dad says so long as it doesn't threaten my future, he's happy for me.'

'Physically threaten or metaphorically threaten?'

'Career-wise, as long as my career options aren't irrevocably threatened.'

'Sounds like it's an abstract fear that your dad has over any physical threat.'

'You think?'

'Sure. It's a CV thing. Your dad doesn't want you coming home as an amputee and so he's glad that you're a combat medic and not on the frontline.'

'I'm often on the frontline. It's where I rescue people.'

'Of course you are. I meant that your dad doesn't *think* you're fighting. But I presume he also has post-war aspirations for you.'

'He'd like me to wake up from this shit and work in the city.'

Adam steals another crooked glance at me.

'I'm joking. I never had the stockbroker option. I'm OK with this. I'm doing my best to add up.'

'To add up?'

'Yeah, to tot up to who we're meant to be.'

'And that person is a 68 Whiskey?'

'I guess so. The job keeps me dangerous. And danger is my occupation.'

I only say this for the sake of having something to say, as he stares down the empty road.

'Doc, do you like danger?'

'I don't know if I'll see tomorrow, and that makes my life dangerous. You never know when you're going to take fire. It makes living unpredictable.'

'But you didn't enlist for the danger?'

'Sure I did.'

'Why?'

'It makes girls love me.'

'You mean, it *forces* girls to love you, as they fear that you mightn't last.'

'Yep.'

'So who have you got?'

'My girlfriend back home, for starters. There's always an uncertainty that I'll not come back, so she can't fight so freely with me. Her conscience would kill her.'

'Emotional blackmail?'

'The ways of love.'

We laugh, though I'm not sure that we're laughing about the same thing.

The night of the massacre in the Sarajevo market I called Becky by Satphone. I needed a grounding sensation, somebody sympathetic. Instead I learned from the answering machine that she ditched me and already had someone new. The machine's message said: 'If this is Scott,

I'm probably down in the Brewer's Bar,' she giggled. Who was Scott? Her future ex-husband, that's who. I thought we might have been real. So much for Becky and I going abroad together. So much for hope.

In Dubrovnik, Adam marvels at the walled city. He tells me that the fortress walls are as useful today as in wars of old, the castle walls withstanding bombardment from tank rounds and mortars. After coffee, cafés, and beer we adapt to the non-war environment. It's strange how you can drive a few hours and it's suddenly the norm that nobody is out to kill you. Lazy days take time to understand. Sometimes the harmony has me break out in fits of giggles as it dawns on me that there won't be the sound of gunfire.

Downtime from war makes everything seem like it's in slow motion, like a stage set without actors, before the theatre begins. Birds dive off rooftops, warbling and teasing the city's wildcats. The water laps gently at the shoreline as I keep a lookout for signs of blood. I might have been on a Greek island, such is the white light and parched stone blocks that make up the old town's promenade. It's there that I sit in a café, watching a sliver of moon emerge and glow.

After the weekend, it's back to reality.

Back in Sarajevo, we're revitalized and hung-over. On the return journey, we share passing smiles, Adam and I, the fun we had, chewing the fat, shooting the breeze, bonding.

I almost forget about my treat, my temptation, my dungeon nymph. It was the real reason I pushed Adam to interview me. In case of last-minute doubts and to ensure that my dick runs on autopilot, I swallow a tab of Viagra. I do this when I have to perform and don't feel like it. It's often the case that I have to sleep with girls when I'm not hungry for sex. The life of being a handsome man. And when I fuck them, I feel an out of body sensation, as though I'm watching an actor perform. With Viagra, there's no stage fright, no shyly retracted cock.

She's in bed when I pay a visit. I cautiously descend the stairs, a candle in one hand and a baton in the other. Just in case.

'Girl? Hello, dear.'

Her smell is the only reply. I march over to the bed and, under the candlelight, see her slit wrists and a pool of dried blood soaked on the mattress. She smashed the mirror, and used a shard to slice her thin wrists. The headstrong bitch leaves me with a twisted smile.

Robbed of my prize, I feel sorry for myself. There's nothing I can do: *how could I have protected her from herself?* What a waste. I might have groomed her for my pleasure, my concubine. We could have talked it over, worked it out, had a future together. *Was it something I did?* Too late to ask.

First, I feel a pang of anger, and then I feel crushed, cheated. I envy her. I was also meant to die young and am embarrassed that I did not.

The scoundrel killed herself against my wishes, without explanation, revealing only a lack of will to live. *But why?* Only I had the right to kill her. She was mine, my souvenir, my catch. I earned her. Hadn't I saved her? I rescued her from the jaws of certain death. Now this pitiful wretch, who hasn't left any mark on the world, dominates me, another suicide controlling my life. Another girl torturing me.

Pitying her won't help. Nevertheless, I feel tricked. Cheated. She forces my hand. I'm not done with her yet. There's a twitch in my pants. I'm not in control; Viagra is. It's difficult to retreat. My cock is primed, ready for action. *What to do?* The girl may be gone but her corpse remains. It's still her. I bury my face in her hair. There's a trace of shampoo. Her childish voice floods back. I sit up and find myself whispering gently while stroking her hair, willing her back to life. It's difficult to proposition the dead, but so too is it difficult to halt a drug-induced eruption in one's pants. My cock is on autopilot.

I hoist her stiff cadaver up off the bed, and lay her face down on the table. With some rope, I lash her wrists to the table legs, letting her body slide towards the ground. Her pencil-thin legs dangle over the table's edge. I hike up her dress, pull down her panties and go to work on myself. With a hand I make myself come alive and, with the other, I feel my way into her. She's cold. Life is heat. That's all that's missing – warmth, and a buck or two.

My overtures are unrequited. It matters not. My cock is drugged erect. I force myself into her, feeling her tightness resist penetration. Tighter than rape. The friction keeps up all the way in; there are no involuntary juices. It makes me harder, my rod like a weapon. After a few frantic strokes, I unload into her, feeding her some much-needed protein.

Just then, mid-orgasm, she grumbles or at least makes a biological sound. Though she's dead, she's not entirely dead within. It suddenly becomes clear – her internal organs are fermenting. She farts then shits, exploding some kind of liquid jam over my pubes. I'm still inside her, helpless, hopelessly unable to detach. When I draw out I feel sick, covered in her feces and my own jism.

I, the sinner, am sinned against. She has the last say. She used me. She exposed my sexuality. I'm a touch confused. I wipe the shit and come off the hem of her dress, pull up my pants and bump into things as I retreat in the darkness.

An eventful evening.

Chapter 5

9/11

2001

Across the road, Gloria is walking her dog. Her voluminous hair bounces behind her. She's nondescript or, at least, if she weren't the only woman around, I wouldn't notice her. As I cross the road to her sidewalk, I see my reflection in a shop window and it makes me feel good. Khaki pants and army t-shirt; I look fit. I'm about to be on my way, when it happens.

Gloria stops to give a bum some money and offer consoling words. She hunkers down to listen to the rabble coming from the wino's mouth. In that instant, the beggar and she are bound as one, as tramps. Her dog tugs at the leash, recoiling from the sharp ammonia stench. Just then, a well-dressed passer-by, approaching from behind and clipping along in patent leather shoes, is put off his stride by the dog and gives it a kick in the loin. It lets out a whelp and Gloria spins around only to receive more condemnation.

'Control your rat, you loser.'

As the man flounces off I'm on him, closing in fast. I line him up, aiming for the coccyx, and kick him up the backside. His hands go to his rear-end as he lets out a roar. I follow up with a kick to the groin - which he blocks - and, for good measure, open-handedly slap him across the face. Only now do I notice his protruding chin. He suffers underbite, his lower teeth protruding in front of the upper ones, and accentuating a pointy chin.

He's flabbergasted, clearly never in his life been treated so. After all, who kicks and slaps a fifty-ish-year-old professional in broad daylight? In life, there are the kickable and un-kickable.

'You cowardly fuck. You hurt an animal.'

'Why did you kick me?' he wails, confused, as he dances around clutching his butt.

'You kicked the dog.'

'What's it to you?'

'Recycle the pain.'

'I'm calling the cops.'

I snatch the cellphone from his hands.

'You hurt an animal, so you must eat it.'

'You're insane.'

'I'm going to kick you around the street if you don't.'

'If I don't what?'

'Eat it.'

'Eat what?'

'The dog. Either that, or apologize. Decide. You have three seconds.'

'You're out of your mind.'

'I repeat: either eat the dog or you apologize and mean it.'

'Soldier, I didn't know it was yours.'

'It's not.'

'Well then?'

'Eat it or apologize. I'm counting: one, two'

He watches me as I scrunch my face in preparation to unleash further violence. He feels my rage. He knows our little chat is over.

'Apologize. I'll apologize.'

With that, he turns about and waddles up to Gloria and company like a constipated man. They've been silently looking on, astounded, and unsure if they're about to witness a carve-up or an apology.

'I'm sorry, I shouldn't have kicked your dog.'

'To the dog,' I bark. 'Address the dog, not her.'

Everyone looks a touch confused, but nobody dares interfere. A terse silence remains.

'I'm sorry.'

'To the dog, I said.'

He turns around, and with a stern downcast gaze, repeats his apology to the dog.

'Pat it, and say it again.'

He looks at me, but has figured out that the easiest way to be done with me is to comply. The dog growls as he nears. Gloria holds it fast and crouches down to pat it, telling it that everything is fine. The man in the suit approaches cautiously, whispering sweet nothings to the mutt. He gives it a little pat while apologizing. Then he stands up and turns to me.

'I've complied.'

'Then fuck off.'

The transaction complete, he turns on his heels and strides away. It's a surreal comedy. There's nothing to be done for it but to go for a celebratory drink. Gloria insists. Apparently, I've shown a courageous act of chivalry even though, for me, it isn't about her, but the dog. It's a point of principle.

Waste not, want not.

At a nearby coffee shop we're a sight. Gloria blathers on as I maintain a vacuous stare. The dog, Rex, the runt, gives me a stunned look, looking from the hobo, to Gloria, and then back to me. The bum wheezes a little, emitting a sound commonly associated with the emptying of bagpipes. He keeps a downcast gaze as he rolls a cigarette and then, suddenly, might look up, and give a darting glance about, as though checking that he isn't being followed. Is he on the run or merely unaccustomed to forming part of society? For my part, I'm unaccustomed to listening to shit in my free time.

What am I thinking as Gloria whittles on? Easy. Why do bums carry on? Why do they persist in putting down time, drifting along – for what? The futility. Do they not have the gumption to end it, or is it that they don't know how to? Perhaps the government could offer a new service - free bullets to the back of the head of a weekday evening.

I get up to leave. But Gloria puts her hand on my arm. I give her my phone number.

∞

Until that point, I was good in bed (B+), but not so good with women in their complete form (D-). I never imagined chatting in a relationship, like, actually talking, like, having bar stool talk in bed. Perhaps I'll work on this (C+).

I begin playing a new role: coy or shy. Whatever. I take on a different personality to entertain myself. After all, I'm bored with pussy. I've stopped following girls on the street. On my cell, I've a harem of girls stored under the surname 'Booty Call'. But I'm tired of my phonebook. I put my non-sexualized self down to being burnt out, to spending too much time on tour. Once back home, I land on the couch and watch TV. Wildlife documentaries are more interesting than chatting to pussy. It's a continuation of the life and death kick that I get from warzones. Or else I've reached my quota in life and, after eighty-nine pussies, that's it, I've done all I can do to them, and there's nothing further to experience, the novelty is gone. Women won. They wore me out. I've become carnally indifferent. It occurs to me that, all along, it was I who had been their object, not the reverse. I was just a dick filling a hole. Girls looked out for themselves, wanting their cropped pussies admired. Dildo or dick, what's it going to be tonight? I feel dirty and used.

Pussy left a moral. The key to self-sustainability is not to want them. To have no need for anybody. At best, a companion may provide temporary joy and short-term distraction. We die alone. Only I have my back. I must reduce my vulnerability and be like a tree shedding leaves in winter. Except a leaf is a metaphor for pussy.

Gloria doesn't fuck me right away, and I don't invite her to. I'm calm about it, indeed indifferent. I feel sluggish, worn out, as though I'm carrying the weight of the world. In maintaining a moody distance from women, I've become curious: curious about seduction, curious to know if I might establish a different sort of communion with the opposite sex, curious to know if I can go on three dates without demanding sex.

I happen to be free, so I take Gloria to dinner.

It's no biggie, I'm bored, and it beats sitting at home. Who knows, maybe at the least expected moment I'll find someone real. Plus, I'm curious to see if I can talk to a girl, not for pussy's sake but for nothing's sake, talking just for the sake of talking – the bar stool way. And plus, being with Gloria is like sampling nothing. There's no tension, no great attraction, no need to impress. She's in my league, not above it.

The restaurant is nothing special, an Italian in Queens. The waiter comes and I insist he gives Gloria a menu before me. Gloria thinks me cute and old-fashioned. I indulge her. I've had a few long-term loves, I say, nothing serious and now, in hindsight, all inconsequential. I'm not damaged goods, is what I'm implying. I leave such obvious clues, cautious to impart an impression of a balanced me. I'm entertaining myself, playing a new game, humming a new tune. But why bother? Gloria hardly casts a spell over me – she is, after all, relatively plain, with mousey brown hair, and of average build and height. She's shapely, less a girl and more a woman.

So.

Is a man not allowed to be curious about himself, intrigued that there might be something more, something deeper? I continuously martyr myself to this hope, though, in truth, it's boredom that feeds me. I've time on my hands but I'm not in a hurry to be used again, to be some doll's billy goat. It occurs to me that with the advent of the sexual revolution, the urge to possess, to keep, is lost to the sexes. Everyone thinks the same thing: why own a cesspit? Piss in it and be off. Other people are urinals.

Gloria and I.

We chat without agenda while feeding eggplant into our faces. With high amusement I'm experimenting, walking myself down different avenues, not being so goal focused, and being less mercenary. Gloria is flashy without needing to reveal much skin. Modest. She's an account's clerk in a non-descript multinational. It's obvious that my work intrigues her. Greek archaeologists, tennis pros, heads of state and flying doctors are some of the only careers in which you have a divine right to score a leggy young broad. A war medic trumps the lot. The more mainstream professions provide few illusions of heroics or adventure, although, despite this, secretaries are happy to bang these plodders. The pity of impoverished minds.

'What's it like being a combat medic? It must be exciting.'

I've been here many times before. How can Gloria imagine that she's being anything other than ordinary, asking such standard fare? She has clearly never seen nor tasted death. I will myself onwards.

'It's violence mixed with peace. I try my best to save people.'

'But you must see horrific things.'

'I try not to.'

'Come on, Doc. Share. Show me who you are,' she gushes.

Deciding to humor myself, I warm to my theme.

'I know things.'

'Like what?'

'Things,' I smugly confirm.

Gloria thinks we're entering a conspiracy. But then she clicks. She knows better than to be teased, and with a smirk, moves our conversation off in a different direction as we discuss growing up in New York. But wait. The way Gloria smirked caught my interest; it was sexy how she scrunched up her nose and snaffled. It's like she was sniffing the air or snorting like a pig. Yes, it's sexy. I wish I could do a pig so easily.

I row back to our earlier conversation – war. Our patter resumes. I'm curious if she might surprise me, challenge me. As we talk, Gloria constantly gestures, her hands flying. I worry for the safety of the items on the table and reshuffle them.

'Mexico is a mess. They act strong but because of the strength of its neighbor, America. I spent time there, in Mexico. I was on the scene after a cartel tortured some dude. It was terrible. I didn't sleep for weeks.'

'I'm sorry,' Gloria says, as though she's to blame, guilty for pressing me on dark subjects.

'How can people do these things and sleep at night?'

'Doc, what you do is important. It's relevant.'

I nod solemnly, feigning belief. I try to veer away from cliché in my reply.

'Should we only look at pleasant things, things that don't disturb, and pretend that ugly things like war never happen?' I ask.

'I agree. But I'm sad that it makes you sad.'

'It's real life. There's a bad-side to humans that's part of our make-up.'

'I hear what you're saying. You're so brave,' she says, fluttering her eyelids.

'I'm not fighting on the frontline, not that I'm any shrinking violet. I'm on the frontline alright, but only as a pair of eyes.'

'Mister Eye-spy, that's who you are.'

'I don't contribute to a fighting scene. I just bandage up our side.'

'Doc, I get you. I do. It's not your fault. You're trying to fix things but you can't save the world.'

She thinks I'm shouldering the blame for war. She places her hand on mine. My eyes go from her hand to her face. Our eyes meet. I fix her a meaningful look.

'I'll tell you something, these fundamentalists with their faces covered and lopping off people's heads: they're cowards. You can't be a hero hiding who you are. Be proud of your actions. I'm a fan of Muslims, but where in the Koran does it say to cover up your face? Those half-bred fanatics think they're the religious police. I'd be embarrassed to have them as guardians of my religion. Why don't self respecting Muslims speak out? Cowards. '

I try not to laugh as I summarize my rant. Gloria gives me a confused look and then it's back to role-playing. She restores me to greatness.

'Doc, you're so modest. You're more than the sum of what you do.'

So touching, so sincere – I feel as if I could be on a movie set. There I'd be, waiting for the movie director to shout: 'Cut. We got it in the can'. I'd make a very convincing Leonardo DiCaprio.

Dessert arrives, and we move to safer ground, chatting more generally and offering tit-bits about ourselves. After eight years with her Jewish boyfriend, Aaron, he left her for a younger girl. For my part, I give off the impression that I'm long celibate. Truthfully, I do feel flaccid. She blushes, then smiles, when I drop these hints. She's grateful for my chastity. She acts equally untouched. We must be keeping ourselves for one another, she thinks. I imagine her sex, squashed in her jeans, shriveled as a scorched fig, dry as a bone. We're both sex-starved. Across the table, she takes my hand in hers and gently squeezes. Our eyes meet, we say nothing, then we smile.

∞

I'm Gloria's boyfriend. Maybe it was peer pressure, as all my friends are settled, leaving me sticking out like a sore thumb. Overnight, I forgive other couples kissing in the street or walking hand in hand. I'm one of them, assimilated into society.

Gloria's friends are harmless – workers who live for the weekend. I piggyback on them and think nothing of meeting her friends for a coffee to discuss mundane things, like landlord problems or which car to buy, as we slowly become an extended family. My own friends I have to filter, making the ones that don't matter, matter, and vice versa. I've always been a bad friend, friends only lasting for as long as they persist.

She meets the '3 apostles' – Stan, Dwayne and Phil – who I jokingly refer to as the GG Club (the guns and God crew). My military friends impart a sense of normality. They're secure in their life's mission and have all settled down.

The stage is set.

But for what?

∞

I'm an adapter, quick to change my spots, or to at least act like I've changed. That's why I keep different sets of friends, people who can reinforce the person that I'm pretending to be: friends from the army or else hoodlums from Queens. Since I turned thirty, I figure that I'm nearing that stage where I'll have to side with one group of friends over another.

'Bull's eye. Right in the head. Nice shot, Doc.'

'Thanks Dwayne. It felt crisp.'

'It's all in the wrist, buddy,' he adds.

'A lot of life is in the wrist,' Phil throws in.

'Popping off rounds is for wankers,' I agree.

We're at Woodland Park firing range. I ordinarily wouldn't meet grunts from my company so soon after returning from a tour but it's a ritual in honor of our fallen comrade, Lance Corporal Metcalf. Unbeknownst to all, I had been banging Misses Metcalf in an effort to help her forget her dead husband. Call it charity.

There's no harm in a bit of guns and God. Yes, you guessed it; I plan featuring my army buddies in my life a lot more. I'm all for fake bonding. They'll make me look like a safe bet. Patriotic too. So here I am, focusing on a target: the outline of a man. I pull the trigger and crack off another round. It's simply a matter of putting a hole in a guy's head. Shooting practice is slow torture, but what else am I to do? I'm bored of my drug dealing buddies in Queens, I'm too burned out for ball sports, and I'm not toned up enough to be seen swimming. It's true, I'm getting on. The shooting range is all I've left but it makes me feel pro-establishment and republican.

That I fit in with this bunch makes me uncomfortable. Why don't I look out of place standing alongside my moronic buddies? We could be in a cartoon. We don't look so dangerous now, wearing Pringle sweaters and khaki pants. We've reached that stage in life where we watch the news, and no longer dream of making it.

News is other people.

Our crumble came quickly. The stars and stripes drape from our balconies. We dress up on Sundays to eat salads. Although we're back from the desert, we're slathered in sunscreen, despite how it's a mild day in New York. Two of my friends wear sun hats to protect their bald patches. They mention burn time. We're creatures of habit. We could be yuppies from the City, no different to the middle-aged shooters in the port beside us, who can't see their dicks over their bellies.

The thought runs through my head again: *it disappoints me that I don't look out of place.* I understand mass shooters. I get them. I do. I feel disconnected from my life, from the reality that I want. I look around me and notice other people getting older but fail to realize that I'm also aging.

'Doc, a man lives for his loves.'

'Was it always guns, Phil?'

'There was a time when my wife was in the frame. I got over her, now it's only firearms I can't cure myself of.'

'You're not inspiring much hope.'

'Doc, relax, Gloria is a keeper.'

What is Phil talking about? I don't care. Yet I smile and nod in agreement at every opportunity. We're crossing wires; there's interference in my head. My head is fit to burst. We talk in circles, bolstering each other, to hide from being average. Yes, we are great. But it's a lie. I know that I've failed. Proof? I'm not disappointed enough in myself to put a gun in my mouth. I wonder if they realize this, that we haven't so much as ruffled a hair in the world. We grew up and went nowhere. Indeed, we've no unfulfilled dreams to pine after.

In some respects I envy this bunch. There they are, having dealt their hand, shuffling through life and scoring decent wives. When we go out, I think their wives are relatively easy to operate. They seem like practical types, whereas when I look at my Gloria, I just see plain.

Sometimes I imagine fucking Stan's wife, Belinda. She always throws me that look – a look that says she's up for it. The pouting slut. In my dreams of plugging her, she doesn't have a voice. Not that her tongue is cut out - but not a bad idea - it's just that she's breathless as I take her from behind.

In the SUV back to New York we stop at Brewer's Bar where, Dwayne, as the loser on the firing range, buys a round of beers. Conversation is inoffensive. Where I'd happily sit silent, they feel it necessary to resonate and be heard.

'Do you ever think we're doing the wrong thing?' Phil asks.

'Shooting jihadis? The T-ban, I'd happily put my last cap in them,' Stan says.

'What Phil means is: are we jerks for having enlisted?'

'I didn't say that, Doc.'

'But you did mean that we're retarded as we never figured out when it was time to grow-the-fuck-up.'

'Doc, you're wild. You're always fighting shit.'

'Dwayne, I'm just saying that we bowled over too easily.'

Suddenly, words are laden with meaning. Everyone knows that I've got the goods. There's a certain quality in my career-path that they envy. It goes with the territory. A 68 Whiskey is respected. I have post-military career options. So, in some respects, I'm the star attraction. Meantime, they'd love to trawl through old war stories. But if that were on the menu, I'd rather tell *real* stories and open up about the unspoken things I've done. But why play the hero? Instead I settle for amnesia, ignoring my past and sipping my beer.

Head doctors say it's good to rake over the past. That's bullshit. It's just because they're on the clock. I'm happy to leave my life's experiences undisturbed, in therapy-free wonderland. After all, doors are also made for closing.

How can we bear to get like this in our thirties? There we are, beaten, and although there's still time, they do nothing but twitter on, too afraid to turn their backs and walk out the door to start life over anew. Perhaps they don't have the imagination to reinvent themselves. They hold no answers and have nothing but acerbic repartees, so here we sit, slowly getting fat.

I shouldn't get my back up. After all, shooting guns isn't about life but lifelessness. Killing. I close my eyes, tilt my head back, and look up to the ceiling.

'God help me,' I sigh aloud.

'Worried about Gloria and her gang?' Phil says.

'We'll be on our best behavior tonight,' Stan promises.

'How tragic,' I say.

A contemplative silence reigns. Nobody dares to question me. Then Stan surprises me with a failed dream.

'I would have been a great pilot. If it weren't for my eyesight I'd be flying F16s.'

With an index finger, Stan pushes the bridge of his glasses against his nose, punishing his eyes for letting him down.

'Operating a track isn't what I'd call a failure,' I console.

'Yeah, a tank operator has the best of all worlds. You act like a pilot, except you're grounded. Saves you having to learn about parachutes,' Phil jokes.

'How about you Doc? Was it an addiction to seeing blood?' Dwayne asks.

'Maybe. Show me what a knife can do to a jugular and I'm excited.'

Nobody laughs. And I don't water down my words. They lack the presence of mind to quiz me properly. Brain-dead meat. Hamsters on a treadmill.

'Doc, why be a medic? I mean, what made you think it might be you?'

I can't tell Dwayne that I'm caught in the trap of being good at something I don't like, but can ill afford to leave. That would make me like them. If I heard myself sounding so pathetic I'd tie up a noose. I accept that I'm without a life's mission. But I also know that my life is a front, and if I don't keep it up, I'll collapse in a heap.

'After High School I knew I had to shake things up. I was either going to put a bullet in my dad or myself. A buddy wanted to be an EMT. He put me onto it. I just tagged along. Dad was blind. He'd ask me to read the newspaper at dinner every night. I got to read about all the shit going on in the world. Enlisting seemed like a good way to see some of it.'

'You didn't choose to become an EMT?

'It started out as a joke. I'm an accidental pre-hospital care provider.'

'It makes sense. You've no empathy.'

We laugh at Stan.

'It's all much of a muchness,' I say.

'Being a medic?' Stan asks.

'Everything. Life.'

'Doc, thinks we're on the road to hell,' Dwayne says.

'It's why we make babies, to be distracted on the way to dying,' I say.

No one replies. I mumble something about refills, and make for the bar. My head is scrambled. And then there's this: *how the fuck did Stan pull Belinda? Was it his family's money?* I'm no longer an oil painting, but surely I'm more of a catch.

I'm irritated by my own lack of daring in choosing a partner. How could the most gifted person in the group be the one found wanting? I made Gloria – lending her a position and dubious status as a war medic's doll – and she just makes me look ordinary. There's an inner grating. There's acid in me. Maybe the fault is mine. I'm no longer worthy of a better class of girl, as I've left it too late.

I wonder if my buddies still love their wives, or if hooking-up with them was a habit too hard to break. Surely, by now, with the honeymoon phase long gone, they're too high-minded for animal attraction and sex. So, what's left? Maybe they use their partners to help them feel half-human. I know I do. But is it worth the other half?

When I rejoin them, all of us with refills, I feel the urge to roar the truth: that the lack of war breaks me out in cold sweats, that without sight of death I don't feel alive, that the smell of charred bodies forces me to live, that death drives me on.

How could they understand? They carry no crosses. They behave as though they're already dead. Might they relate to the twinkle in my eye, or does it ever cross their minds that I deal in death and not in trying to save people? Alas, no. They'd laugh at the truth of me.

The truth is that I also am an ant. I've lost faith in myself. I'm frightened of the way I'm withering away and losing my potency. And this is why I've snagged Gloria; I'm selling out.

Selling out of me.

And buying in to hope.

Later on, we're hooking up with Gloria's friends to celebrate her thirtieth birthday. We move to the advice phase of our conversation.

'Doc, don't go launching in tonight and mouthing off. You're still on probation. Scope them out and let them throw their chips on the table first.'

So that's how Stan bagged Belinda – he played it safe, stalked her out. Cowboys yesterday, grunts today. We're no longer beasts of passion, we just talk tough and, if tonight goes well, wives will be boned.

∞

Gloria has limp biscuits and wet lemons for friends. And they're the nice ones. Many of them chew their fingernails. At the house party, her friends - the ones I haven't yet met - check me out, to see if I'm suitable. But suitable for what?

'You're a soldier. That's like a calling. So, what do you believe in?' a black-haired girl asks.

I give the girl the once-over. She's wearing all the colors of the rainbow. My mouth tightens. I bet she's a Green Peace warrior.

'You assume that I serve a cause? But I've none; I just serve.'

'You don't believe in anything?'

'Correct. I believe in nothing.'

'Because nothing is worth believing in?'

'You nailed it. I'm headache-free.'

Her friend joins in. She was tucked behind the black-haired girl but now comes to the fore. Her face is brutally ugly, her body worse. She's a shapeless dumpling, dressed head to toe in shades of brown. She looks like a nobody so let's call her that – Ms Nobody.

'If you don't believe in anything it means that you don't want anything.'

Ms Nobody forces me to think for a moment. When my military buddies describe how lucky we are and how far we've come, they're implying marriage and children. Whereas I think my life's achievement is simply being alive.

'Is the mere act of being alive not enough?'

'But how can you go through life not wanting anything?' Ms Nobody asks.

'Easy. I'm no marketing foil. I have no false wants.'

'But do you not want to be anyone?'

How ironic the question, a Ms Nobody asking if I want to be somebody. She has let her own demons out of the bag.

'Speak for yourself. I know this is as good as it gets.'

'You sound very clinical,' says the black-haired witch.

'But you must have some principles,' Ms Nobody interjects.

'A few policies, yes. For protection.'

'Protection?'

'Self-preservation – for protection of my own interests.'

'But I thought that you didn't have any interests.'

'Self-interests.'

'Like what exactly?'

Two or three people have gathered around, entertained by the evident friction. Gloria also joins, placing a hand on my shoulder as I'm seated on a chair. I feel cornered. How to escape? Shutting my mouth might help. Fuck that.

'Number one' I say. 'Never eat cake made by a man. Number two: don't trust an adult who learns Arabic. And, number three: don't date a woman over thirty.'

A hushed silence descends. My last policy is the stinger.

'You wouldn't fuck a pensioner. Brittle bones. You'd be done for assault.'

I look around but nobody is laughing. I stay resolute.

'You meet a woman of that age – thirty plus – and she speaks a different language.'

'What language?' the witch asks.

'The language of babies and mortgages.'

She gives a blank look. Maybe she doesn't understand.

'Women after thirty only have one thing on their mind: an expensive diamond.'

In a blink, I have her down. She's clearly over the 30-mark and, without wedding ring, is happy to egg me on. Fine, I'll hang myself. But when I wake up tomorrow at least I'll have a dick.

'Getting serious with a woman over 30: just don't do it.'

'Do what?'

'Do her.'

'*Do* her?'

'Okay, we're being politically correct – don't *be* with her.'

We're getting on each other's nerves.

'It sounds like you're afraid.'

I pause to consider as the black-haired girl scowls, scrunching up her face, and showing crow's feet. Then she lets out a triumphant sigh, as though justifying her suspicions that it's entirely man's fault that she's been left on the shelf.

'I'm not afraid of love,' I say. 'It's just that I don't trust it to catch my fall.'

The disparity of opinion in the room makes for a hostile silence. Men and women stare. I feel heat – no, hate – on my face, and try to ignore it. My buddies shake their heads like I've gone mad. The gathering thins out, everyone suddenly sitting miles apart. There's no consensus: we're all individuals sitting on different planets. I play it cool, and lean back in my chair, self-satisfied, clasping my hands behind my head.

'But aren't you in your thirties?'

'What has that got to do with anything?'

'It's not parity.'

'Sorry, what isn't?'

The witch is insulted that I can't be bothered remembering her point. She resupplies me with the details.

'You can't insist on having someone younger than you.'

'Can't I?'

'No, you can't.'

'Actually, I can and do.'

'But that's manifestly wrong.'

'I'm not an employer – equal opportunities don't apply.'

Everyone thinks I'm being insensitive. Maybe. But only because I told the truth. Maybe I should have held my tongue. But in a war, when someone's shooting at you, you don't stop to consider if you're a pacifist. You pick up a gun. Anyway, I hate people who act like they're gunning for sainthood.

All the while, Gloria is shaping up to interject, but never actually does so. I know I'm slow to it - it being her thirtieth birthday - but it didn't strike me that she would be offended. I keep forgetting her age due to her youthful coating of baby fat.

Until that point, Gloria and I had made huge progress in our relationship. But after that evening, she cooled on me, holding me in contempt, perhaps seeing me as a wasted investment. A poor bet for a diamond.

In our time together, Gloria seemed happy to soak up my rants, and accept being trodden upon in the same fashion that her dad had bullied her mom. Alas, no more. She finally bucked and dumped me. Gloria is reluctant to continue, sees no point, as I can't be cured. My brand of companionship is wrong. Overnight the bed is cold. It's the first time that she dumped anyone. Her friends must have rallied around her, and forced her to show some gumption.

Maybe I asked for it. Maybe it was my fault. Whatever. She didn't matter that much. After all, she was an ordinary sort (she didn't even know how to use chopsticks, appreciate rare steak or Stilton cheese). I liked the way that I put her calf muscles through a workout – she had to stand on her tippy toes to kiss me. They were nice, her calves, but over

135

time, they'd fill out. This was something I had to consider. Over the years, like the rings on a tree, did I want to be able to measure her bulging calves to calculate how often she had kissed me? Sure, it boosted my ego. It intrigued me, that she spent such considerable effort satisfying her longing for my lips.

Gloria even got to my stomach: she could cook up magic on a wok. She reminded me of my mother, before Mom was sent to a home for the deranged. I also liked that I had brought her along in bed. I was her personal coach: she became more expressive, screaming things she never thought she'd hear herself say: 'Fuck me. Buck me. Destroy me.'

I went back to wanking for a while, which was a relief in many respects, as I didn't have to whisper sweet nothings to my hand. It's easier to have sex on one's own. The self-ownership, the autonomy of it, is liberating. And nobody is offended in the morning.

∞

The world is falling down. It lands on a heap at the foot of the Twin Towers. I'm covered in a layer of dust that's evermore known as 9/11.

Earlier that morning, Dad rang. Before picking up I turned on porn for background sound. Anything to rattle his cage.

'What's that noise?' he asks.

'I'm multi-tasking: pleasure and pain all at once.'

I have the sniffles.

'Dad, I've a cold.'

'Take lemon and sugar.'

'Dad, I'm in the middle of something. Can we talk later?'

I hang up without allowing him another word. I look at my watch. I'm late for my weekly session with Doctor Bernard, the psychiatrist. Work pays for it. I've caved in, doing what I said I'd never do: opening doors that are meant to remain shut.

I'm in the habit of bringing along some foible or other, some little trauma that I invent for him to work on, to help him feel useful, successful. He thinks I'm blocked up, that I suffer deep-seated guilt. Today I'm chewing gum.

'Do you have an ashtray?' I ask.

'No smoking in here. You know that.'

'It's for the gum.'

He hands me a tissue. I hand him back the tissue-wrapped gum. He places it in an ashtray. Weirdo.

He doesn't mind me talking to Doctor, and says a second opinion may help. Sometimes I mix real stories with fake ones. It brings me back to my youth with Dad when I had to read him the newspaper and would make things up. Other times I think Doctor Bernard is onto me, as he sits there nodding along, wearing the trace of a tight smile. I persist, regardless, and empty myself out as he continues to play along. There's respect between us: intelligent people always respect one another.

'You should think of life as something to experience, and not a game to play.'

'But life is a game.'

Then comes his twisted smile. I know what it means. He's trying to lend meaning to things, to add interest to events, to make things more than mere things. We're shadowboxing, both of us afraid to connect. And we're both glad when the session is up. The poor doctor, I've learned more about him, than he can ever know about me.

After our meeting I stop at a café. It's then I witness the Twin Towers coming down. I watch it on a television and alight onto 24th Street to watch it for real. It does very little to me. People run past me as I walk towards the madness. I'm mouthing: *I told you, I told you so.* I feel vindicated for my behavior in staring at brown faces.

That afternoon I ring Gloria. We haven't spoken in two weeks and it seems like the appropriate thing to do.

'What are we going to do?' she asks.

'Who is "us"?'

'Americans. Christians.'

'Then I'm with the Iraqis.'

137

'Iraq? Why?'
'Or the Arabs.'
'You're for the Muslims?'
'Whatever. It's all about oil and money.'
'Doc, you must be more American.'
'I fucking serve America.'
'But you sound so foreign.'

∞

9/11 makes me wonder if I could bring things down on myself. I'm standing stock-still, staring at four brown men when the thought occurs. Become a wounded animal. And be loved.

It's dark. It's a lonely street. I shouldn't be here. The outcome is a given. The intention was to lose, to take a beating. Since Gloria dumped me, I became irritated by myself, by my ways. I needed a jolt. For something real to happen. So I went and had my jaw broken. A year earlier and fed-up with Captain Sloan treating me like a schoolboy, I threw myself down the stairs and broke an arm. That got me a two-week holiday in Florida on sick leave.

There's a shelter of some kind not far from Brewer's Bar. I passed it a few times and noted its whereabouts, knowing that I might need to call on its services someday.

I never had visions of my death, but I have seen myself slaughtered many times. Slaughtered, yet still, inexplicably, among the living. Fantasies like these started in the aftermath of seeing people jump from the Twin Towers. Did they think they could fly? Maybe we have superpowers that we never considered. I daydreamed of being slaughtered, of being carved into neat little pieces: separating limbs and organs. Of course, dreams aside and ignoring minor self-inflicted cuts, I've never actually acted upon this urge.

Still.

I can't deny that it isn't there, lurking beneath the surface. I want violence enacted upon me. To be pitied. Is that such a crime?

I want to know what it *feels* like to be cut up into dainty little portions. Does it feel any different having a hand cut off, as opposed to a foot? What is the phantom feeling like, of having an amputated limb? Is a cut penis more painful than slicing off an arm? Perhaps it's all to do with how close the injury is to the core?

I often use glass to keep in touch with my senses. Of a weekday evening, I might punch or head-butt the windows of a derelict building. I always carry a map of Queens, marking out suitable buildings that I stumble upon. I seek them out, store them up and grade them: bay windows, single or double glazing, wood or composite frame.

You never can tell when you'll need an object to fight.

A lone-standing house that I cased might linger on me for days, as I leave a shard of glass in my hand. It's to study the quality of pain, to allow it niggle at me, until I give in and pull it out.

∞

The shelter across the road caters for refugees from Pakistan, Afghanistan, and Bangladesh. I think they're on to me. One night I spoke to security and the dude laughed when I asked him what it would take for me to be allowed in. It was a stupid move as I was caught on the security cameras.

In a back alley, two blocks from the shelter, is where I encounter four brown men. I whistle at them like they're hookers and they get their backs up. One cracks a joke and their dirty faces smile, their white teeth gleaming in the night. It angers me.

'Hey Paki, want a well-paying job?'

'Oh yeah?' one says, approaching with a white smile.

'Oh sorry, you're brown. No $50,000 for Arabs.'

Tickle and get a laugh, but prod and be poked.

'What did you say?'

'You heard me. I mistook you for humans, but you're rats. Vermin like you don't deserve this. You sleep on our charity and think you deserve everything without effort. Brown worms.'

∞

Alone I come to my senses.
Alone I expect to be left.
Not so.
A passer-by rings 911. But nobody can identify me. Sure enough, I've no wallet on me, nor indeed any clothes. The immigrants must have been so riled by me that all they left were a few quarters on my chicken-pink skin. There I was, knocked unconscious and left for dead, clothed only in blood. Jesus-like.

After three days in intensive care, the army becomes curious. A phone call multiplies like semen. The local newspaper reports my disappearance, and the police track me down. My parents are in separate homes and, in any case, don't really know who I am. I become a minor news item.

Gloria isn't long showing up.

The brown men really worked me over. They almost did me in; my jaw is broken in two places, my face invaded, violated, screws drilled into my jawbone. A slab of steel architecture surrounds me. My mouth is pinned into position by a steel cage; it's an immovable thing, screwed into my jaw. Mastication is a far-fetched dream. Saliva drools down the sides of my face.

Pain reaches a threshold previously unknown to me. Gloria is its antidote. She cheers me up. She sits by the bedside, the whole day long, a calming presence. She carefully picks the vomit from my mouth, gingerly working her way through the metal cage, careful not to touch it and hear an imaginary buzzer go off, like the game.

The police who come to extract a statement find me unable to speak. They fetch pen and paper. I write:

Dark night. Silhouette. Four men. Brown. I only saw shadows.

Everything went black.

No disquieting revelations from me. The cops share a look and take off. 'We'll do our best,' they say. Invisible assailants; another unsolved assault.

Gloria is my protector. She's like a mother bird feeding and cleaning her young. I can only sip on soup and milkshakes, and swallow scrambled egg. It would be easier to snort food.

Vomit. Snot. Blood. Why would anyone lower herself? When I manage to focus on something other than the pain, I become curious about her. I marvel that Gloria doesn't abandon me. She won't let me hit rock bottom. Why?

Then it hits me. Gloria's mom was a slave at home. And now that her own mom is unwell, she's happy to nurse her. Gloria is a Murphy, just like her mom. A carer. Then there's the deformed friend, plasticine face, who she also nurses. The portents are good. Gloria likes administering pain relief.

Plasticine girl looks like wolves ate her skin. She has no nose, lips, cheeks – nothing. She left a lit cigarette by her bedside. The apartment went up in flames, and she suffered 95 percent burns, and needed to be surgically remade. Rebirth by scalpel. Her face now looks like a two-year-old tried to remold it using melted plastic. It's truly gross. It has no symmetry, with unnatural contours that misrepresent a mouth, ears, nose and cheekbones. It's an abomination. And yet, Gloria greets her with a kiss on the cheek. I'm repulsed. No way that I'll let her touch my cock with those lips, not until she rinses her mouth.

What amuses me about Gloria is the way she carries on with her friends, although they failed. And even though she can't save everybody from himself or herself, she still persists. She can't recognize pathetic people. The burnt girl who lit a cigarette and cooked herself alive – she's still a smoker. Maybe Gloria enjoys the irony of being with those who don't learn from their mistakes. I can't figure it out. Does she enjoy the pain of others? Perhaps she's trapped in the same *pain versus plain* dichotomy that I am.

Then it then hits me. Gloria must love me. It can't be money – I have none. And so it seems that she's willing to sacrifice her prime for me. To risk her future gambling on me.

I'm not love-struck. A wave of practicality kicks in. If I can't return to the womb, then, at least, I might be babied for the rest of my days. My eyes open up to this opportunity: if I live to be old, Gloria will care for me. I can count on her. She would put up with me, put manners on me, domesticate me, be the earth mama who reforms me. The thought brightens. As arbitrarily as I considered her love for me, I think: I'll take her if I get through this.

And though I never saw myself as hubby material, I think – let this be her test – can she cope with me when I'm at rock bottom? If so, I'll allow myself to want again, to want her. I'll end my love affair with myself, or at least downgrade it to a secondary role. But first, let's test her loyalty.

I have a chalkboard tablet on which to write.

'I'm sorry. The things I said, they weren't me.'

Gloria snatches the chalk away from me, halting my apology in its tracks.

'Doc, I know,' she whispers.

We look at one another. I swallow. I plead for the chalk. She returns it to me.

'What do you understand?'

She's already pointing as she mouths: 'You.' In that case, she understands things I don't.

'Doc, you just need to allow yourself.'

'Allow myself what?'

'Me.'

'But how?'

'Open your heart.'

She confiscates the chalk, as though everything that I write is getting in the way. It's said that communication between lovers is non-verbal? I ape her finger, pointing back at her, as though saying that she is the one. *You, yes, you.* I reach for her hand. Hands clasped, we are bound as one, united.

Then, as the notion of marriage develops in my mind, before leaving the hospital, Gloria gifts me a little treat: a flavor of what's to come. She lovingly clasps her lips around my cheesy knob and I shoot into her and, as she draws back, a drop of salty semen splashes in her eye. I nearly break my steel cage laughing.

We're back to the us of old.

∞

Back at home, reality kicks in. As I get better, I have my doubts. I take a backwards step: forestalling, kicking and screaming. Was the cage around my face a mask? Do I really need to become solidified in all of this, to fake normality, in order to gain a foothold in the world? And if so, is marrying the only answer? I argue with myself, but there are counter-arguments.

Argument 1: Marriage isn't in my five-year plan.

Counter-argument: Time happens.

Argument 2: People slow me down.

Counter-argument: Maybe slow is the new fast.

I'll admit that sometimes I need to talk to somebody. Even murderers and thieves feel the need to share their guilt. They often confess to absolute strangers. Me, I confide all to a local simpleton. At fifty years old, he's mentally equivalent to an eight-year-old boy. The things that I tell him.

'I saw a goose's egg,' the idiot tells me.

'Have you ever seen a girl's egg?'

'Girls don't have eggs.'

'Yes, they do. You must look for them.'

'Where?'

'You must investigate.'

'How?'

'Be more promiscuous.'

He laughs but I think he understands. Alas no, he merely finds the word 'promiscuous' funny.

'What's that? Prom-cus'

'Look under a girl's dress and see what you find.'

I've struck a chord. He cocks his head. I wonder if when I leave his mind goes blank, or if his curiosity remains tweaked. Can he think things? Does he have a memory?

'Two plus two?' I ask.

'You're funny.'

The fucking retard, I'm wasting my time. Of course he can't think. I walk away.

I try talking to Gloria. It's a first. Like, really talking. She knows nothing about my serious transgressions. She wouldn't understand. I'm not a textbook case. We keep it touchy-feely. Gloria meets me at Brewer's Bar, where I'm habitually propped at the bar. We move to a quiet table.

'You shouldn't drink alone.'

'I'm not comfortable in company. Apart from yours,' I quickly correct.

'You should live in the woods.'

'I'll consider it.'

'Stop being an oddball. It's not good to be alone.'

'Why?'

'It's the beginning of the end.'

'Really?'

'If you like your own company so much, who knows where it'll end.'

'It sounds like a promising date.'

I enjoy our slow pace. It gives us time to breathe, to unite as one. I've come to value – no – *to long* for it. It's like a sealed-off private world known only to us.

'I love you,' Gloria announces.

She catches me off guard. I look at her, then furtively glance around lest anyone heard.

'Me too,' I confide.

She absorbs my delayed response. It's an affront, a slap across the face. Love ought to be a certainty. She twitches her face and rights her blouse, removing her cleavage from sight.

'Want to visit a firearms store?'

'Gun shops are closed.'

Anyway, I'm having none of it. I have to show feeling. I reach under her hair and massage her nape. Then I slide my hand down, past her slim neck, and towards her breasts. She smiles.

'You have such a long neck. So exquisite. You speak from here.'

I use my finger to tap the base of her throat.

'You're never afraid of being vulnerable. I want to learn from you.'

This message of faith in her is appreciated.

'What makes you happy?' she asks.

'You do.'

'There you go then.'

There it is, then.

'Mom says that I've a swan's neck. Maybe I'm as nasty as…'

We're primed to talk properly. My relationships with girls up until then were based on animal needs. But now I must plan beyond that.

'Gloria, I wonder where I'm going and how it's supposed to turn out.'

'It's natural to think so. The eighth wonder of the world is the mind. Some people think they have all the answers. Others don't know what they're about. It doesn't matter either way. Life is for first timers.'

'Man meets girl: they've been doing it for millennia. Yet I make it so complicated,' I muse.

She knows better than to compound matters. We're bonding. She confirms that, yes, you can tamper with fate. How does she know things I can't? It's baffling. I throw out a question, curious how she might answer.

'I don't know what I'm supposed to do, how to act. It might be that

I'm mis-calibrated. I feel out of step with everyone.'

'It's not about acting, just be. That's the secret.'

For her, it's that straightforward. She has none of my existential depth. She places her hand on mine, and isn't afraid to stare into my eyes and smile.

She'll make someone a happy home. I remember her devotion when she nursed me during my broken jaw episode. The promise I made. A wave of practicality kicks in – do I evermore wish to be alone? If so, am I content knowing that there won't be any new chapters? If I want to get tangled up in life, is it good enough to merely *like* Gloria? With her the journey won't be too messy, as she's tolerant. And though there mightn't be any great shift in feelings, we'll quickly settle into coupledom – without any great highs or lows.

Plodders

Keepers.

Gloria does me an act of kindness by wanting me, and I'm only returning the favor by taking a chance on her. My reason is simple – I owe her one.

'I like being with you,' I say.

'I like being with you too.'

'No, that's not true. I mean, that's not it. Not fully. There's more.'

'Go on,' she prompts.

'Well, I feel normal.'

'Normal? And that's supposed to make me feel special?'

'It's special for me that you can make me feel normal. It's unusual that someone can affect me that way.'

'Make you feel normal?'

'Yeah.'

'Doc, nobody knows what normal is. But go on, what makes being normal so special for you?'

'It makes things meaningful.'

'What things?'

'Things like you.'

She has prompted my words. She smiles.

'That *is* a compliment,' she coos.

I go for the knockout line.

'Gloria, will you marry me?'

She falters a moment, then smiles.

'Is that a proposal?'

'Have I not made myself clear?'

A hesitation ensues, a formidable pregnant pause. For a moment I think she won't have me. My lack of worth is something I try not to question. And though I routinely end up with lesser beings, doubt fires up in my mind. *Am I a fit suitor?*

'I will marry you, Doc.'

'Oh, thank God,' I hear my ego speak.

The bartering is over. Her eyes well up, and I hand her a napkin. They're the last happy tears I'll ever see. I've interrupted my life, my autonomy, and become a collector of titles - husband and wife. We give ourselves to one another and lock our freedom in a cell, each the other person's slave.

Sold.

I never imagined that I'd be gifted a license to marry. How can she rely on me, when I can't rely on myself? Is love necessary for the marriage contract? No. But then why marry? Because I can. I can have what I don't want. Moments later, Gloria has her doubts.

'Doc, are you sure you're not just in one of your fucked-up moods?'

'No, really, let's get married' I say, somewhat absentmindedly.

We have a new motive. She smiles, then kisses me. I wipe her lipstick from my lips. Gloria gushes sweetly. I get a semi, all on its own, without hands.

'Come on, let's go.'

'Where to?'

'Where we can get something decent.'

'Where's that?'

'Somewhere posh.'

I take her to an up-market restaurant where I feel ill at ease, and order the expensive things at the bottom of the menu. A conjugal tone establishes itself and Gloria has no qualms in taking a doggy bag home.

'Doc, who are you?'

'I'm just me.'

'But what's your real name?'

'Are you after the name I was born with or the one I'll be buried with?'

'I know how your tombstone will read – a sexy man lies here. Let's start at birth.'

And so we start at the beginning. I've boxed away so much of who I am, where I came from. I'm slow opening up. But her patience is comforting and, eventually, I tell her the truth, the tragedy of being me. She insists on meeting my parents.

First we first visit Mom's psychiatric home. Mom throws sugar lumps, then a cup of tea at Gloria, all the while shouting: 'Run, run, save, save'. Gloria pats Mom's hand, trying to quieten her. Mom calms down, but as Gloria hugs her goodbye, she sinks her teeth into Gloria's neck. She draws a little blood. Later on, Gloria remarks that she really likes my mom and I believe her.

At Dad's nursing home in Elmhurst, I take the cane from him – just in case. He motions for Gloria to come near, and feels her face. Then he smiles. It's so weird having Dad's approval. I haven't seen Dad's smiling teeth in decades, and didn't know if they were worn down or wolfish.

Answer: wolfish.

∞

The build-up to the wedding almost breaks me. It's so tedious that it becomes extremely difficult to feign rapture. Though also a non-believer, Gloria is too afraid to break with convention and we book a chapel. The wedding menu is salmon or beef. As I'm banking on it being the end of my decision-making as regards menial chores, I insist that it be trout or lamb. Just to be awkward. The menus are reprinted.

We celebrate a solemn wedding, a small Prod one. So upright, so righteous. The flower arrangement is imaginative. Gloria even made sure that, aside from chrysanthemums and orchids, there are wreaths of heather for decorating the pews.

∞

During the wedding ceremony, I think about the stupidity of the marriage contract: *through thick and thin and until death do us part*. It's all a bit over the top, and then there's the fidelity bullshit.

I'm only getting married out of curiosity, but apathy prevails and the rest of the day is a thick fog. I interrupt my indifference by shedding a tear during my wedding speech. 'Someday you have to settle on somebody, to couple up.' They're Stan's words, the ones he delivered at his own wedding. I repeat them. Then I zone out.

The job is done and our papers are in order. We're officially one entity, Gloria and I. For two weeks I feel like I can do no wrong. Gloria squeezes me dry on our honeymoon. She fucks me so hard that I think I might break her pussy. When we get home we still haven't recovered. I'm almost relieved that our life's worth of fucking is over.

She vomits all the time. Gloria is delighted, says it's a baby. We're spawning. More property. I didn't heed the warning: 'you could have a child together but then she'll own you forever.' We strike a deal. She gets a baby and I get my War on Terror. Afghanistan is around the corner.

We stop being who we are. Gloria needs more love; I give less. I take what lovers I can. I'm not on for fucking a fatty, so I go back to paying for it. I like seeing my prick as it sits encircled in some strange girl's mouth-hole.

Chapter 6

Covid-19

2020

On the subway home I'm pensive. Disturbed. My hair is damp. Did I run a hand through it after touching the girl? It means that I've the spittle of a coronavirus victim on me. I rub my hand against the underside of the seat. If I'd a knife, I'd lop off my arm. To distract myself for another four stops, I hum a tune. It doesn't work.

Karma is a bitch.

Once home, I run the shower. I don't calm down until I've shampooed my hair twice. I take it for granted, my hair. I overlook its vitality. I've an excellent head of hair for my age. In the mirror I say it aloud. I've a fine head of thick brown hair at the age of 48¾. But when I run my hand through it, it feels like my fingers are counting each remaining strand. My face is full of pockmarked lines; wrinkles are like streams that join up with broad rivers. I don't know which is worse: Covid-19 or the thought of growing old.

In the kitchen, I crack open a bottle of JB and neck a thimbleful before sinking into the sofa in the living room. I think about it, the scolding that I gave myself in the bathroom mirror. I'm larger than my reflection. An hour later and I feel sedated. Two hours later and I'm comatose.

The next morning I lie in bed and wonder. Maybe I have coronavirus and maybe not. I behave like it's the latter. Regardless, I call in sick.

'Doc, what you doing?'

'I can't face another day of coronavirus deaths. I'm staying at home.'

'For real?'

'I could drive the kids to school.'

'School is closed. Lockdown.'

Gloria heads outside, whereto, I don't know. She acted strange when she found me in the kitchen. Why? I was only trying to guess how many thimblefuls of JB were left. I do some rooting in a cupboard and come up with a handwritten note. I laugh out loud as I read it.

Gloria's core competencies have increased: she can deceive. The polygamous cow has kept herself busy as I try to keep my shit together, responding to 911 calls. Her egotism stuns me – how she looked after herself without leaving a scent. Husband bravely goes to work during a global pandemic and, for the first time ever, things at home don't stand still. This is news to me. I thought that domestic life just plodded along. That it doesn't, makes me feel weary, too tired to continue, too tired for the drama of life. Time has caught up with me and I feel an inner sadness. There's barely a morsel of undeadness left in me.

There's poison at home.

Gloria is putting out. The thought of it. Of offering her naked self to somebody. Of someone actually wanting her. To cry or laugh? And do you know with whom my wife is having an affair? Postman, butcher, neighbor?

Nope.

With Dad's septuagenarian mate. And how do I find out? Nursing home, neighbor, Dad?

Nope.

The food deliveryman from *Meals on Wheels*. Un-fucking-believable. It's beyond cliché.

∞

'Nice day,' says Mister *Meals on Wheels*, when I open the door.

'Yes, it is.'

'Is the wife out?'

'Sorry?'

'Your wife. Is she not in?'

'Gloria? Yes. I mean, no. She's out.'

'I'll call back tomorrow.'

For some reason something niggles me. I never imagined that I'd actually listen to a man who deals in free food for the elderly, but suddenly I want him to talk.

'Do you know my wife? To be asking for her like that, there must be a reason.'

'I'm just the deliveryman.'

'So I gathered.'

'It's just that, ordinarily, I deal with her.'

I find myself sizing up his looks. No way – small, bald, fat and greasy.

'Ordinarily, you deal with her?'

'Settle the score.'

'What score?'

'She cashes up for Misses Bennett.'

'Misses Bennett?'

'Your neighbor.'

The deliveryman acts like I'm the weird one.

'Let me guess: the old woman is on a free food scheme but has to pay a token something?'

'One dollar per meal.'

'Do I know you?'

'Know me?'

'Have I seen you before?'

It turns out that the deliveryman does some kind of overlap at Elmhurst Care Home where Dad used to boast that his friend was fucking my wife.

What to do?

When Gloria arrives home I make enquires.

'Where were you?'

'I went to see your dad.'

'Really?'

'You should go.'

'We're not on speaking terms, because Dad is dead.'

'I know, honey,' she says.

'You were at the graveyard then?'

'I keep it so pretty. You should visit.'

'So, you weren't at the senile center?'

'Elmhurst Care Home?'

'Yeah.'

'Funny you ask, as I was. I'd arranged to collect some things of his – mementos. The nurse said you never dropped by. You must let it go, Doc.'

'A month after his death and you're dropping by to collect his things.'

'I made friends there. In case you forgot, I visited your dad for decades.'

We lock eyes. She looks away. I let out a heavy sigh.

Caught.

She's clearly lying: her supposed 'friends' is a code word for lovers. Although I'm on to her, I conceal my discovery. I don't feel comfortable barging in on her private life, or abandoning her just yet. And anyway, the thought of it all exhausts me. I need a strategy. A come-good.

A year or two ago and I might have acted differently; it might have bothered me. Back then, I broke up with a girlfriend and was in the habit of running back to my wife to help me get over my secret affairs. But now I'm so removed from myself, from who I used be, and, it seems, I'm far away from the goings on around me, and I wonder why I don't care. I know that I'm on my own, so why bother confronting Gloria to confirm this? Instead I wing it, wing being us.

The day doesn't drag. I'm busy. I have a new mission. I don't want to die just yet, at least not before knowing the details. I become more vigilant: I watch her comings and goings; policing her expressions. Then I take to following her at a distance, renting a car to fulfill my investigative role.

The word 'intercourse' persists in my mind. Fucking who? Which old codger? Or might she be consorting with one of the young carers? Does she want to hurt me, or is it for her own amusement, to experiment, and merely for daring's sake? I'm indignant that my fat-assed housewife is getting plugged, jealous that her cunt has found a gardener. I presumed we had a kind of mono-directional monogamy. I never figured on this: her infidelity and my jealousy. The axis of control has shifted.

Then there's the matter of my father.

So pious.

Pontius *Pious*.

The traitor.

Why didn't Dad look out for me? By keeping the affair secret he not only acted against my interests, but treated me with contempt. Perhaps my (unremarkable) success threatened him. Did it irk him, how I managed to rise above our station in life? Or, maybe it was his way of exerting power over me, to show me that he was still the man.

The answer might be simpler.

The bedeviling old bastard probably wasn't quite with it, as he shuffled along to his next stop, his final stop, and all the while hindering me. Just as in life. Hadn't I once asked him to look after Gloria while I was away at war? Naïve me. No matter the task, he never failed to disappoint. Now, with Dad dead from coronavirus, I've become like him, with an inability to forgive.

With Gloria too pathetic to confront, I decide to approach the Casanova directly, and have a man-to-man chat.

I visit the residential-care home suited up in paramedic attire and like I'm on the job. I'm not driving an ambulance but have taken Gloria's car. I take Corona Avenue and pigeons occupy the street. I feel like I'm starring in an apocalyptic movie. It's a sad irony that Corona is the worst hit area by the coronavirus. With no traffic coming against me, I swing into the middle of the road, hoping to mow down the birds. They scatter. The vision of a lockdown pandemic is a beauty to behold, if only because there's space to think. I think, at least I christened my kids right; they have solid names. I think, I had no choice about who I became. I think, my wife or I must die for things to get better.

'Doc Cage. What's up? We didn't call you guys,' the security guard says.

'It's something that was left behind.'

'You forgot something? Personal shit? Gloria took your dad's things.'

'It's not about him. Jamaica Hospital sent me down to collect a sample.'

Past security, without a thermometer check, and I make my way to the open-air quadrangle as I pull off my facemask. There he is, the fucker, fixing a wheel on a rusty bike that should have been tossed away.

'Is it true?'

'It's definitely true,' he says, not bothering to interrupt his labor.

'You admit that you have been fucking my wife?'

'Sorry?' he asks, as he creaks himself upright, squinting a look at me. 'The wheel is true. I don't know nothing about your wife.'

'Do you know who might?'

'Depends who your wife is.'

'I'm Antonio Rivera's son. Gloria Cage is my wife.'

'You're Antonio Rivera Junior. That would be Bingo who's banging her.'

'Bingo? Where can I find him, Mister Bingo?'

'Nickname is Bingo. Big Bingo, actually. Garden – most probably.'

He too is bent over, sunk in the ground a meter deep, in a hole he dug to uproot a tree. From way off, I hear his hacking cough, heavy, I presume, with tar. Big Bingo is in his mid-seventies, large-framed, broad-shouldered and rotund, as tall as me. Doubtless in his youth he was quite the specimen. I throw the lover's note that I found in the kitchen into the pit and circle around him like I'm a badass. He sees the note and raises his head as though trying to sniff the air over my head. It feels like high noon. Where is the sound of church bells so we can draw guns? He doesn't follow me with his eyes as I circle the hole that he's stood in. Instead, he clears his throat and spits out phlegm. *Gloria was with this ignorant animal?*

Bingo strikes me as being a war veteran, what with the dehumanized scowl. I know the type. Or perhaps it's prison that he survived. He has beady eyes and a protruding lower lip. Above it, he has a cropped moustache – a Hitler-ish thing. I don't know if it's meant to make him look stern or educated, the facial hair. On level ground, Bingo would surely stand a good inch or two over me. When he stands, he stands as if to attention, ramrod straight, square on, barrel-chested, as though I'm an artist about to sketch him. He has on a light blue singlet, over which sprouts grey chest hair. Across his right bicep I take in a tattoo that reads: 'Dying to Live'.

Keeping his imposing stature, Bingo delivers what he has to say via a process of digestion, first mulching his words, before spitting them out through wheezing sighs. Maybe he has some kind of stutter. Or was he damaged at war? He has a demonic look about him, such that I imagine if he were to become upset he would fly into a rage and trash me. There I am, afraid of a man heading towards eighty.

I let my guard down to issue a health warning.

'You should be wearing a mask.'

'Shouldn't you also be wearing one?'

'I'll take my chances.'

I imagine Gloria blowing his cock and am done with small talk.

'Are you going to confess?'

'To Gloria and I? We're done.'

'Done?'

'Just back to being old friends.'

'Fuck buddies no longer?'

He ignores me, preferring to pick at the tree stump. I feel cheapened. After having his wicked way with Gloria he no longer gets turned on by her and hopes to hand her back to me. He'd rather whack off. We both would. Still. It's insulting. Only now does the real fucking begin, the fucking *me* over.

'At my age, the spark doesn't burn so bright. Lead in the pencil stuff.'

'Too much information.'

'I thought you wanted to know,' he says, bewildered, shooting me a cock-eyed look.

Once Bingo realizes that I don't actually want to know about his sex life with my wife, he seems to take stock of me as a person and not as a threat.

'You're a bit out of shape. Losing your vitality, I dare say.'

I feel self-conscious and tuck in my belly and square my chest. This is ridiculous. Here I am, taking it, getting fucked all over again as I listen to his bullshit. I could rush at him, storm the pit, or upend a garden bench on him. But if I did, I know that I'd be fighting over someone I don't love. I'm not sore about their fucking – no, my pride is hurt. There's little point in admonishing Bingo, and anyway, it's he who's in control.

Guilt is inverted, as things weigh on me. Though cosmic law suggests we should fight, he makes it so that I don't know how to wage war.

'She was sad,' he offers by way of apology. 'She said you weren't looking after her.'

Bingo speaks about Gloria with disquieting candor. It doesn't feel right.

'I know my marital duties.'

'I was only obliging. I didn't mean any harm. I was scared at first. I thought it mightn't be good for my heart. You see, I'm on these tablets.'

'I don't need to know.'

'I thought that you did. Isn't that why you came to see me?'

'All I needed to know was that Gloria was being unfaithful.'

He changes tack by trying to fill in my own back-story.

'Why did you marry her?'

'Loneliness,' I find myself saying.

'Your dad said that you were a combat medic and became a paramedic?'

'So what?'

'I don't know about first aid but I do know something about killing.'
He eyeballs me.

'I like soldiers,' he says. 'The things they believe in are the things they die for.'

'And more often than not, we get killed by friendly fire.'

'You could get killed doing this. The coronavirus is the unseen enemy.'

'Dying is only a question of when.'

Bingo scowls at my blasé nature. Here we go, another person who wants to lecture me about life. But no, born in 1945, it turns out that Bingo served in Vietnam.

'Were you drafted?'

'Volunteered. Nixon got in by promising to end formal call-ups. I was deployed to South Vietnam. Didn't have a choice over military occupational specialty. Just picked up a gun.'

Bingo knows about mortars and rockets, their range and capability. Indeed, he's something of a handgun historian. He speaks about a buddy that he fought alongside, L.Cpl. Todds, who lost a leg and, once home, was knocked down by a bus crossing the road.

'The prosthetic leg froze on him. He saw the bus but could only move in slow-motion.'

'Leg jammed up, just like a gun. It costs so many lives.'

'Are you being funny?'

'Not intentionally.'

'In Vietnam, hundreds were killed on any given day. They left no stories. They just vanished.'

In a bizarre twist, our chat comforts me. I never say much to Gloria - she finds death more boring than discussing washing powder - but I think Bingo gets me. I dish it to him, as he pays me full attention.

'Nobody gives a shit about war. The only killing people see comes out of Hollywood.'

I have him now. Bingo nods along with me. I become curious as I watch him care about stories of strangers dying. He starts grinding his teeth, disturbed.

'They don't count them, these current people?'

'Coronavirus deaths? No. We're not at war. They're casualties of life. Mere fatalities.'

'My friend got buried in Hart Island last week. Nobody to claim him. There's not even a head count up there. They throw them in a mass grave like at Auschwitz.'

'Death is a spectacle, that's all it is, Bingo.'

I'm half a world away, as I indulge Bingo in my macabre deeds. Remember the time jihadists set fire to a church and everyone trapped inside? I watched from a distance. Anyone who escaped was shot. On I continue, unloading my life's horrors on Bingo, glossing over details that would show I had a hand in things. Remember the burning forest? A child ran out of the raging flames and collided with a wild boar, even before my eyes could understand it – the sound of bone on bone. Gristle on skin. The boy's mouth was open in shock, as he was raised into the air and skewered. All the while, the enemy was pinning down any survivors. I don't tell Bingo that, out of mercy, I finished the boy off with a bullet. The boar got away.

'Did you ever think of joining in, of taking up arms?'

'My MOS was 68W but I carried a gun. I wasn't just a bystander.'

'Which was the worst?'

'The worst war?'

'No. Warlord.'

'There are so many – Milosevic, Karadic. Al Baghdadi trumps Bin Laden.'

We touch on the reasons for war – nationalism, land grabbing, religion or oil – and the difference between religious wars and authentic land-grabs like Russia in Ukraine. The Crimea invasion was obvious as the Russian's lease of Sevastopol was up for renewal and the Ukrainian government was in transition. But does anyone take any notice? Not a tap. Everyone is too afraid to change now, never mind tomorrow.

'What can I do for you?' Bingo finally asks.

He stumps me, suddenly leveling me with a superior attitude. The cheek. He tries to soften the blow, once he realizes that I'm taken aback.

'She's a fine woman, that girl of yours.'

'Gloria? Yes, she is. She snores a bit, though.'

'Don't know how you stick that.'

'Was that what did it?'

'Did what?'

'Broke you two up?'

Bingo reminisces, as though he's trying to jog his memory about something that happened decades ago.

'No, it wasn't that.'

'Then what finished you?'

I fear he might mention the way Gloria sweats during sex. I almost feel embarrassed for her.

'There were different things.'

'But there must be something?'

'No offence, and it's just as you are pressing me. The thing is, she's a bit of a talker. But enough about us. What was it that made you ignore her?'

I look at the plants around the garden, and then back to Bingo, trying to contemplate him at some remove. It's all very odd, yet feels remarkably ordinary. For him, everything – everyone – has a start, middle and end. For him, my wife's usefulness has simply come to an end.

I never thought about the end, until now.

'Tickles,' Bingo announces.

'The tickles?'

'Yeah. She tipped a pot of tea over the bed once. Look here.'

He raises his t-shirt and reveals what looks like a birthmark on his ribs. I let out a laugh. Bingo frowns at me.

'If you touch her, she gets jumpy like a horse.'

'She did that,' he cries. 'And it's only because you're wanting to know all the personal details, so then have it: the ammonia smell.'

'Pee?'

'I'd rather not be vulgar,' Bingo says.

'Ever since the second kid it got worse. She used to say that holding in pee was good for the vaginal muscles.'

'Pelvic floor rehabilitation.'

'What's that?' I ask.

'The cure.'

'For what?'

'Incontinence. My wife had it and it's not rubbish.'

Bingo pauses, looks to the heavens and blesses himself.

'I'm sorry,' I say.

'Nothing to be sorry about. She's long dead and was well looked after.'

Bingo delivers this last line with a twinkle in his eye and, for the first time, reveals a gold tooth.

I don't have it in me to condemn him, despite how I sought him out, to have someone to fight: a target. In a strange way, the entire drama is cathartic. I was tired of things happening all around me and never actually *to* me. I had long felt outside everything, hovering above daily life, like an angel. But now that I'm brought back down to earth, and now that Bingo and I are no longer strangers and both play a part in Gloria's life, I don't have it in me to hate him. Instead I find myself trying to relate to him.

'Do you have kids?'

'The wife couldn't. I'm the end of the line.'

'I'm sorry.'

'But you, you have fine children.'

'Yes. I do,' I say.

'Keep you grounded, kids do. Keep you plugged into life.'

'I'm not programmed that way.'

'How so?'

'I feel like I'm living a fake life. I don't get the subtleties of living. I'm immune to feeling things. I'm a manufacturing malfunction.'

'They're strange things you're saying. You talk like you're not from this world. You're not a machine. Life has no formula to follow; everybody is different.'

I'm in a pre-mourning phase. Blame the fever that I'm keeping at bay thanks to Tylenol. I'm slowly losing grip over myself. I'm also losing them – the kids, my family. In some ways, it's thrilling not knowing how life will carry on after I'm gone.

'Are you a misogynist?' Bingo asks.

'Me? No.'

'Disfavor women. Or are you gay?'

'Homosexual? No. I hate humans, but as I only interact with women it's only then noticeable.'

Bingo touches his moustache as though checking it's there.

'What do you live for?'

'Escape,' I say.

'From what?'

'It's odd but, when I used go to war, as soon as I got there I'd long to be far away from it. It's the same working in the ambulance. I never want to be where I am. When I'm at home, I'm not at home, if you know what I mean. And between these two places I shuttle all my life.'

'That doesn't make sense.'

'I'm never at home in my own skin.'

'That's called *weltschmerz*.'

'What's it mean?' I ask.

'It's German for world-weary. In my day we used shoot them. Germans.'

And there it is. Bingo shoots straight from the hip. No angst, no bullshit, no analysis. It's as though he's here to clear up my mind, telling me the what and how. Then he seals my miserable fate.

'Doc, if you feel that way about life then you should do something big and die young. Be really alive at your death.'

'It's a bit late for that, dying young, no?'

'Then do something big and die right now.'

I wipe my feverish brow and smile. Does Bingo mean it or is he just

Doc Cage

trying to be high-minded? I hold out a hand. He looks at it. I smile, like I'm safe. We shake. He turns his back on me and resumes digging.

'Bingo, be sure that you get all the roots out before planting something else.'

'Will do.'

What he really means is: fuck off and stop bothering me.

∞

We're watching the news. Donald Trump is up in arms. He blames the Chinese for the coronavirus pandemic. The world is imploding. The lockdown objectors are getting vocal and storming government buildings. War floods onto the street and into my head. It baffles, war coming home does. I thought I left all that behind. A spark of ignition is all it takes to start a movement. That night, there's a hullabaloo of some kind out on the street. A car is on fire. There's a riot. It's odd having warlike mayhem at home.

Gunfire. Destruction. And violence. I feel it coming. I do.

The following night, I lie in bed and I'm listening for the sound of Armageddon: a loud bang, sirens wailing, or a stray gunshot. Gloria thinks I'm paranoid. But there it is: gunfire. There it is again. Boom. It's past 2am and I laugh out loud as the world goes to pot. It weirds Gloria out as she heard nothing.

'What's so funny?' she asks.

'The world's patience is timing out.'

But the charade is all in my head. Outside, there isn't a sound. I'm sweating. I have dizzy spells. My laughter turns to tears, catching me off guard. I must be dying.

'Doc, what's wrong?'

'Coming home to roost.'

'Who is?'

'The ghosts are coming. The boy in my dreams.'

'What boy?'

'Coming home to roost,' I repeat.

'Who, Doc?'

'The boy in the well.'

I try explaining it to Gloria. Apocalypse Now. She's having none of it – she only knows peace. She doesn't know the animal urge that lays dormant in civilized society; the caveman lurking in us. Everyone is on edge as it's a psychological war, the killer virus being invisible. Coronavirus statistics to date: every two minutes, the virus kills someone in the tri-state area. The death toll in New York City has passed 20,000. My neighborhood of Queens is the county with the most fatalities in America.

In the morning, I receive a call.

'Doc, we need you.'

'I can't work. I'm sick.'

'Are you sure that you don't have the rona?'

'No. My back is out. I can't even stand up.'

Fuck the lot of them. I'd rather die at home. I must write this faster as time is a luxury. I even have a title. Ah, the life in my notebooks, the ambiguity of being me. Scribble this and into the sunset I'll go…

I get a second wind. Although I feel better, my life hits a three-o'clock slump. I'm in the doldrums, with no urge to snap out of it. Compassion fatigue, or, in colloquial parlance, I don't give a shit. I tell work that I slipped a few discs. Gloria ignores me. She's an emotionless fish. Look at what she's doing: making a lie of us, as we can't talk for real. She says I'm not open to the world so why bother communicating. I'm sick of it. For my part, the energy of hate is too much bother. I'm not going to kick up a fuss over someone making use of my wife's pussy. After all, her pussy, when last I saw it, was an overgrown hedge.

Gloria is slumped on the couch, barely watching the television. She seems meditative. Stuff is on both of our minds. We're shaping up for a fight, I feel it. All is revealed in her sigh. I wish I had complained about it to Bingo. There may yet be a way - I'll go back and tell him. We could strike up a secret rapport. When we chatted, I felt our conversation was a puzzle, a mystery I didn't have a complete picture of.

'Gloria, was it the rose?' I ask.

'Huh?'

We talk in a distracted time-delay. At best, we're only half interested in one another. I think it's prudent to clear the air in case... Just in case.

'Are you sure?'

'Doc, it wasn't the rose.'

'But you do see my point?'

'About the rose?'

It's an artificial conversation we're having. Our eyes are trained on the TV where we are watching a lover present a rose to his girlfriend at dinner. That very same scene was the source of our last fight.

We had gone out to dinner, the two of us, to a cheap Italian. A brown dude came in with a bucket of roses. Maybe I was short with him, as we had barely been seated when he stuffed a bouquet between us and demanded that I buy a rose. I refused and, ever since, Gloria has been in a huff. Yes, even now, weeks later.

'Gloria, a complete stranger doesn't have the right to define our love.'

'Define our love?'

She turns to look at me, as though I'm admitting to being an alien.

'OK, to put a price on our love.'

'Was it not worth five bucks?'

'Of course. It's worth much more, and that's the point.'

'What's the point?'

'The point is that he knows love is priceless, so he can ask for the moon.'

'But if love is equivalent to the moon then five dollars was a steal.'

'Gloria, we've lost the real value of things if money is the benchmark to be applied.'

'He wasn't selling love but a token gesture.'

'Yes, a cheap tokenistic gesture.'

'Exactly, Doc. It was cheap. As in, it was affordable.'

'Fine, you win. The rose was a metaphor. I didn't like the cut of the guy. OK? I'm sure he was Syrian or mujahedeen.'

Of course, we're not talking about what we appear to be talking about. Anything but. I've been casting about, digging behind her and trying to see the things about her that I've stopped noticing. Indifferent to her existence for so long, I had to force myself to become perceptive by treating her as a jigsaw puzzle. And what did I learn from spying on her?

This.

Although Gloria and I fucked thousands of times in every conceivable position, I never really seemed to know her. Not carnally knowing, but *knowing* knowing, if you know what I mean. Next: as part of survival during lockdown, her friend is teaching her how to bake bread. Making bread in this era of mass production. It can't go unchallenged.

'You got through life so far without wanting to make bread,' I say.

'Doc, are you investigating me? Since when did you care what I do?'

'Since this self-improvement thing, I decided to become more aware.'

'By spying on me?'

There's no point becoming indignant about bread, roses, or love, as our union is pointless. A mere front. We're so lonely together. And if I am going to fight with her over Bingo, it's going to be a fight over nothing. Over nobody. The line rings true: it was for the children's sake that we remained together. I look for reasons for us and come up with a blank. Sure, she manages my life. Gloria is my organizer and house cleaner. But if only she went to her own home when she clocked off and left me alone. The way things stand, it's as though I'm married to the housemaid.

Amidst all of this, out of the blue, Gloria wonders why we didn't have another child. I always wanted one less. It's lucky that Kurtz and Bob aren't around to hear. Hear what? To hear me say that I never wanted any. That the kids made me old, that they ruined me. That it became all about them.

'Gloria, you're almost fifty. You're menopausal.'

'We should have had a girl.'
'Why?'
'Because we don't.'
'So what? We don't have a horse either.'
'It might have softened you up.'
'What, have a daughter instead of taking Alka-Seltzer?'
'A girl would have dazzled you.'
'Yeah, with baby dolls and maternal feelings at four years of age.'
'It beats football and fighting.'
'Fighting is human nature.'
'Oh, not this again.'
'You started it. But Gloria, just so you know, there'll be no fucking and no daughter.'
'Unless you can have a horse?'
'Yeah. Unless we throw a horse into the equation.'
'Doc, all I got from you was a surname, and the wrong one at that.'

∞

A shrink is on TV, telling a story about a girl with bad dreams who gets up one day, murders her parents and then goes back to watching TV to look for more inspiration. What follows is a debate about the way television and the Internet has become a substitute for our imagination. Then the shrink says something that resonates with me:

'If you think about a thing often enough, it will come to pass. It's possible to will a thing into being, yes, even sub-consciously.'

A subconscious power. Intriguing. But can it be undone, as wish I wasn't killing Bingo.

There's no enmity between us, between Bingo and I. I have the urge to see him, to have his disapproving comments, and hear his prosecuting tone. I know it's odd, but it's all that jars me alive, his scorn. It's like talking to the gut. His gut to my gut. Or maybe it's because we're both outsiders, and understand each other's strangeness.

I worm my way into Elmhurst Care Home, dressed as a paramedic, suited up and full of infection. Bingo is with hammer and chisel, seated in front of a block of stone in the quadrangle. He used to work stone, being something of a self-taught sculptor.

'Stone is honest. You hit it, and it chips. If it doesn't, you've flawed technique. The force is soaked up by the stone and shatters when you least expect.'

As if to make his point, he blows the dust off the stone and wipes it with his sleeve. What do I care about stone?

'Know how I started?' Bingo asks, noting my disinterest.

'How?'

'The wife did yoga. I saw that it was a charade. So, I got into body weather.'

'Body weather? What's that, walking in the rain?'

He laughs, pleased to have awoken my interest.

'Body weather is less hierarchical.'

'Than what? Walking in the rain?'

'Take your body, for example: you look and you move.'

'So what?' I say.

'The eyes look, and the body follows. So your body follows the eyes. Get it? Your body is a servant. But in body weather, you don't need to look. You lead with an ankle or a rib. You forget looking. You just throw your body out, throw a shape. There's no politics or purpose about moving body parts. You just do it.'

Bingo shuffles, throws his hip my way, and then does a flourish with his ankle. It's utterly ridiculous. It's like watching a coalminer do ballet in boots and overalls. I can't contain my laughter. He's pleased.

'In body weather, it's the body that is the instrument. Not the eyes. Min Tanaka says the body is a force of nature. Just like a tree sways in the wind, your body can also shake in unorganized ways. Call it outdoor improvisation.'

With that, Bingo reaches out a hand like he's picking an apple off an imaginary tree, then he throws a hip out in a feminine way, before

Doc Cage

crouching low, arms raised high, jumping up, and finishes with a ridiculous pirouette. I can't contain my laughter, yet the nurses passing by hardly notice him.

'There's also body landscape. That's a totally different movement ideology.'

'Let me guess, that's where you behave like a rock?'

'No. But you're getting there. Body landscape is where you dance among stones. It's how I got into carving, chipping away at them, and sculpting rocks.'

'Like whittling a piece of wood?'

'Exactly. But here's the thing: the rocks find me.'

'The rocks come to you?'

'Sometimes, yeah.'

'Dad was into stones,' I find myself saying.

'I know,' Bingo smiles.

I need to move away from this and push off in a new direction.

'Bingo, can you tell me why the marital bed has moved?'

'Moved?'

'Gloria positioned it differently in the room.'

'How so?'

'It's not between the bedside lockers anymore. It's lurking down by the door.'

'Which way is north?'

'That way,' I say, pointing in the direction of Canada.

'Not here, in your house, stupid.'

Bingo called me stupid, and I just took it.

'North is the direction of the main wardrobe.'

'And how has the bed moved?'

'The head is now at the wardrobe; I can barely open it.'

'That's right.'

'Right?' I say.

'Yes, your head to the north and feet facing south.'

'Why?'

'Electromagnetic forces. The iron at the Earth's core rotates in a given direction, and the iron in our blood must move in the same direction and not go against the earth's flow.'

'Is that why you're always digging? To get to the earth's core?'

In many respects, meeting Bingo was a blessing. He knows things; he has answers, about humans and life. I wonder if he might help me engineer a reconciliation with Gloria, now that he's finished with her. He seems to get me, almost without explanation. He knows the way I am and, crucially, the whys and wherefores of me that I can't even figure out.

∞

May Day and I borrow my wife's bicycle. Actually, I think it belongs to one of her friends. No matter, it's a good way to get around the stay-at-home order as exercise is allowed. I have a clear sight of all that lies in front of me, as the streets lie empty. Outside Jamaica Hospital, nurses have taken to the street to protest the lack of personal protective equipment. But with hat and mask on, nobody recognizes me.

During my dash to the church, I feel alive, like a runner during the great wars of old. His white skin is like a traffic light and I roll to a stop. His greeting is an apology, as though he has something to confess. He does.

'I'm sorry that I didn't contact you before.'

Before my father's death? I don't ask.

'*Mea culpa*' he continues, his hands raised high as though I'm holding him at gunpoint.

He notices my indifference to his confession and looks to the heavens.

'It's a lovely day.'

'Is it?'

'Care to come inside?'

'Isn't it prohibited?'

'The church is officially closed. But there are exceptions.'
'Aren't you afraid?'
'The Lord protects me, Antonio. I feel invincible.'

Father Ryan shouts this in a gay theatrical manner. I look around in embarrassment but, as usual, the world is empty and only pigeons loiter. Although I'm not gone on priests, what really bugs me is how he tinkers with my name. Catholic priests are suspect. I mean, is Father Ryan really celibate and on the path to sainthood or is he just another pedophile? I look at his overflowing girth and think: where's the solidarity with hungry people?

'Did you know that before I was posted here that I was a missionary in Africa?'

'I didn't, Father.'

I don't know what, if anything, I want to get from him and strain my neck, looking up at the height of the church. Father Ryan observes my interest with pride.

'Are you not curious?'

He's like a puppy waiting to be patted and I indulge him, following him inside. The air is cool and stale. Father Ryan motions with a hand for me to look around and take it all in. Left and right are wooden pews, catering for hundreds of believers. Beneath stain glass windows, the Stations of the Cross line both walls. There's no denying that the place instills calm. Halfway down the center aisle and Father Ryan stops.

'Would you like me to hear your confession?'
'I've nothing to confess.'
'My son, even Jesus had sins.'
'I came to collect something, it's what the lawyer said.'

Father Ryan smiles and in a low voice invites me to sit and reflect.

'I'll be in the confession box if you change your mind.'

I sit on a pew, feeling neither bullied nor threatened. I fall into a trance of sorts and don't notice time passing. The tingle of a bell summons me to a confession box fitted against the wall like a lean-to.

I stand up, genuflect, and walk to the confession box. I'm curious.

Inside there's a cushioned step. I dutifully obey and kneel. On cue, a curtain draws back, leaving us separated by a mesh grill. I'm reminded of jail. I face Father Ryan, who sits side-on, and sports a white sash around his neck. Can I afford the price of a clean soul?

'In the name of the Father…'

On auto-cue, I join in, mumbling the odd few words that I remember. We come to a silence, one I'm happy to keep. Father Ryan prompts me with a cough. No reaction. More nudging follows.

'What you say is between you and the Lord. I'm only a conduit to God.'

'I told my wife that I would be faithful to her, but I haven't been. Ever.'

Finding my feet, I'm uncertain of what category of sin to open with.

'Very good. Keep going,' Father Ryan encourages.

'I told my wife that I'd do things but didn't.'

'What things?'

Although the light is scarce, I see him nodding, the light catching his bald pate.

'I said that I'd visit my father.'

'And you didn't?'

'Not yet.'

'One of the Ten Commandments is to respect your mother and father.'

'But he's dead. She wants me to visit his grave. Surely, it's my wife I let down and not my father.'

'Is there anything else, any other wrongdoing?'

'I visited Isabella Geriatric Center and Elmhurst Care Home.'

He looks corrupt, so I wink at him. He pauses to think about this.

'Are you sick with coronavirus?'

I don't say. He slumps back on his stool and covers his mouth and nose with the sash. Then he prays to himself.

'Is it a sin to kill yourself, even if you don't really mean it?'

A blank look follows. I leave the confession box with a reasonable deal: one Our Father and three Hail Marys. But when I look at my watch, I see how much time I've lost. Penance must wait another day. I explain this to Father Ryan and insist he fetches what I came for. He returns with an envelope. I don't open it in his presence but know that it contains a black barrel key.

'Your father was a good man.'

'I know.'

I freewheel around New York like I'm the last man alive. As I cycle home, I wonder if Father Ryan will inform the authorities about my confession. When I get home, I feel alive and giddy. A weight has lifted. It being a while since I felt any way healthy, I go for a lie-down and jack off. Is that something that I should have confessed, my libido? I float off into a deep sleep. When I wake up, the events of the day are still on my mind. I reach my hand under the bed and take out my notebook. I read my thoughts, which you are now also reading.

∞

We've long ceased confiding in one another but, out of curiosity, I try to lure Gloria back.

'There's a fish that attacks its enemies. Scientists discovered that when all the enemy fish are removed, the fish turns on its own species.'

'Doc, is there a point to your wisdom?'

'Violence is natural. It's in our make-up. We don't have a say in it.'

'So accept that New York is going to explode and go up in smoke? Doc, lay off the chaos theory and be grateful that you haven't caught the virus.'

'War is life. Peace is slavery. Violence is the ultimate expression of free will, but peace is a crime of inaction.

'So, harmless people are cruel?'

'Gloria, they shout: we want peace. But it achieves nothing.'

'Man the slayer. Okay, Doc, you win. Now what?'

'We wait to be conquered.'

'By the virus?'

Gloria sighs. The gulf between us widens. How to reach her? The bottom line is that home decoration and fashion magazines define who she is. There's no middle ground. For me, the excitement of Armageddon is a calmative. It shows that we evolve. By contrast, Gloria loves false drama. She might reply to a horror story by saying that we need new curtains. How much more can I take?

'Doc, the only thing I find interesting about you of late is how, for the first time in your life, you can't tolerate yourself. Did something happen? Has an awareness of your mortality kicked in? Do you hate yourself more now?'

'More than what?'

'More than others hate you.'

I don't hold her gaze. Instead I mumble under my breath.

'You're a fucking witch. And I hope the plague nukes us all.'

Her scolding tone depresses me. She says I'm my own worst enemy, that I should stop buying into myself.

'Doc, you need to pull your head out of your ass and take up jogging or something.'

'Jogging? And be like someone in Central Park?'

'OK. Swimming then.'

I wake from a nightmare covered in sweat. I take double the recommended dose of Tylenol to bring the fever down. The nightmare wasn't the one about the boy locked in a well. Instead, it was a dream about the girl with the coronavirus that I ferried to Elmhurst Hospital. The one I touched as I brushed the hair off her face. The one who reminded me of Erin.

In my nightmare, I was the only patient in a ward at Elmhurst Hospital. The fire brigade pulled up outside and honked their horns, giving thanks to the medical staff for getting us through the Covid-19 pandemic. The siren woke me up. From my hospital bed, and still in my nightmare, I was looking up at the ceiling but saw black clouds, dark portents. Standing outside the ward, in the dark corridor, a girl was waiting for me. Although the door was closed, I *sensed* her waiting for me. I *felt* her existence boring into my skull. It drove me mad, her waiting, and I reached the point where I had to have her message.

I got out of bed and looked for a weapon – a stick or a tennis racket – and, despite finding none, I braved opening the door. She wasn't directly outside, but stood at the end of the corridor. She must have only been about twelve years old, and wore a faded blue nightdress. We stood a few moments, assessing one another. I tried to say something, to ask what she wanted, but discovered that I was hoarse and without a voice.

I walked down the corridor. She didn't move or blink, her eyes just bore into mine. An angel or the devil? Standing in front of her, over her, I re-found my voice: 'What do you want?' I asked. I knew she had a message for me. She murmured something.

'Can you repeat, please?'

'You need protection.'

And then I'm running, running back down the corridor and slamming the door shut. I sit with my back to the door, my hands cupped around my ears, singing to myself, and trying to deny her existence. The fortuneteller in Mexico is back in mind. Nobody can tell me anything. I keep repeating it, over and over.

Nobody can tell me anything.

Nobody can tell me anything.

Nobody can tell me anything.

Still in my nightmare, I jump back into bed. Through the night I'm bursting for a piss, but too afraid to stir. I finally manage to doze off a little, and in the morning wake up with doctors looking down at me.

Did it happen? Was it all real? At 6am in the morning, I look for answers. I look to the ceiling at home. The clouds are gone. I get up, go to the kitchen, neck a quart of whiskey, and the little girl in the nightdress is consigned to history. I go back to bed, roll over, and cuddle into Gloria, and she lets me.

∞

The day after the little-girl nightmare and I go downtown to meet Abigail. Doctor thinks it might help. To go back to the source. To try and undo any blockage.

Back in the day, back in Afghanistan, I was too young to have ideas about myself. I wasn't after grand outcomes. I was just trying to keep my head on. But I was only so-so about my existence and it allowed me to be reckless. I didn't think I was mortal and so I tried to get my head shot off. That I always came back alive only reaffirmed my immortality. What flew over my head in all of this, wasn't my bravado, but how emotionally unavailable I was.

Though she's a way off and wearing a facemask, I recognize Abigail by her stride. It's only when she's up close do I notice that a dozen years have passed since we were in Afghanistan. Her eyes are pinched and she has crow's feet. We nudge elbows and laugh that we can't hug for fear of passing on the coronavirus. We sit at an outdoor café. As though we're playing a kinky game, I reveal my face by slowly removing my facemask. She follows suit. Her lipstick is smudged and what powder she had on her nose is wiped off and the tip of her nose shines. I can't help noticing how translucent she appears, how pale she is without a lick of Afghanistan sunshine. I never saw her out of military uniform and she dresses like a frumpy woman in a skirt and cardigan. Just like Gloria. I wonder about me, if time kills us all equally.

'Doc, you've a cough.'
'Not really.'
'But you have the sniffles.'
'I ate a lethal curry. Spicy. Lack of sleep is all I have.'

I place the black barrel key on the table between us and say nothing. I'm going back there and am bringing Abigail with me.

'What's it for?'
'It went missing from my things. My father took it. It's to unlock me.'
'What does it open?'
'Me. You see, I'm blocked.'
'Doc, you're weirding me out.'

'Azizabad.'

'Afghanistan?'

'August 22, 2008.'

'Operation Commando Riot. The Oliver North thing. Sure, I remember it. The Afghan guys who we nicknamed Mister White and Mister Pink.'

'Jubor Shah and Afran Khan. They were employed by the private security company, ArmorGroup, under a Pentagon subcontract.'

'The warlords on the military payroll who provided security for the airfield we were building. They shared the contract 50/50 until each wanted it all. Then Mister Pink killed Mister White on our watch.'

'Abigail, this black key is about the aftermath.'

'I remember that too. Jubor Shah's surviving brother becomes Mister White II. We dump Mister Pink from our payroll and keep Mister White II on as airfield security. He gets all the guns and money in the world, although he was connected to the Taliban.'

'And then we lost our loyalties.'

'Doc, you're losing me.'

'The night we dropped the 500-pound bomb on Mister White's house and found ArmorGroup ID badges littered around the dead.'

'But CENTCOM said that….

'Abigail, the CENTCOM report was bullshit. It didn't mention that the Pentagon was killing it's own employees.'

'Mister White was Taliban. And we got Mullah Sadeq.'

'Mister Pink bluffed us. He fed us intel on Mullah Sadeq and knew that we'd go in. He took out the first Mr White and we took out the second one for him.'

'Doc, after 12 years you want to discuss this?'

She forces a tight smile, hiding mild boredom.

'I just got the key and wonder how you guys live one way and act the other.'

'Us guys?'

'Goodies. I mean, we were in Afghanistan to do good. But we didn't.'

'I seem to remember that you were there too. Are you a goodie?'
'Do you ever have nightmares?'
'Doc, why don't you tell me about your nightmare?'
'It's about a boy in a well… I was there after it happened.'
'Where?'
'After we bombed the shit out of our own security guards. It was a cleanup operation. Hide the civilian casualties. I dumped a few bodies in a well. A teenager sprung up out of nowhere and started beating me. Maybe his brother or sister went in the well. I fought with him and he fell in. I locked the well with this key.'
'And the casualties appeared lower?'
Abigail doesn't think me a monster. She puts her hand on mine. We remain silent for a minute or more.
'Doc, we live with what we do.'
'My wife says war achieves nothing. Do you think our choices are ours?'
'Doc, we served. We obeyed orders.'
'But outside of military stuff. I'm curious about the choices that our subconscious makes, and the things it makes us do.'
'Doc, shit just happens.'
'My wife says we want peace but our subconscious makes us fuck it up. But I think we love chaos. It beats boredom.'
'Doc, why did your father confiscate the key?'
I shrug.
'Doc, was there something that you wanted to tell me?'
I shake my head, no. But it's not true.
'I've got to ask: where are you from?'
Abigail bursts out in laughter. I quickly change my mind and jump in before she can answer.
'Forget that question.'
I bark at a waiter and order the bill. I'm confused how in the decade since we saw one another how she managed to become a real person.
'Doc, nobody matters to you, do they?'

'What about you?'

'My husband.'

'You're married a long time. What did you tell him?'

'When I went on tour? He's paralyzed from the waist down. Car crash.'

'Does he know the story?'

'What story? Us? Doc, he doesn't know soldier life.'

'What did you telling him when you were deployed?'

'That I was going to work. He's a great guy. He's not afraid of being vulnerable.'

'What's so great about being weak?'

'You'll never experience the miracle of living, at least, not fully.'

'Sounds like you're preaching religion.'

'Doc, you must let in the unexpected and let people connect with you.'

'Or?'

'It makes you a bad friend.'

Know what she does? She pulls a book out of her handbag. It's a wishy-washy thing about enneagrams and how to divine what type of human you are. After asking me a few cursory questions, Abigail noses through the book and trots out the antidote to being me. The summary is this: my enneagram reading says I'm not my own type, that I don't fit into me, or, at least, I'm not who I'm supposed to be. My real type is hopeful and is a happy-go-lucky sort, whereas I 'suffocate myself' and 'stifle my growth'.

A silence descends. I'm thinking, what the fuck would she know? Her pop-psychology is slapdash and touchy-feelie. Who is she to tell me who I am?

'I'm a paramedic nowadays.'

'So you said, Doc. How many certified saves?'

I shrug.

'It's all I was good for afterwards.'

'And where are you now?'

'I'm still up in Queens.'

'I mean, mentally. Doc, are you crashing?'

'Immortal me? Get real. You sound like a shrink.'

I spit out a laugh. Does Abigail think she can help me? My laugh insults her. I right myself to make an apology. I sit up in my chair but the words don't come out.

'Doc, I'll catch you if you fall. If you let me.'

Solidarity. It's pathetic. A nobody wants to rescue my life, just as my life means nothing to me. Abigail is asking me something, but I've tuned out. She stands up to leave. It's my one chance, my last chance. I have to say it.

'Abigail, if I didn't love you, I wouldn't hate you so much.'

There. I've said it. Finally. Abigail is stumped. She looks down at my face as I stare at my empty coffee cup. Abigail, you are my Erin. She kisses my head and walks off.

∞

Enough is enough.

It's time for action.

I'm at war with myself and civilians can't understand. I go to see Bingo at Elmhurst Care Home. But he's not there. He's slowly losing himself. They carted him off to Jamaica Hospital; intensive care, I believe.

Fully kitted out in Covid-19 personal protective equipment, I get back on the bicycle and cycle to Jamaica. I can hardly breathe so I remove the facemask and hairnet. I'm sweating. Is it from the coronavirus or is the plastic suit to blame? I flash my credentials at A&E and make my way up to intensive care but am refused entry. Pre-hospital care providers only gain entry if carting someone in. Fortunately, I discover that Bingo is actually in a ward.

I'm surprised he recognizes me as I'm wearing full PPE. I must have a distinguishing gait. Bingo talks through his ventilator mask.

'Did my tree die?'

'No. It's doing well.'

'Then what is it?'

'I just thought that I'd say hello.'

He looks at me like he doesn't believe me. So, I tell him about my nightmares.

The nightmare about the girl in the hospital corridor.

'Bingo, she was real but she was also see-through. She was luminous, radiant blue.'

'The Virgin Mary?'

The nightmare about the boy in the well.

'Bingo, I looked down into the well. I saw his eyes looking up at me. He asked for help but I locked the well and left him there to die.'

The nightmare in the graveyard.

'Bingo, I'm walking away from a church. As a child, I used to jump into empty graves. But now I'm carrying skeletons I dug up. I think it's a premonition that something bad is going to happen.'

'Once you carry a dead person, they always stay with you. You need to find a way to grieve.'

'I've nobody to grieve.'

'Then why are you telling me?'

'You know about people who feel they are strangers to themselves.'

'Doc, your nerves are shot. Go home to bed, or pray.'

'I've nothing to believe in.'

'If you don't believe in an outside force, then life is your own fault.'

'War and coronavirus is my fault?'

'Doc, an atheist thinks we kill because we are animals. To mark our patch. We kill our rivals so they don't procreate.'

'And if I was religious what would you have said?'

'That God asks us to kill.'

'Bingo, I'm at war with myself. I can't do this until my hair falls out. I'm flat. I've no new fix. There's nothing to prop me up. I run on adrenaline, and that needle is gone.'

It's true. Life is shit. Gloria thinks we'll persist but I don't want to become the settled person that I'm sliding into. I'm tired of it. I'm tired of following my every impulse and getting away with it.

I came to Jamaica Hospital looking for a message of some kind. Something to cling to. But all I hear is emptiness. There's a dull ringing in my ears. Another coronavirus symptom? I can't deceive myself any longer. Nothing is holding me together. I pull off my facemask and whisper in Bingo's ear.

'I know all I'm ever going to know about myself and don't like what I see. I'm ready to go.'

'Go where?'

'Poof.'

I make the sound of wind disappearing. He understands.

'You need to listen to different sounds. Try stones. They sing.'

'There's music in rocks?'

'So says Pythagoras. Doc, you must pay attention.'

'To what?'

'Your breathing.'

'I'm out of breath.'

'Things might change.'

'Bingo, I'm not mad at you. I'm mad at me. I'm nothing special. I'm just a worthless man at a crossroads. And I'm done chasing a carrot.'

I put my facemask back on and am almost out the ward when I stop. I'm dead still. Bingo said: stones sink and empty people float. *Doc, feel your weight.* My eyes are slits. *Become a heavy stone.* I'm concentrating on me. *Breathe, in and out.* Without turning around to face Bingo, I stretch out my left arm. *The branch of a tree.* Like an astronaut moonwalking, I shift my feet in slow motion, crisscrossing the ward, taking very deliberate steps. *Move like a stone.* I stop. I throw a dainty move with my left ankle, ending with my toes pointing at the ground. *I'm a tree trunk.* My right arm crosses my body and a finger points down at my left ankle. *The roots are damaged.* I do a half-pirouette and then spread my legs. *A tree splits in two.* I arch my back and then flop forwards, bending my torso, and following my legs down to the floor and roll into a ball. *A stone at rest.* I roll on the ground and jump back up again. A doctor stops to watch, followed by a pair of nurses. And although they cheer me on, I'm not doing it for them. I'm doing it as I'm transcending and becoming at one with nature.

∞

Amazon delivers just as I'm out of air. I've no lungs so it's good that I bought an air pump.

Like an ancient man, I drag myself to the garden and set Kurtz and Bob up with gardening chores. We're at the shrubs. The evergreens are true to their promise. Always green. The red berry and Alberta spruce are also doing fine, but the hydrangea needs work. Unusually for May, there's been a dry spell and things need watering. Using trowels, Kurtz and Bob feed compost to the hydrangea. I sit by my pride and joy, the crabapple tree, and watch them mucking about. They feel my eyes on them and are confused when they see me smiling.

Doctor watches from inside the kitchen door, his eyes flitting from me to them. He's frustrated. Doctor knows that I should be scolding the kids for making a mud bath. Doctor senses that something is up. That I'm not in my right mind. Feeling obliged to do something, I sit on the grass beside my sons.

'Do you know how to chop down a tree so that it doesn't fall on you?'

'You learn that in school,' Kurtz says.

'It's a handy thing to know. You must plan your retreat in advance. The key to felling a tree is to cut your first notch in the tree trunk in the direction that you want the tree to fall. You must watch the wind, especially if the tree is carrying leaves. And as it falls, you must yell "timber".'

'Like shouting "four"?'

'Good boy, Bob. But "four" is for golf.'

'One, two, three, four,' Bob shouts. 'Sir, why don't we play golf?'

'The same way we don't have a horse.'

'But I want a horse,' Bob says.

'If you chop down all the trees, maybe you'll get a horse. Deal?'

'Yes,' they chime in unison.

'Get the saw and do it. I want every tree chopped down when I return.'

'Really, sir? Why would we chop down your trees?'

'Repeating day after day isn't enough reason to go on. So, today you get to do something new.'

I open Gloria's present. I want her to have something to remember me by. It's a piebald plastic horse. I connect the air pump and am breathless from pumping it with my foot. As it expands, I realize that the living room was missing a centerpiece. Something other than the sofa and TV. Something that Gloria might actually grasp. She wanted a girl. Well, everyone else wanted a horse.

I take a look around the kitchen – all the cups of tea that I drank here. I rub Doctor's head.

'Give me the paw.'

He does. We shake goodbye. His ears are perked. Doctor wags his tail. He's all that loves me. I crouch down and pat his head.

'Look after Mom when I'm gone.'

I leave Doctor in the living room with the inflatable black and white horse. I put my keys on the hall table, in case somebody needs them, and go upstairs to bed. I hear a tree creak. Kurtz shouts "timber", but Bob shouts "four". The tree hits the side of the house and a branch full of leaves presses against the window. I smile. Living things are finite. We materialize and dematerialize. Infinity is not for us.

Chapter 7

Roots

1986

Despite being an only child, I'm rarely alone. It's hard to be invisible. Others have you in their sightline. We're a flock, a gang of eight. We're young and hot. And we don't give a fuck. But just because we don't have a care in the world doesn't mean that we don't know how to.

'Fuck?'

'No, only a finger,' Paul says.

'What a bitch. Was she tight?' I ask.

'Tight as,' he smiles.

'I know. High five, brother.'

I'm happy with Paul's failure. For some reason I thought that Erin would only let me touch her, and that for others she was only on display. I had her down as a sensitive, sensible sort. Now look what she's gone and done. The slut.

It's a hot summer, and so warm that if you lie on the grass it sticks to your back. Everything underground comes to the surface for air: ants and worms. It's a micro-zoo heaven, and attracts all kinds of hungry birds.

Paul waded towards me, through the long meadow grass, wearing a big grin. Erin took longer to appear, but when she stood up, I was momentarily paralyzed. *How could she?* As she approached, she righted her bra strap, leaving a bare shoulder showing. Then, with her fingers, she began combing her long blonde hair, as though some of the tinged grass was caught in it. She was making a point.

How do you pretend to your best friend that getting his dick wet and fingering the girl of your dreams is okay?

I consider beating him up, but no, it was Erin's choice. She wanted to be touched. I'm just miffed that she could fancy that four-eyed toad, and enjoy shining his dick until it pulsed red. Paul has nothing interesting to say, he's a bore and a nerd. I scold myself, nothing I say to her counts for anything. Girls don't care about words. Yet Mom insists that words can be used for theatre or truth. Well, we'll see which…

∞

Loosely speaking, there are eight of us, an even mix of boys and girls. In many respects we're the rejects, the outcasts who are friends of circumstance. We try to act cool, mess about, drinking cans of cider, sharing a spliff, or going into the long grass to see what you can get: a finger or a dry fuck.

It's around this time that I discover who I am. The summer that I turned fifteen.

I'm not the intimidating sort, being both un-athletic and scrawny, but I have my way. Wordlessly, I invite insults or violence, and all just by staring. My stare is harder than my fists as, in my look, is read grievous bodily harm, something my fists are manifestly unable to engineer.

Today, I'm tired. In the school canteen I find myself unwittingly staring at the girlfriend of the linebacker.

'Dude, stop leering at my girl,' the football ace shouts.

I don't even hear him or realize I'm ogling the girl until a spoon hits my forehead, catching my attention. I become angry. Paul, who is sitting beside me, starts to fret.

'Antonio. Don't do it. Please.'

Paul's hands are clasped between his knees, as though he needs to pee.

'I'm standing my ground.'

'Antonio, back down, or he'll hurt you.'

'How do you know?'

'Because he's bigger.'

'So what? He mightn't know how to hurt me.'

'Stop being stupid.'

'If he can't make me feel pain then he can't touch me.'

I'm resolute. I had never shirked a stare, and shift my gaze to the jock. I'm dumb enough to think that my scowl might be as sore as a punch in the face. Not so. Behind the school shed, I get fixed up with a black eye, as a crowd cheers him on.

'Get the freak.'

'Kill the weirdo.'

I hear the heckling although I'm busy getting beaten up. I force myself to laugh, and start laughing louder, until finally I'm hysterical. Blood spits from my mouth. It puts the frighteners up everyone. The bully eases up and we stand apart, me, bloody and bruised. For a few seconds there's an eerie calm. The crowd falls hush as I laugh hysterically, and pouring blood.

'You're fucked up, Rivera,' he says, before walking off.

I weird everyone out and the crowd disperse. Paul hangs back to offer me consoling words. I never had many school friends. Paul never had any either, although he has no excuse for being lame.

That day, I learn that I must prepare for real life.

In the video shop I buy a video called *'How to Get Big. FAST'*. For the coming days and weeks, I watch it every afternoon. Once I've the routine memorized, I go to by bedroom and do sit-ups, press-ups and bicep curls, with a kilo of sugar and eight tins of cat food tied to each end of a broom handle. I also do static strength exercises, clenching my fists for two minutes, repeating the exercise six times, until my wrists hurt. After a fortnight, I can hold myself in a press-up position for up to four minutes before collapsing in a heap. All in all, despite not noticeably growing – although my body is harder – I'm able to tolerate more pain. I've become more resilient, physically-speaking. Mentally, I was always a rock.

∞

Paul and I go to the swimming pool. Swimming is a good tonic to loosen up exercised muscles. The unisex changing room has private cubicles, but there are separate male and female showers. After swimming, I steal Paul's towel. Stark naked, he hares after me, around the changing room, to the glee of a few pensioners. Paul is so furious that he changes quickly and goes home. I go for a shower, and there he is, waiting, standing alone in the shower, with his back arched slightly, his head thrown back and his hands shampooing his hair. His penis is erect, outstretched in front of him, and ready for business.

I put him at fortyish. Lean and proud of himself. He pretends not to notice me, then, suddenly, turns about and stares at me with piercing blue eyes. He's pleased with my disgust, pleased with his hard-on, a shaft on a mission, and eager to ram it home.

He moves towards me, trying to look seductive. I push the faggot away.

'Fuck off, weirdo.'

'You no like a Frenchman?' he asks, patting his ass checks with both hands.

'Back off or you're dead.'

'If you can't engage with weird fetishes with a stranger, then you never will, *garçon*.'

Garçon? Me, a boy at fifteen? It's true that I'm smooth-chested, but surely with my developed musculature he can tell that I'm almost a man.

Unexpectedly, he runs at me just as I turn to walk away. I swing around and thump him in the chest. Then, to both our surprise, he slaps me across the face, letting out a shriek as he does so. I'm stunned that he whacked me like my Mom, while he, surprised by his actions, leaps backwards like a gazelle.

I flex my muscles, primed for battle, and charge at him. He protects his balls, cupping them lovingly in both hands, so I land a kick to his midriff. I punch him squarely in the face, knocking his head against the wall, and as he buckles, blood spurts, and it's my turn to take a backwards jump.

He sinks to the floor, onto his haunches, and the shower raining down on him. He revels in the steady flow of water and blood. All the while, his cock remains hard.

∞

The ingredients of life fascinate me. And it's not that I consciously choose to apply myself, but more a case of school acting as a go-between, between me and my curiosity with the world.

Although I'm surrounded by other kids, I don't need them. I'm getting on just fine with myself, as so many questions occupy me. Rather than communication with humans, it's my own communication with the physical world that becomes all-consuming.

Chemistry is my favorite subject. Air is made up of hydrogen, nitrogen and oxygen, while planet Earth is made up of mineral ingredients. I get to grips with different types of stones and rocks. We learn about the magical powers of minerals and the Cherokee, a type of mountain inhabitants.

Above all, water is my thing. The meniscus around the rim of a glass, or the way a liquid's viscosity can be altered, are some of the things that intrigue me. My water fascination began when I watched a single droplet drip from my nose, slide down my thigh and land on the floor. Water doesn't break on impact. It bounces. I thought a droplet of mucous would wet the first thing it touched, but no. The drop deflected off my trouser leg – it had its own sense of being.

A drop doesn't give itself up to the first thing it meets.

A weakling, neither.

Perhaps it's the stage I'm at, the age of inquisitiveness. Although my curiosity is insatiable – around that time, I was also big into power: conductors, electricity and heat – nothing holds me the way liquids do. I study the rain and marvel at the way individual raindrops align themselves and end up in a stream gushing down the street. The clouds overhead even draw me in: cumulonimbus, cumulostratus. Then there are bodies of water: rivers and oceans, tides, waves and estuaries. Differing water types also fascinate: salt and freshwater, saliva and saline solutions. On and on it goes, my bank of knowledge of the Earth's terrain ever increasing.

With mischievous intent I accept an invitation from Paul to spend a week in their RV by the sea at Floyd Bennett Field in Brooklyn. Paul's parents are both teachers and, with the long holidays, it makes sense for them to have a second home, albeit in an RV by the sea.

It's a pretty fishing town we're in, Georgetown, with a deep port that allows yachts and fishing boats to dock. I love watching the fishing boats approach from afar, the sense of scale growing before my eyes, a little dot on the horizon becoming an enormous steel vessel with squalling seagulls in its wake.

Daily we fish from the pier, and return to the campsite with more mackerel than we can eat. One day I decide to test the equation: water or air. Which is a stronger force? I tell Paul my plan.

'You're mental,' he says.

'Elemental, you mean.'

Once we've gutted enough mackerel to take home for dinner, we recommence fishing, but this time we keep the fish alive in an underwater net. Then we take ages blowing up balloons. We tie the balloons to fishing gut, and knot hooks on the other end. One by one, we take out the mackerel, and lodge a hook in each one's mouth so that it's attached to the balloon. Then we throw the fish back in the sea.

All of a sudden the fishing port comes alive, like a computer game. Thirty balloons are propelled around the pier by the mackerel, who find it impossible to submerge or swim away at speed due to towing the balloons which are like buoys with the fish moored to them.

Now we have moving targets. We perch ourselves on the pier's edge, lying flat on the ground, and take turns shooting at the fish with my air gun. Sometimes we hit the mackerel and roar in delight. Other times we accidentally hit the balloon and allow a fish to escape. The winner is the one who can kill a fish so that its dead body floats on the water. Yet, no matter how often we shoot the fish, they never seem to die. Eventually, after an hour's shooting, one fish gives up, perhaps through exhaustion, floating belly up, and the balloon gently blowing it out to sea.

I win.

I don't know what happened, but later that evening there's a strange silence in the RV. What did Paul say? I catch a few looks, and then Paul and his mom make an excuse to go into town. It's just me and Paul's father, Mister Reardon.

'Antonio, I'm friendly with your parents.'

'Yes, I know, Mister Reardon.'

'I also know the dilemma.'

'Mexico or America?'

'That too, but also the choice: Catholic or Protestant. Which are you?'

'I don't know, I haven't decided yet, Mister Reardon.'

'Antonio…'

'I prefer Tony.'

'Tony, do you know about original sin?'

'I don't, sir.'

'In essence, the story is that when Adam and Eve did things in Eden that they were forbidden, they condemned mankind. We are evermore sinners, born sinners. But it's OK. It's hereditary. Sinning is natural and the animal instinct is also. Do you understand, Antonio?'

'I do, sir.'

'We're Catholics in our family, although many people in America are Protestants, WASPs like your mom. But we're all Christians and share the same God, however, there are subtle differences. Antonio, as humans we are frustrated creatures and sometimes do bad things. But that doesn't make us bad people. It's why we have confession, to be absolved. By confessing, we gain complete forgiveness. Do you know the key difference between Catholics and Protestants?'

'I don't, sir.'

'Catholics allow confession, but Protestants don't. They don't have the sacrament of penance.'

'Protestants don't want to be forgiven, sir?'

'Let's just say that they have to be more careful about their sins. Catholics are better sinners.'

'Better than Protestants, sir?'

'They've more license to do wrong. Know why the Italian mafia has the most ruthless killers in the world? Because they *are* Catholics. Nothing holds them back from doing their killing, as they can repent later. Once the sin is satisfied, their soul is healed and the guilt is gone. Sins are natural, but it's about having the right kind of religion to support your sins.'

∞

I've an air gun but I'm out of lead. Paul has a Black Widow slingshot, but its rubber is broken. We're short of pocket money to remedy the situation. Anyway, money is better spent on cigarettes and cider. So it's back to more primitive ways we go.

To one end of a thin slat of wood we fix a clothes peg. Then we dismantle lots of clothes pegs and remove the steel springs. To each steel coil we attach an elastic band. The steel spring is then fed into the mouth of the clothes peg, which is fastened to the strip of wood, and the elastic band is stretched over the far end. This becomes our new weapon. A rudimentary crossbow that fires the steel coil of a clothes peg. A nasty thing to catch in the eye.

Sometimes we aim at bottles, but more often we target animals. We might sit for hours in the long grass as we wait for an unsuspecting blackbird to fly past. I hit a crow flying overhead once and, unable to fly with a broken wing, it nosedived on top of us. Another time, Paul hit a dog, but that wasn't funny.

American Slaughterhouse

∞

Back home in Queens, all eight of us listen to Michael McDonald, Toto, and Kenny Loggins. June is hot, sticky and boring. But then I hit a rabbit. I'm on it before it escapes. I hear Paul cry after me: 'Cream it. Cream it.' I've raced up to the rabbit and there I stand, looking down at it in the long grass as it wheels about in circles, its leg broken. It's futile, yet it persists. It's programmed to try and save itself. All animals are. My friends have gathered around just as I land a rock on the rabbit, crushing its head.

'It's pregnant,' shrieks Erin.

'It's dead now,' says Paul.

'Maybe you shouldn't have done that, Tony,' another boy says.

I feel them ganging up on me, acting as one.

'Fuck you Paul. I didn't know.'

'You didn't care,' Erin says.

'I had to finish it off. I had no choice.'

'You could have checked first. Consulted.'

It's Paul. He's being bookish; it's something he's good at. It's only when I take out my penknife and start gutting the rabbit that I become repulsed. When I slit its stomach, three blind bunnies, days short of delivery, emerge. They squirm, unused to such freedom.

'You're a disgusting animal, Tony,' cries Erin, before running away in tears.

'You're gross,' Paul agrees.

'Shut-up and give me your lighter,' I say.

'Fuck you, psycho,' Paul says.

I give him a look, but he's hardened to my stare. I snap.

'She doesn't like you anyway. She said you're shit,' I blurt, nodding my head in the direction of the absent Erin.

'Erin called you spotty dick,' he retaliates.

'Yeah, and you're a five-second wonder. She told me you're her charity case.'

They're harmless words but words that nevertheless ferment over time and leave lasting doubts. Girls have the upper hand, only they know the answers, knowing how long we last. The adjudicators of our ejaculations.

I could have settled it then and there if I had challenged Paul in front of the others to a round of soggy biscuit. But I have torn underpants, and don't want to be further humiliated. The baby rabbits stand between us. They squirm, asking for attention. Paul returns to the immediate.

'What you going to do?'

'I told you, give me your lighter.'

'Why?'

'Just give it here. I'm responsible for this mess.'

'No way.'

I grab Paul by the collar and try to intimidate him with a look. With no reaction, I have to spell it out:

'Paul, it's fine if you cop out, but I'm not leaving them squirming. We need to do something fast.'

Suddenly, I have four lighters in my hand. I don't know why, but I push aside the mother rabbit from the baby bunnies. With a stick, I push the baby rabbits closer together. Then I pour fluid from our lighters over the bunnies, and set them alight. For a brief moment, their squirms become livelier. The grass burns and a little clearing forms around them. One by one, everyone runs off, as I force myself to watch it all, to honor what I've done, to watch the bunnies sizzle until they fuse as one, congealed by the flames. They're little more than interwoven twigs, tiny empty nests. Shells. And they smell of burnt meat.

∞

Brute force.

Dad beats me over the smallest of things – a crumb left on my plate, brushing my teeth while letting the cold tap run, not appreciating a plate of offal boiled in onions and milk, washing too often (myself or my clothes), or not walking the meat bones down the road, out of harm's way, for the wild animals to gnaw.

Waste not, want not.

Dad says it every thirty minutes of his life.

Waste not, want not.

He celebrates his out-of-court settlement over his eyes by beating me. He rings in Christmas by beating me. A beating always comes on the back of Mexico losing some sport or another. And before all of the beatings, when I was too small to beat properly, he said that the boogeyman would get me. I couldn't sleep and became afraid of the dark. I stared at the ceiling for hours, waiting to hear a door creak. Dad limited Mom's cuddles. He stopped me from being hugged. He said I needed toughening up.

The reason for the beatings? I was Dad's American son, and he carried a chip. A look in his direction and I might set him off. It's something in my eyes that he doesn't like. I'm not a credit to him but a cost. Mom would look on as we fought, pained, but afraid to intervene. As Dad beats me, and as I grow bigger, I become emboldened and taunt him, calling him a greaser.

'What did you say?' he asks in disbelief.

My bravado fails me as soon as he has me on the ground. Then I'm a helpless football, and he's playing for Mexico against the enemy, the US.

'You think you're American royalty? I'll knock the Cage out of you. I'll make a Rivera of you yet, gringo.'

I stare up at him with my demented stare that he hates. Anything to get my revenge. It has the desired effect. He beats me harder and harder until I look away so he can't see my tears.

'Think you're better than us Mexicans?'

∞

Dad possesses heavy knowledge. It's an unusual skill to a boy's eyes: he can size up a stone block and tell its weight. Any block, any size, even the enormous ones embedded in the stone arches on the Bronx side of High Bridge. Stones and rocks are his thing. The caveman.

'See that there?' he'd say.

'The house?' I ask.

'No. We're looking at the bridge. The stones. It's granite.'

'Oh.'

'How heavy is it?' he asks.

'The bridge?' I ask.

'No, not the whole thing. How heavy do you think each block is?'

Of course it's about the blocks. I'm only humoring myself.

'No clue. Would each stone be four tons?'

Dad looks at me like I'm mad.

'8,000 pounds? Are you a simpleton? Guess again and guess properly. Don't be fooled; it's only stone-clad, it's a cheap trick. Each block, in my estimation, is at best a ton.'

America needed blocks laying and roads paved. Dad came running over from Culiacán. Dad does Mom's parents' driveway, and a while later is doing Mom.

If the US army called, he might have gone there, disregarding his proud loyalties for a regular salary. He should have gone anyway. Their loss. My loss, too. Instead, at home, he's the bullying boss, where at work he isn't. Home is his empire.

Dad moves into metallurgy: welding and panel beating. That does him in. He isn't made for appliances – blowtorches and gas bottles – he's more a demolition-and-hammer man. For him, earth is important. He needs grounding.

Just as with the stones, he now quizzes me about his latest trade.

'What kind of alloys are they?' he asks.

'On the car wheels, Dad?'

A car passed by. I noticed the brand, whereas Dad merely noticed the wheels that he so often mends.

'Aluminum and steel rims,' I say.

'You're not bad.'

Dad backs up the rare compliment by offering to buy me an ice cream.

'Eat slowly and spare it,' he says.

'But it's an ice cream. It'll melt.'

'Give it here then; give me a bite.'

He didn't buy himself an ice-lolly, and munches half of mine with a single bite. The only positive is the pain that his sensitive teeth give him. And this is us bonding. And this is the extent of his fatherly advice: know a stone's weight, and know your alloys.

He's too 'big' a man to wear a welding mask. He sees searing white light in the dark. He runs around the house bumping into things and roaring, his head bursting with migraines. It's madness for a while, until he finally settles into blindness.

Dad always believed that the world was everything his eyes could see. If the eye can't catch it, it doesn't exist, it's a non-happening, an untruth. But once blind, Dad's memory has to tell him where things are, and overnight his world becomes very small.

The compensation claim helps Dad to understand his blindness; it puts a measure on it, a price tag. But it isn't enough money – it never is. We still have to save. He won't have a guide dog; they're too costly to keep. He'll never even learn how to spell the word 'Braille'. It's Mom who suffers most.

Everything that moves is Dad's enemy. He hates to touch things; touching is work, it forces him consider what the strange object might be.

Out he goes into the street, fanning his white cane in front of him like a fly swat. He ploughs on ahead of Mom, only to be upended by a garbage can. He cusses the thing, and whacks it with his cane. Depending on Mom's mood, she might take her time helping him up. She has to be careful – his ways of old have resumed. Frustrated and violent, he once knocked out her front tooth as she helped him up. The ogre.

∞

I'm adamant that the pregnant rabbit episode not get the better of us. We agree to meet later the same evening, down by the disused rail track and the overgrown field. To keep up the summer vibe, I play 'Sweet Freedom' on my cassette player.

I make a clearing on top of a train track sleeper and build a fire. Four boys and three girls show up. Erin is missing. I take it as a personal affront, but say nothing. She's from a good family and wears designer clothes. My escapades don't go down well with her kind. In Erin's absence, the other girls seize the opportunity to shove themselves into the limelight, mocking Erin and how sensitive she is. I'll get revenge on Erin in my own discreet way – when I get home I'll make sure that I don't wank over her. Instead I'll think of Maisie.

I sharpen a stick and poke it through the head and ass of the mother rabbit, which I gutted and skinned. I place the skewered rabbit over the flames, slowly turning it. Shorn of fur, it browns nicely. But then, the rabbit's corpse reminds me of its offspring, which I scorched to death. Maybe the others are thinking the same thing, but I'm afraid to look at them. Trust a bunny rabbit to fuck things up. I'm going to eat it out of revenge for the way it affected my relationship with Erin.

Waste not, want not.

Once cooked, I flick open my penknife and hack the meat into chunks. I insist that everyone take a piece and, for a few moments, we all stand looking at one another, waiting for somebody to take the lead.

'Screw it, let's chew it,' says Maisie.

'I don't know about this,' tempers Paul.

'You don't know much about anything, Paul, but it doesn't stop you doing stupid things,' I say. 'Waste not, want not.'

'Yeah, screw it,' Maisie says, backing me up.

Maisie dares everyone with a smile before biting in. We're stood around in a circle, chowing down and pretending that the rabbit tastes OK. A bottle of cider is passed around to help us swallow it down. By now, not even a spliff can calm me. I'm possessed, restless. I feel like flies are swarming inside me, and my face is on fire. For no apparent reason, I blush. My face has gone red. I'm ashamed. I need distraction.

Frantically, I urge everyone to follow me as I hare off in the direction of the old rectory. Maisie, who I know likes me, urges everyone to follow and seek me out. I hurdle the graveyard wall ahead of the posse. I dart among shimmering tombstones and step over the dead.

I jump into a freshly dug grave, and pop up and surprise the others. They shriek in outrage and fear.

'Show some respect,' says Paul.

'To who? It's empty.'

And I'm off again, running around the graveyard with Paul fast on my heels, and the others strung out behind us. I stop at the little church. When Paul catches up, I ask him if he thinks we should break in.

'There's lots of wine in there. We could get twisted on the Good Lord.'

'But we still have drink.'

'That's not the point.'

'Then what is?' Paul asks.

'It's to test God. To see if he's real? If so, we can confess and be forgiven.'

I throw Paul a wicked grin. I don't know if he knows about the talk that his dad gave me, but I let him know that to sin is one half of being absolved.

'Tony, we'd better not. It's probably alarmed,' Paul says.

'It's not a fucking bank.'

There's a howl, a shriek of cats, then panting. One by one, the others catch up with us and they've taken to mimicking my animal howls. But I've moved on. I'm too impatient, too wired (to what, the moon?), to bother discussing our next move. Up I climb, in between the ivy, up the church wall. The grooved stones offer enough affordance to stick a finger in, and get a toehold. I don't know where I'm going, anywhere but here. Up and up I go, climbing up into heaven.

Blood throbs in my forearms, as I get weaker. I stop to regain strength. Then I showboat. I release a hand from the wall to turn and look down. I'm ten meters off the ground and only have a split second to appreciate the view, before my hand slips off the wall. I go into free-fall. It takes two and a half seconds before I crash on the ground.

I land on my back. For a moment, I'm blinded. Maybe I'm dead, I think. However, I'm just winded, though I can't move. I have to double-check to see that I'm alive. Perhaps this is the in-between phase that Paul's dad spoke of – purgatory. Once satisfied that I'm in the land of the living I wonder about broken bones or, worse, internal bleeding.

They gather around.

'Is he conscious?'

'Don't move him.'

'He's breathing.'

'Call an ambulance.'

They're looking down at me as I'm facing upwards. I don't look them in the eye or respond. I'm too busy trying to breathe, to focus on living. Once I reach a level of equanimity and the pain eases up, I force myself to focus, not on me, but on the world out there, up there. I begin looking outwards, into the spectral sky. Amid masses of stars, and slowly inching along, I spy a shooting star. Everything slowly slots back into its own place. The ingredients of life. The stars fluttering around my head realign. Nothing traumatic has happened.

I still exist.

I'm here.

On Earth.

Grounded.

What was I doing clambering up a church wall? Why was I so manic? Why, it's because I want to experience danger alone and without a parachute to break my fall. Yes, I killed the rabbits but it all seemed so arbitrary. Random. Mortality has left me unconvinced and I'm testing it, checking to see if it will bend for me and let me off the hook. And it does. And yes, I can be sinful now, confess later, and be absolved. If I fake being a Catholic, everything is permissible. Innocence regained after devilment.

From my prone position, I begin laughing, then coughing, choking almost. Everyone think its blood that I'm hocking up, not life. They don't understand that I'm answerable to nobody, to no higher realm. If I had been flat on my back looking up at the sun, I'd have been blinded. But no, not for me: I have the moon, I survived. It's right then, at that very moment, that I realize that I will always survive. I'm a survivor. A cat. And because I get up off the ground and dust myself down, I know that I'll never have to compromise with life. It doesn't have the power to destroy me.

Nothing can happen *to* me, things may only happen *from* me, by my hand. I must be brave enough to stand outside the system, to remain raw and feral and not be mollified by home comforts and, most of all, to keep an edge. Though this is the precise moment in my life that I first feel immortal and imagine that I'm destined for greatness, I accept there are still some things that I don't understand.

Things like Erin.

∞

Every generation has its brute.

I dreamed of being bigger and older. A grown-up. Now my time has come. It coincides with the day that rabbit and lamb is on the menu and it's not a pot roast I'm having.

Once inside the front door, a birdcage is laid out on the floor. It stands in my way. A budgie shrills in warning. Mom has sprung a trap to allow me a second's grace.

At the vet's clinic, where Mom grooms animals, she habitually brings home a recovering animal to nurse. They're usually caged birds, as they can be kept out of Dad's way. Though we've no pets of our own, Mom often brings home a few tins of dog or cat food – the perks of the job. I don't know what she does with them; sells them or gives them away, I suppose.

Only yesterday, Mom assisted with the emergency surgery of a ten-kilo dog, removing four kilos of pus from its womb. She tried to explain to me something about the rancid smell of necrotic pyometra. Now, tonight she's putting budgies in harm's way.

It's teamwork, and we have it down to an art-form: I draw Dad on me to spare Mom. She always ensures there's a knuckle of lamb in the fridge when Dad begins showing signs of stress. It's all she can do. Mom and I leave our routine unspoken. I know it's coming when a joint of lamb is in the fridge – and that's no small thing in our family. Over the coming days I have to be ready, to fight, to protect.

Ever since I failed to return home on one occasion, I swore to myself that I'd be extra vigilant. That time, Dad broke Mom's arm by flinging her down the stairs. It was the crazy bee buzzing inside his head, the piercing white light scratching at the back of his cornea. I plotted his murder but Mom second-guessed the man I was becoming and assured me that she had genuinely lost her footing on the stairs, and that she alone was to blame.

Of course Dad was violent, but what saddened me was his lack of emotion. He had no depth. No empathy. No come good. There were no debriefing conversations or apologies to explain his nature. Simply put, I don't think the brainless twit could think at all. Inside his head was a blank – no questions, no baggage. He's like a dog – on to the next trick, the next meal, his next walk.

Anyway.

As I say, so there I am, at the front door, I see the birdcage, feel the heat of the oven from the kitchen and then Dad barks.

'The posh American, who calls himself Tony Cage'.

'The beaner is already yapping about the homeland. You thick Mex.'

I don't hesitate to reply, to keep his focus on me. Mom guessed his mood that morning and I notice that Dad hasn't a belt on, and is without anything to whip off and hit me with. Nothing but his fists. Or so I thought. Luckily, I hold up my school bag and use it as a shield, as he whacks me with his walking cane. Then over goes the birdcage, which startles Dad and sends him crashing into a chair. Suddenly, everything is out of control.

I skip around the dining-room table to the kitchen where Mom is waiting for me. I squeeze my hands into a pair of oven gloves and, on cue, Mom hands me the joint of lamb, enabling me to storm out and do battle with Dad.

A musketeer is nothing. I'm the best.

I call out to give Dad a mark, and he swings wildly, beating the meat and laughing when he hears contact with the knucklebone. I dutifully let out a yelp, as though he made contact with me rather than the joint of lamb. On it goes, the pantomime, saliva forming in Dad's mouth as the demons emerge.

When all is done, an hour later, we act like nothing had happened and settle down to a lovely roast lamb. These are the best of memories.

The sacrificial lamb.

Waste not, want not.

∞

In many respects, I consider myself more mature and developed than I really am, and certainly as regards the physical aspects of life; drinking, smoking and dry humping early on. But like the majority of boys, I suffer a degree of emotional retardation and an abject unwillingness to comprehend serious things.

For example, I can't believe they ever did it, Mom and Dad. I guess Mom can't either. Maybe they didn't. Me, the immaculate child.

Whatever the case, I was their first and last. Dad had no say. Not long after having me, Mom had a hysterectomy without consulting Dad. As I grew up, sometimes Mom would freeze in her tracks and stare at other mothers laden down with children. I never plucked up the courage to ask if she wished she had more kids or if it was pity she had for these child-heavy mothers. I also never asked Mom why she had a hysterectomy. Growing up there were dos and don'ts, and we were the kind of family that didn't go looking for trouble. We knew the next disaster was only around the corner.

Perhaps my being the only child is what affected their marriage. Maybe it explains Dad's anger towards me. He treated me like I had killed his unborn. Apparently, in their courting days, they struck a deal: the first child would be American, the second Mexican and so on it would go. Mom ruined that. Thereafter it became America versus Mexico, Antonio versus Tony, him versus us, the Cages.

They can't escape each other. They're broken down together, afraid of being together, yet afraid to go at it alone. Dad can't so easily return to his ways of old; he needs Mom to interpret everything for him. Yet he doesn't want Mom disturbing his way of life. He wants to be his own man and go his own way. Except, once blind, he can't.

Mom, for her part, didn't know how to break the habit of who she had become, and wasn't cruel enough to leave the blind old bat. Still. Their unspoken arrangement was killing them - her mercy and his acceptance of it. I suppose it must be difficult to disassemble and start over. After half a lifetime spent together, they were too accustomed to living in a certain manner to consider any kind of change. It would require undoing routines. It was too late for re-starts, or for untying themselves from each other. They could never fight the odds and re-originate alone. This is particularly so for Dad, who finds it nigh impossible to re-formulate habits even if they're simple matters like going for a shit, finding his shoes, or knowing when he can pick his nose in private. Mom has to perform his most routine tasks: choosing clothes, cutting up his food, how to go, where to go, even, it seems, what to discuss as, without his eyes, Dad's imagination is a blank. And a lot of this is how things were *before* Dad's blindness. They had somehow managed to plough through the years, establish a working relationship, and keep a semi-functional home, and *then* Dad goes and becomes a blind baby.

He can't handle his dwindling power. He's like Hitler without the murder, only that Dad's concentration camp is in his mind, as all he sees in his empty head is a raging white sun. Sometimes, his suffering is too much for us. We've learned to read the telltale signs and how to spot the rising tension. Motion is our rescue.

A drive in the countryside.

Though Dad can't see, the soft squelch of the land does wonders for his temperament. He sits in the back seat – it makes him feel grand, like a member of the landed gentry. Though I'm only fifteen, with Dad now at Mom's mercy, she loosens up and isn't averse to sharing the odd prank or two with me. Out on the open road, we swap seats in the car as I take the wheel. Dad hasn't a clue.

I might have fared better with a hippy sort of Dad. That being so, I buy him bright Jamaican shirts in a second-hand shop. Anyway, Dad probably can't even remember what colors are. I'd put him in a dress, except he'd know that there's something fishy without having deep pockets to bury his hands in.

∞

Everyone acts like Erin has been murdered. Some say it would have been better if she had been.

People speak about her in the past tense. But for me, and with Erin out of sight, she's more in my mind. I always think about her. The things that she gets up to on her own, her secret life, her daring, and the way she put her life in peril.

Erin returns to school after a month's absence. Nobody has seen her since the fateful bunny-burning incident. Everyone says she was lucky and that she got off lightly, that it could have been worse. We're told to act normally around her, and let on that everything is the same. Only it isn't, of course. Amongst ourselves we speak about it. I keep my distance from the conversations. I try and work it out on my own, who he was, and if she knew him and whatnot.

Some of our group looks to me. They expect me to know certain things about girls. We've reached that age – the stage at which our bodies have become public property.

'Dude, in case you don't know, I don't have a period,' I say.

207

That shuts them up. But the truth is, just because you can have sex doesn't mean you understand it.

Erin looks sullen. She's downtrodden. Gone are the tight-fitting bright clothes of old; she doesn't care how she looks anymore. It's disappointing. She's much thinner, and wears clothes that are two sizes too big for her.

For me, she's still the same old Erin, with long blonde hair, pert breasts and long skinny legs that used to be beaten into a faded pair of denims. But now she drapes a jumper over her butt as though she's hiding something other than perfection. Why? She'll never be a fat-assed girl. It's not that. It's that Erin has lost all self-respect. My festering curiosity mounts. A day after she returns and I collar her by the lockers.

'I thought you didn't like to do it.'

'Do what?' Erin asks.

'Hump.'

'I don't.'

'You're all talk.'

It was an outburst. At least I refrained from boasting about our dry fuck. And Erin can't deny that – we were both there. Still, it irritates me how blasé she behaves. The next day I get in another dig.

'Erin, we dry humped.'

'It's not the same.'

'And you'd know.'

She doesn't respond. I have her snared. I presumed right. Erin wanted to engage in a spot of darkness. She was asking for it. Up for it. At least, that's how I have it down. I'd heard the rumors: that she vaguely knew him, that they secretly met, that she drew him on her, that it was a welcome trespass, that she wanted it.

'I get it. I'm not classy enough for you. That's why you didn't turn up that night to eat the rabbit.'

I'm ranting, and slam the locker door shut. The bang shocks her, and she collapses in a ball of tears on the corridor floor. I'm furious with her, and stand over her waiting for a satisfactory explanation.

'Tony, I didn't ask for it to happen.'

'That's a technicality. I heard the stories. Like Mrs Murphy says: seek and you shall find.'

'For Christ's sake, I was raped. I was on my way to see you when it happened.'

'Using the Lord's name in vain – tut, tut.'

Rape, lust – it's all sex, just with different toppings. I can't understand why she opened her legs for somebody else. She probably led him on; she definitely asked for it. That will teach her to fan her ass around, teasing people. Though she deserved what she got, it only makes me more jealous and mad.

I walk off, leaving Erin slumped on the ground. But I remain incensed. When next I confront I raise my concerns.

'You always thought you were above me, didn't you?' I ask.

'How so?'

'Not fucking.'

'But I don't.'

'Yet you did.'

'Not by choice.'

I don't read enough protest in her eyes, and turn away. Erin was only ever toying with me. I amused her. I was never good enough to take her virginity.

'I don't go to school by choice, but I still go,' I say.

'What's your point, Rivera?'

'It doesn't mean that I deny going. Doing it is still doing it.'

Calling me by my surname is what does it, what really makes me flip. Rivera. I hate every inch of the Mexican in me. A greater distance is forged between us, we aren't friends any more. When next I see Erin she's my enemy.

'Miss Special One, you're a hooker the same as everyone else. Did you come?'

For once, Erin has no smart riposte. First the sniffles, and then come the waterworks. She looks so vulnerable that it's no wonder a stranger wanted to put an arm around her. She really is a stunner – so feisty and yet so weak. I need time to think, so I bunk off school for the afternoon and go down to the train track where we hung out before.

I need to think things through; to understand the way things are. I'm conflicted: I love her and hate her, and I don't know which feeling is stronger. And I don't know what Erin thinks of me. Distracted, I start picking flowers and have soon collected a bunch. I look at my watch and decide to intercept Erin on her way home from school. Yes, I think, I need to press my advantage on her as she only complies with men when they demand things of her. There are things I need to know, and if it goes badly I can always deny it later. My version of events will be more credible. Erin clearly can no longer be trusted.

She's traumatized when I jump out from behind a bush. She crumbles in a heap once more, and starts bawling crying.

'Why are you torturing me?' she asks.

'Stop being so hysterical, I only wanted to give you these flowers, that's all. I picked them.'

I place the flowers on the ground beside her. But Erin grabs the flowers, and throws them back at me. There's fire in her eyes.

'Did you to it to our song, *Sweet Freedom*?'

'Go away, Rivera, you're twisted.'

'Do you dream about him?'

'I've nightmares, you stupid fuck.'

Then, holding her hands either side of her head, her eyes all puffy and teardrops rolling, she screeches:

'What the fuck do you want from me?'

'I just wanted to say that plants are sacred. Not humans.'

And then I'm running down the road as fast as I can, and more confused than ever. Erin has put the frighteners up me – it's the first time I ever saw her lose the plot. So, there is another side to her.

Nothing makes sense, and anything that does has resigned from being useful. I've nothing to draw on to explain the confusion, and have no one to talk to.

It's time to get my own cock out.

I'm sucked back to the swimming pool.

I end up in the female showers. My move bears the hallmark of a genuine mistake, save for the fact that I'm fully erect. It takes three girls a few moments to spot me. They scream, and I become firmer. A third girl, who is shampooing her hair and has soap in her eyes, tries to rinse away the suds so that she can see where to run. Then, stumbling blind and without time to towel off, she darts away. I run around the changing room after her until she locks herself in a cubicle. Stroking myself wildly, I come all over the cubicle door.

Could I make up such theatrics, my first public indiscretion, my erotic awakening?

I needed to figure it out, to learn what was what, to understand my latent desires, my sexual predilections. Living with such reckless abandon, and getting bent on perverted tendencies and debased urges was still a dimension unknown to me. And then there was the slight matter of nobody sharing my exquisite tastes. I felt like a freak, or a rapist who hasn't yet raped. Yet, new avenues open up as I ejaculate more and more.

So?

I know that I'm becoming unrecognizable as my life moves off in a new direction. I'm searching for something. Knowledge. Awareness. Answers. I'm seeing clearer, as if in slow motion. I see the finer details as things converge and conspire: a dog squatting to shit, a bum zealously hoarding an unopened packet of cigarettes, a shifty-looking black man watching to see who is sneaking a look at him. Everyone is on my radar and every girl is a sexual possibility. I can read desires, too: a couple walking down the road eager to get home and copulate. Smells, once overlooked, I become perceptive to.

I take it further, and pay closer attention to objects – the smoothness of china teacups, the coarseness of wood, the viscosity of liquids. I'm alert to things that might titillate me. All told, it's like a new awakening, a rebirth, as I become hyper-sensitized to life. Anything I touch or that touches me triggers my senses.

I go for a haircut. Hovering millimeters from my scalp, I feel the warmth from the tips of the hairdresser's fingers, in stark contrast to the cold touch of the scissors. With a cutthroat razor, the barber trims the hairs from the back of my neck. Then he blows the hairs away. At first, it's irritating – the blowing – but when he stops it's even more tantalizing.

∞

With the pain of it all, Mom can take no more. She finally implodes.

I vividly remember the day of her breakdown. It was the same day I went to the swimming pool.

Mom had being double-jobbing, looking after Dad, while also holding down her position at the veterinary practice. At the time, Mom was on antibiotics as she was driven half-demented with cat scratch fever. One of her hands was nibbled raw, and trebled in size. It looked like the mauled arm of a boxer put through a crusher. At any minute, the flesh might burst through her skin and spill onto the floor.

Dad was listening to the radio, and I could hear the shower on upstairs. I couldn't smell any dinner cooking and had an eerie premonition that something wasn't right.

I go upstairs and notice the bathroom door is ajar. I call out, but Mom doesn't reply. She just carries on humming to herself. I stand a minute or two outside the bathroom door, and ask if she's all right. Still, nothing. I implore her to respond. But no, Mom is humming away to herself, and leaves my calls unanswered. I have to go in.

There she is, standing fully clothed and under the shower in a sort of trance, using one hand to wash away the other, elephantine-sized one. I call the doctor. Mom is sent to a psychiatric hospital. First for tests and then to stay, indefinitely. Dad is indifferent to it all, probably preoccupied and wondering how he'll get by.

I want to go crazy. I want to go on some kind of murderous rampage. Dad is first in my line of fire. I put Mom's going mad down to his obsessiveness, his bullying and his parsimony. If she wasn't under so much pressure and kept on such a tight leash, maybe she wouldn't have been tipped over the edge.

My time has come. It's only Dad and I left at home. We sit silently in the house, me brooding, he listening for the giveaway floorboard creaks of my attack. He never shouts. I have the upper hand. It's me who is the boogeyman.

There he is, seated on the couch, the blind old bat. I look at the pitiful fool, and decide that he's too old to beat up. There would be no satisfaction in it and, anyway, it might only allow him feel like the victim.

Instead, I erase him from my life. Right there, standing in the living room before him, I swear it to myself: I will change my surname, and wipe 'Rivera' from my existence. I'll start calling myself by Mom's maiden name, 'Cage'. When I'm old enough, I'll make the formal name change. I will; you'll see.

∞

Christmas Day, and the words 'Merry Christmas' fail us. Dad gives me $10 and I give him a pair of socks.

I never much saw my Mexican grandparents. Mom and I refused to travel down. Mom said the people weren't welcoming. For their part, it wasn't that my Mexican grandparents were too old and infirm to visit, but it was more a case of America being hostile territory.

Mom's parents gave up on Dad long ago, and were frustrated that Mom never plucked up the courage to leave him. But with Mom gone, the ring of the telephone brings constant anticipation. My American grandparents are concerned and check up on me, and various phone calls bring different outcomes:

Call Number 1: 'Yes, grandma, I'll come for Christmas dinner.'

Call Number 2: Dad grabs the phone. A heated exchange follows with granddad. The outcome: I'm staying put.

Call Number 3: I get to the phone. Grandma tells me that Dad won't allow me to celebrate Christmas with them, but asks what I'd like as a present.

Call Number 4: Dad gets to the phone first. I'm disappointed, as I knew the call was to enquire after the present that I'd decided upon. Dad overrules me and says there'll be no presents, that it would spoil me.

I'm too literal, I thought Christmas was supposed to be about something, like a new air gun, but it's not to be. Now Christmas is about nothing.

Christmas Eve, and I celebrate my first full-blown depression. I don't have the heart to turn on the TV and hear Christmas carols. *Scrooge* would send me over the edge. I go to bed early. I make a long list of promises to myself, promises involving revenge and promises of getting people back. And then promises to the world.

It's the first Christmas without Mom. No home cooking, but I put a fix to that. For Christmas dinner I make a cat food stew. In the attic I discovered hundreds of tins saved up by Mom, and there's even a seasonal cat food special – Christmas turkey. Thrush pie, I call it. I tell Dad that it's the remains of turkey cuts from the butcher. He admires my ingenuity. I watch him eat, as I push my fork across my own plate, scraping loudly. Dad eats, and releases a satisfied grin. The cat that got the cream.

I wanted to get him back for what he did to Mom. In a way, I think he'd understand.

Waste not, want not.

∞

Erin becomes pregnant by the rapist. The problem is that she was raised by a strict Catholic family and they want her to see it through.

Although I cool towards Erin, I blush when she catches me looking at her belly. She has filled out. I imagine squirming bunny rabbits wriggling insider her.

Erin has become a woman, but somebody else's woman. I wonder if rapists demand blowjobs? Surely they don't, as mouths have teeth. It's the first time that I understand sex as serving a higher function – offspring. I wonder if Erin goes home and touches herself, and thinks about him in the way I go home and touch myself and think about her. I wonder if she knows how much she offended me.

I go home, make Dad a cat-food sandwich and lock myself in the bedroom. I strip naked, and stand before the full-length mirror that I requisitioned from my parent's room.

'Am I not fit enough to be her rapist,' I ask the mirror. 'Could I not have done this to her, might she not instead be having my child?'

My dick rises in tune with notions of raping Erin, and I jerk off. Then I begin my calisthenics: burpees, squat thrusts and jumping jacks. Then I do sit-ups, more than I've ever done: three sets of forty repetitions. Then I look at myself in the mirror again, studying where I've grown. I jerk off again. This time, my ejaculate sticks to the mirror higher up than the last time. I wipe away the lower come stain and leave my new personal best on the mirror.

At school, the next day, I ask Erin aside for a quick word.

'I forgive you,' I say.

But I don't forgive her. I just think it's fair that she has my pardon. I figure that I have the upper hand on her now. Indeed, I pity her.

Erin gets the better of everyone. She won't be forced into delivering a stranger. That evening, she commits suicide. Self-delivery.

I've nowhere left to turn. I stare at the wall. Fuck catholic cunts. And fuck confession.

CPSIA information can be obtained
at www.ICGtesting.com
Printed in the USA
BVHW041656150720
583834BV00010B/128